TALES FROM HAUNTED SCOTLAND

By

GRAEME MILNE

Tales from Haunted Scotland

Published by Landon Publishing

First Edition

ISBN 978-1-9995827-0-8

DEDICATION

For Tertia

With Thanks

Thanks to all our contributors who in no particular order, have included Exploring Scotland's History with my Dog Facebook page, Aberdeen History and Photos from the Past Facebook page, Aberdeen Stories from the Past Facebook page, Aberdeen Forever Facebook page, Helen McKinnon, Chris Willet and staff at the Old Kings Highway Aberdeen, The Scotsman Newspaper, The Evening Express, Keiran Begg at Eerie Earth, Oor Wee Toon (Paisley) Facebook page, the Daily Record, Laura Mahady, Catriona Platten, Kelly Brooks, Lisa Murray, Anders Buaas, John S. Tantalon, Kerrie Powell, Scott Lyal, Wayne Gilbert, Joss Cameron, Amy Dudley, Craigentinny Community Centre, Stuart Simpson, Inch House Community Centre, Liam Shand, Andrew Cuthbert, Vikki Cavanagh, Paranormal Scotland Investigations(PSI) Michael Scott, The Tulloch Institute Perth, Stuart Simpson, Jane Toye, Broughty Ferry History Facebook Page, The Real Banff and Macduff Community Group Facebook page, Secret Scotland Facebook page, Mark Fernyhough, Haunted Perthshire Facebook page, Ian MacDonald, John Irwin, Angela Short, Dr Fiona Jane-Brown, Aberdeen Press and

Journal, Perth Auld Bairns Facebook page, Highland Paranormal Facebook page, Aberdeen Old Shops Facebook page, Linda Whiteford and staff at Culross Palace, Paranormal Scotland, Spooky Isles, Chris Lothian, Tabitha, Geri, Carol and to any other contributors who I may have shamefully omitted but without whom this book would not exist. Many blessings!

Table of Contents

INTRODUCTION

Initially I toyed with the idea of calling this book, 'Something Old, Something New, Something Borrowed, Something Boo.' On reflection, it was perhaps a little flippant, so I settled for 'Tales from Haunted Scotland.' In the following pages you will read true experiences many of which follow the expected tropes of the ghost story, while others defy the norm, if such a description can be applied to the subject. Either way I hope you enjoy these offerings which are all purported to be true. Writing a book on haunted Scotland was never going to be easy, it's a small country but with an embarrassment of riches, so my first challenge was to find a way of organising the stories. By type of haunting seemed a little prescriptive and would have probably created more of a headache for me. The thematic approach might have been good, but for the casual explorer it would have meant jumping back and forth across the country with each new tale. I remained undecided but after further debate I plumped for region. Anyhow it works for me and hopefully for you too. I have, as you would expect, covered the requisite pubs, hotels, and theatres but I am confident in saying there are a few surprises also. As in previous outings I have endeavoured to speak to as many people as possible during my research. Sometimes this has been impossible due to the historic nature of the stories, sometimes the locations themselves no longer exist or have changed radically. On another note, when receiving stories for inclusion there is obviously a level of trust between narrator and listener therefore one must retain a degree of faith. They are to all intents and purposes true stories though of course that very definition will come down to the reader's personal beliefs. As a believer with a sceptical nature, I am quite open to all possibilities, others may of course find some of the material stretches credulity. Of course, one must question the veracity of certain stories, it would be absurd not too and in these moments of doubt, I ask myself what would the witness gain from telling their tale? Usually very little and in fact while collecting stories many witnesses have been quite reticent to share their experiences. Perhaps they fear ridicule and because of this I expect many a good story remains bottled inside never to be spoken of. Some promised tales much like the ghosts also never materialised due to cold feet no doubt and it is a pity as there were some interesting ones I would have loved to have included. Saying that I have been blessed, for example, to have received new information on a building I had previously covered, and many genuinely unsettling tales I had never heard before. I am, as always, grateful for those who have taken the time to do this.

It was the Swiss cleric Ludwig Lavater who argued that ghosts were deceptions, sent by the devil or brought on by drunkenness and melancholy. Our own James VI took it a stage further on publishing Demonology, a treatise on witchcraft. In the book he claimed that no good spirits had appeared on earth since the time of the bible, why he was convinced of this, God only knows. It was at the time a real page turner and his lurid descriptions of demonic entities, sent by God as a 'rod of correction,' captured the public's imagination. Unlikely as it sounds the idea of spectra, ghosts that haunt lonely places, faeries, succubae and incubi sent to tempt man, worked its devilish magic resulting in several high-profile witch trials. Protestantism adhered to the doctrine that only heaven and hell existed and that no spirit would willingly leave heaven or conversely leave hell, this of course was in direct contrast to purgatory which the Catholic church expounded upon. In this middle ground there was in a sense room to manoeuvre, where a soul in purgatory might cause mischief due to its frustrating predicament. Personally, I think that both these ideologies were inspired by nothing more spiritual than flesh and blood. Ghosts held little sway in those times, but do they fare any better today, or are they still like the product of those times used as a means of keeping the populace upon their knees?

I think perhaps they do, though I am not naïve enough to think that every creaking door and breeze constitutes a haunting. In the following pages I am happy to say I have brought some hitherto unknown contributions to the table and given life to some older stories forgotten through the passing of time. It is tragic to think that while some tales remain in the public consciousness others fade to be wisp-like, much like the ghosts themselves.

As a believer who enjoys a healthy dash of scepticism, forgive me if the tone occasionally slips. Despite this however I do take the subject seriously, after all it deals with big questions, questions many would rather avoid. Are these apparitions able to communicate with us? Do they retain their personality and intellect? Are they just a slowly fading recording from the past or are we just deluded? Scientists will always look for the scientific theory and although no one has yet proven they exist, neither can they disprove. We are as a nation chained to the past, our collective psyche the product of our dark history, it's inescapable.

I have seen ghosts, and I am jolly glad of it, it certainly broadens the horizons, and I consider it a blessing. It is also heartening to know that most appear to be benign however there are exceptions as you will see. Whatever the reason, I hope you enjoy the journey and now invite you on a grand tour of Scotland's haunted heritage.

SHETLAND AND ORKNEY

Shetland, Scotland's most northerly isle with its stark landscape and ancient Viking history is our first port of call. It is without doubt a magical place where myths and legends are deeply embedded in the culture of the island. There are of course ample incidents of ghostly folklore as one would expect from such an ancient land. For me the most interesting is the Busta House Hotel, situated on the Busta coastline. Speaking recently to the manager of the hotel, I felt it was worthy of being the first location of note as the stories are current, and the incidents have been witnessed by multiple people. Many buildings are thought to be haunted, despite the most tenuous of stories but I am happy to report that here they deliver and is a great way to start our journey.

In the hotel witnesses have experienced varying phenomena but specifically sightings of full-bodied apparitions. When I recently spoke to a Shetlander on one of my tours, he informed me that his friend's wife had claimed to have seen a ghost there. I was intrigued but even more so when he went on to say that the correct pronunciation of the hotel was 'Boosta,' probably the most apt name for a haunted building ever. Regarding the history of the property, it will eternally be linked to the name of the Giffords, the original owners whose actions set off a chain of events which some claim still reverberate today. The history of the Giffords is long and complex and it is thought the spirit which haunts the building, or at least one of them, was the victim of a bitter jealousy.

Between the years of 1715 and 1734 Thomas and Elizabeth Gifford (Lady Busta) had between them eight sons and six daughters. Quite a handful though I suspect the servants dealt with the brunt of it. Despite a full household they managed to squeeze in another occupant in the shape of Barbara Pitcairn. Barbara, brought up in Lerwick by her mother, had lost her father before her birth. Described as impoverished relatives they nevertheless were respectable. Lady Busta we must assume saw it as a moral duty to bring up the young woman in surroundings befitting a lady. Barbara however was regarded as being lower in station, a fact borne out by Lady Busta's inability to countenance her eldest son's obvious devotion towards her. Having already lost five of her children to smallpox what followed in 1748 literally haunted the family for generations. It was on a calm clear day when John Gifford set sail to visit relatives nearby and accompanying him in the rowboat were his three brothers, a grieve and their tutor. Casting off from the nearby jetty they set off across Busta Voe. It was a journey they had undertaken on many occasions and so what happened next remains a mystery. Having failed to return the next day a frantic search recovered the empty boat which held nothing more than a few personal belongings. Where were the men? Had they been struck by a freak wave? It seemed unlikely as the water was described as calm on the day of their journey. Had there been a quarrel? Their fate remained a mystery for some days until the bodies of John Gifford and the grieve, were found. It was said that on discovering John's corpse the family gathering around in shock, did not notice Barbara surreptitiously remove a document from the young man's sodden pocket. It was later suggested it was their marriage certificate!

After his funeral the distraught Lady Busta received a further shock, on hearing of Barbara's advanced pregnancy, the father being the late John Gifford. Despite the tragedy one would imagine the whiff of scandal did not sit well within the household but nevertheless they agreed to support the mother, by continuing to put a roof over her head. It must have been a gruelling experience for Barbara now forced to reside in a household that refused to acknowledge her marriage. Six months later the late John Gifford's son was born, whom she named Gideon, who eventually inherited the estate, being the only legitimate or illegitimate heir they had. Barbara fared less well and was eventually ostracised from the family when Gideon was six, spending the rest of her life in Lerwick, where she saw her son only once more, at the age of fourteen. Lady Busta never forgave her. There is much more to the tale as in the ensuing years the house and lands were fought over by various family members resulting in bankruptcy and misery for all involved but that's for another day.

Today the building is regarded as one of Shetland's finest listed buildings and now operates as a hotel where guests can enjoy the same views as the privileged Giffords. It is of course rumoured to be haunted by the tragic figure of Barbara Pitcairn whose sad fate has left an indelible stain in the ether. During my research I spoke to Grant O' Neil, manager of this well-known landmark and he was kind enough to provide a few tantalising tales. Though some have alluded to have seen the figure of Lady Busta herself, it is generally thought that most sightings are those of the tragic Barbara. Why she would choose to still be present in a home that gave her so much unhappiness is anyone's guess, but some say it is because of her eternal search for her long-lost child. Others suggest that her presence is merely a shadow of the past, however as you will see this may not be the case due to certain interactions. Whatever you believe both staff and guests claim to have had experiences including the current head chef who I was told had frequently seen the apparition of a lady clad in white, witnessed in the kitchen area. Her manifestations, I was told, have frequently occurred on the right-hand side and Grant described her last appearance as being around a year ago. I was further told that on one occasion the chef followed the figure out of curiosity but on cornering her as it were, was met with a brick wall.

Guests have also frequently reported being woken in the middle of the night by the feeling of someone sitting on the edge of the bed whose weight on their legs and feet has roused them from their slumbers. Grant stated, that, 'on coming to they have witnessed a sad looking lady sitting on the edge of the bed.' He went on to say that this 'has been going on for many years.'

It was further noted that the most current owners, who lived in the 1730s part of the building, also experienced multiple incidents which included their radio being turned on, lights randomly being turned on and off and an iron being switched on. On one occasion the ghost's exploits reached the tabloids where in a lengthy article various witnesses spoke of their experiences. On one infamous occasion the spirit allegedly ironed some discarded shirts while the owner was out of the room. Some of course may have been grateful for this spiritual intervention as no one particularly likes ironing. The article was accompanied by an illustration of said ghost busy pressing shirts. Fantastical as it sounds Grant backed up the story stating that the scenario did occur some years previously. Perhaps less amusing was the following.

Grant stated: 'The one that stays in my mind was when I was covering reception as duty manager and at the time there were three young girls working in the restaurant. I heard a commotion and assumed they were gossiping or larking about; however, one came through in tears and visibly shaken. I asked her what happened, and she said, "I have seen her." I asked who? "Barbara," she replied, stating she had switched off the dining room light after clearing up and was about to enter the kitchen, but on glancing back noticed the light had been switched back on. She said: 'I walked back to put it off and there was a lady sat at the table closest to the window, she looked at me and smiled, stood up and walked through the wall.'

Lastly during our conversation, he told me that some time ago the subject of refurbishment had come up and there had been a conversation about potential changes to what had been the Laird's room. This is regarded as the best room and there was debate whether to remove some wood panelling. Soon after the hotel suffered a week of incidents in which plumbing and heating went wrong and televisions broke. Co-incidence? Perhaps but Neil suggested to me that maybe he had annoyed Barbara, and she had shown her displeasure in the only way possible. He later told me that sightings of Barbara still occur though they are infrequent.

Another of the islands most haunted houses is the infamous 'Windhouse' in Yell, an apt name indeed if you should witness any of the ghosts thought to reside there. Built in 1707 but remodelled in 1885 the house sits about a mile from the nearest village, Mid Yell. There have been numerous stories connected to the building, some dating from the time of its occupation to those from the last hundred years or so when the building was abandoned. Today it is literally a shell, and the stories bandied around for decades have included sightings of a lady seen wearing a silk dress, a phantom dog and the ghost of a maid. The apparition of the maid is of particular interest as she was allegedly witnessed ascending an invisible staircase. There has also been reports of a tall male figure wearing a long black coat and top hat being seen within the building. In recent times visitors, who have dared to explore the ruins, have allegedly seen figures peering in through the empty window frames. It certainly has a reputation that shows no signs of abating. Unoccupied from the 1930s it nevertheless remained in reasonable condition on the upper floor till the 1980s where one intrepid explorer spent a night only troubled by nesting birds. So, is it haunted, and does it deserve its title of one of the world's most haunted buildings?

It may well be as in recent years several new reports have emerged, most interestingly from previous tenants. Rumours of death have always surrounded the building, and it was thought that at least two skeletons had been found buried secretly there, one being a man the other a child. The man was thought to have been killed by a blow to the head as there was noticeable damage to the skull and rumour has it that he was a partygoer who met his fate during a drinking session many years ago. Or could he be the local tax collector, who was said to have vanished mysteriously one day? No one knows for certain however it came to light recently that the occupants living there in the early part of last century employed a local builder, Gideon Smith, to repair a flooded drain outside the kitchen area. Upon lifting the flooring, he was surprised to find the skeletal remains of a tall man. Said to have been around six foot tall he was found with his arms folded across his breast in a shallow grave.

Going back to the early 1900s the house was in good order despite suffering severe damage in a thunderstorm in 1889 and at that point the building was occupied by a family who by all accounts had several strange encounters there. The accounts, posted by Justine Bainbridge some years back made interesting reading and she had submitted them in response to an article posted in the 'Ghostweather' blog. The blog written by Lynn Cherny was very well researched and included a raft of stories which were new to me. Justine, one of the main contributors described being told these stories by her own father who had lived there. It sounded a terrifying place with the occupants hearing disembodied laughter and witnessing figures walking through the walls. To add to this there was also reputedly the ghost of a dog on the premises which on one occasion was seen by her uncle. In one incident he bent to pat its head but found nothing but thin air. Adding to the mix, a maid was then forced to flee a bedroom as each time she went to make the bed someone began laughing.

Further stories included one in which she described her father attempting to open an old sea chest which sat locked in the hall. As her father deliberated on how to open it, his eyes were drawn to the sight of strange mist which appeared at one of the corners of the chest. According to his testimony it rose up and formed the shape of a man before disappearing. Unfortunately, there was no mention of whether the chest eventually revealed its secrets. On another occasion the family received a visit from a couple who were invited to stay the night and on retiring were given a paraffin lamp for their room. They never made it that far, for as they ascended the stairs, they were met by a supernatural darkness which swallowed up the light, the lamp later being described as disappearing into the dark. Retreating backwards they refused to stay in the property. Lastly after going for a walk the family returned under cover of darkness and were halted in their tracks at the sight of a blazing light appear at each window until the building was aglow. After some moments they then went out one by one. The strangest part of the story is, that the house never had electricity. I daresay there will be many other people who have experienced such things there and if the stories are genuine then it is deserving of its reputation.

To this day it is regarded as a haunted house though the question is why. There have undoubtedly been several deaths attributed to the house, some unnatural, and no doubt many more we don't know of. There have also been suggestions put forward that it might lie near an ancient burial ground or perhaps an energy line. To add to the mystery, it is known that in 1985 an American theology student visited the island with his wife, while working with a local pastor. One day the student, accompanied by the pastor and their respective wives decided to take a walk to 'Windhouse.' As they approached the back of the building they came upon the carcasses of four or five sheep, each bearing a distinct gash across its chest, and stated at the time that it appeared as if a ritual had taken place. They did not linger but for years remained puzzled as to the manner of their passing. It was also reported that some years back 'Windhouse' had been purchased and that a couple had planned to refurbish it. It obviously did not work out as sometime later it was back on the market. Perhaps it was just as well as in more recent times one local claimed to have seen 'the tax collector fellow.' In his account he described that while parked near the building having lunch, he became aware of a tall man wearing a long black coat and top hat who walked across the front of the building before vanishing through the wall.

ORKNEY

Approximately 148 miles south of Shetland lies Scotland's second most northerly isle, Orkney. Naturally the island has borne witness to many tragic events in its history and in turn is the location of several enduring tales. A phantom drummer boy and green lady naturally are present and correct as one would expect however there are several more interesting ones including several from local guide and storyteller Tom Muir. Employed at the Orkney Museum, Tankerness House in the late 1980s he described hearing heavy footsteps clumping around while there was no one there. A common phenomenon, the steps were heard most frequently between the Baikie library and the drawing room and came in sets of five. Multiple people were witness to this. On another occasion the caretaker whose bedroom was in a small room off the library was woken one night and saw what was described as a grey shape at the foot of his bed which vanished.

Another building that needs no introduction on the island is the beautiful Skaill House a 17th century mansion which sits adjacent to Skara Brae. An accredited Visit Scotland attraction it is open to the public as a museum. The 12th laird major Malcom Macrae still resides there and over the years both staff and visitors have reported several uncanny experiences throughout the building. The north wing for example, not open to the public, contains a bedroom known as 'ubby's' room. Who 'ubby' was, remains unclear but he is thought to be small in stature, almost hunchbacked, giving rise to the opinion that he was a member of staff from the late 18th century or the child of a member of staff. His face has reportedly been seen by visitors staring from the windows of the private wing. It has also been reported that he is playful and has occasionally tripped or nipped people on both the legs and bottom while they climb the stairs, which if you forgive the pun is a little cheeky. The present Laird, also convinced he had a run in with him some years back, described what happened while working alone in the house one evening. Hearing footsteps in the corridor outside, his canine companion began to bark furiously and ran from the room. The Laird, obliged to investigate, found nothing. It was noted that footsteps have been frequently heard in that very area while objects are found to have been moved.

The following stories collected by Tina Meldrum and Julie Cassidy were kindly passed on to me and show the extent of the haunting. With the house being built upon an ancient burial ground it is small wonder there has been so much activity and during an excavation in the 1930s skeletons were found beneath the property. One of the areas thought to be haunted is the dining room where one visitor in 2018 claimed to have witnessed the spirt of a young child running around. Quickly taking a photograph, he was disappointed to find her image had not appeared however he was able to pinpoint who the apparition was, as her portrait hung nearby. The painting in oil was that of Elizabeth Scarth, daughter of Walter Scarth, the previous occupant, before the current laird. Elizabeth had died at the age of 90 in 2019.

Another ghost and one described in detail was that of a woman witnessed reading a book. Sitting at a writing desk in the drawing room, she was seen looking towards Skara Brae and was noted as wearing a green jersey, striped blouse, tweed trousers, and brown loafers with toggles. The witnesses companion saw the same figure and quickly took a photograph though on checking the image remained obstinately ghost free. She is thought, by her vivid description, to be the spirit of Kathleen Scarth who died in the house in 1991.

Another a female spirit, but this time a maid has also been seen on a landing and when first witnessed one visitor assumed it was someone in costume. His assumption was quickly dispelled on seeing her walk through a wall. It was said that afterwards he had to sit down with a glass of water due to the shock. It was noted that at the point of her disappearance there once stood a door, now blocked for many years. Speaking of shock, in the bishop's room one member of staff was given a fright on seeing the bishop himself kneeling by the bed, afterwards refusing to enter the room again. There have also been reports of a shrouded figure in the same area which may or may not be the same apparition. To finish off though here are two ghostly interactions which I find the most fascinating. Take for example the following when a visitor entered the shop from the gun room and announced she had been going to ask a question about the house, but an 'old man in tweed who said he lived here, answered my question.' She was naturally the only visitor in the building at the time. There have also been several sightings of, 'the man in black,' a very courteous ghost by all accounts who on occasion was witnessed in the gun room looking out to sea. He may also be the same spirit who was seen one morning by a visitor who remarked, how nice it was to be greeted by someone in period costume, and how it enhanced the tour. Despite the proliferation of apparitions, it was noted that the atmosphere remains cordial. Perhaps that is why so many find it difficult to leave?

There is of course a smattering of lesser-known locations on the island and the following I would imagine is one of them. Unfortunately, the witness would not divulge the name of the hotel though I am led to believe it is in Kirkwall. It is without doubt a creepy tale and when told it some years back it certainly raised a few hairs. It all started when a group of Edinburgh fireman visited the island on a training program and was related to me in person by a friend of the witness who along with his colleagues spent several days in Kirkwall with the Orkney brigade. While there, they were put up in a local hotel and he described to me what took place on the second morning of their stay. At breakfast the next day he noticed one of his colleagues appeared to look tired and very pale. Assuming at the time he had not slept very well, perhaps being in a strange bed, he didn't think too much more on the matter. After work the group met up and after eating spent some time in the bar before heading to their rooms. In the dining room next morning he was alarmed to see his colleague looking even more exhausted than before but after deciding to ask was told that he hadn't slept well. On the third morning however, his co-worker looked as white as a sheet and now increasingly concerned for his wellbeing asked him directly if everything was all right. It was then he told his confidant what had happened, describing that it all began on the first night when woke after having an awful dream. In the dream he saw an upright coffin which opened to reveal the body of an elderly woman. Unsettling to say the least but much worse to come as on the following night he woke to find the same woman now standing in his room. Frozen with terror he lay there, eventually crying out after she attempted to climb into bed with him. On the third night the terrified witness was again woken by the same apparition but on shouting out for the woman to leave, was relieved to see her vanish. After hearing the story, they immediately made enquiries, and it wasn't long before someone grudgingly admitted to the fact the building was meant to be haunted. The ghost was thought to be that of a former bar worker who had once resided in the room where the unwitting guest had spent three sleepless nights. They were then told that some years ago a woman had died in an accident after falling through the hatch leading to the cellar, where she had broken her neck in the fall.

Another venue of interest is the ancient St. Magnus Cathedral. Sightings have included the figure of a man in tweeds seen standing in front of the memorial stone who vanished after some seconds. Several custodians have also reported hearing footsteps and on one occasion a witness who was in the upper floor of the tower heard distinct footsteps approaching up the stairs. Stepping into an alcove to let them pass he was surprised when the footsteps continued past him even though there was no one there. On another occasion two colleagues, a custodian and bell ringer were in the tower and on reaching the ground floor were shocked to find the building lit by candlelight and the walls brightly painted as it had been in the Middle Ages. The image faded from view returning to its present-day incarnation before their startled eyes. An interesting example of a timeslip I would suggest.

THE HIGHLANDS

Now on the mainland, the Highlands, geographically speaking are hard to define and appear to mean many things to many people. In Birnam in Perthshire for example I recently noticed one of the many small tributaries which feed into the River Tay had a sign on the narrow bridge which spans it. On reading it indicated that on the left side lay the lowlands while on the right, began the Highlands. If this is the case, then theoretically anything from there on upwards should have been included in this chapter. However, without wishing to offend anyone I decided to completely disregard this and instead focus on the west coast and most northerly regions including Sutherland which is our first port of call. Bordering Caithness and Moray its largest town is Dornoch. The first location however is the Altancealgach hotel near Inchnadamph (Gaelic for meadow of the stags) a small hamlet in Assynt, Sutherland. The story surfaced some 45 years ago when it made the papers and readers were entertained or scared by the revelations they read therein. The proprietor at the time, Mr Bert Matheson, claimed that the frequent appearances of an apparition was causing such concern among his young staff members that he was finding it difficult retaining them. The focus of the haunting was inconveniently centred around a three-bedroom bungalow used as staff quarters. At the time of the interview, it was thought that several had already refused to sleep there after seeing the apparition of a man in old fashioned clothing. In the report Mrs Olive Marshall the mother of Mr Matheson's partner, was interviewed and described how the terrified employees had felt his presence on several occasions with one being convinced he had sat at the end of their bed pushing the mattress down as it did so. Mrs Marshall vividly recollected seeing the spirit herself and described him as a tall man wearing a long jacket, green velvet knee breeches with lace ruffles at his cuffs and neck. The apparition then further alarmed the witness by walking through her sewing machine before disappearing. After some research it was revealed that the hotel cellars were once the town dungeons, and it was claimed that a poltergeist was active in the building with the obligatory movement of objects and electric pumps being switched on by themselves a regular occurrence. At the time of writing the hotel was thought to have been around 150 years old.

Moving on we reach Dornoch Castle Hotel, this fine building dating from around 1500 was built for the Bishop of Sutherland and over the years repurposed as a jail, a school and now hotel. The ghost which haunts the building is thought to be that of Andrew McCornish a sheep stealer, held in the castle before being hung. It was in the late 18th century when he made his first appearance, the witness being his jailer's daughter, Marion Mackenzie. She later described seeing a grey-haired man sitting in her father's study who wore 'grey stockings and breeches who had a weird face.'

Running from the room to get help he vanished before any other witnesses could see him. Allegedly that same evening her uncle also received a similar visit, but this time, being made of sterner stuff he threated to report the ghost to his brother. The ghost vanished and was never seen again. Or did it? In 1922 the strange phenomena was again reported and the new owner taking no chances had the building exorcised. Shaking walls and unexplained noises were reported including the disembodied sound of furniture being dragged.

In January 2022 the general manager was noted as saying that around three to four unusual things happen yearly. For example, while working in the bar he witnessed a straw jump out of a container and land on the floor which was caught on CCTV camera. On another occasion a girl's loud scream was heard from a private dining room which was found to be locked at the time. It was also noted that one morning a man wearing a bright red shirt was witnessed walking into the reception area who then headed straight into the office. The manager assuming it was the porter followed him to discuss the state of play but found the room empty. Apparently, a few minutes later the real porter arrived who was noted as wearing a white shirt. None of the phenomena points to the suspect being McCornish, which begs the question, who is the ghost?

The following story also concerns a highland hotel though the witness did not disclose the name of the venue for fear of the tale being detrimental to business. I first found it on the 'Outlander Past lives' Blog and though I am not usually keen to include stories that don't have a firm setting, I felt I had to in this instance. I will keep it brief. In November 2014 Diane Nicholson and partner Andy decided to take a small break travelling to several hotels on the west coast. The hotel they chose was in a tiny village at the head of a loch with stunning views of the islands. The owner showed them to their rooms in the oldest part of the building which contained their bedroom and a vacant one opposite. After a relaxing day they slept soundly that is until Diane woke to hear what she perceived to be the sound of long fingernails scratching at her wax jacket hanging two feet away. Lying wide eyed in the dark she then heard footsteps and the creak of floorboards as if someone was pacing at the foot of the bed. The steps stopped at the windowsill before something was placed loudly upon it. This was then followed by a rustling sound to the left. Somewhat frightened she lay staring into the gloom but could discern no one standing near the source of the noise. After a time, the scratching started again before the same footsteps could be heard walking towards the window. This set the pattern for the next two hours. Later once the noise abated and she drifted off, the witness stated that she had what appeared to be an out of body experience in which she travelled to the bedroom opposite. A ghastly feeling of dread then enveloped her before she woke up with a start. In the morning, she asked the owner if there had been any reports of the supernatural to which he alluded there had, but only in those two rooms. Perhaps she should reconsider her civic duty and name the establishment before any other unwitting souls enter.

Moving off the mainland we reach the magical Isle of Skye, one of the most beautiful in the country. It has many ghost stories attached to it but for me the most fascinating is the Skye ghost road. As the name suggests it is a stretch of road thought to be haunted by a phantom car seen driving at speed. Strange as it may seem sightings of such cars are not just confined to the Skye area as there have been numerous such incidents across several areas of the highlands. The question remains whether the sightings are connected to historic tragic accidents, and though there is evidence to back this up, no one can tell for certain. Of course, some suggest the sightings are nothing more supernatural than the ramblings of overtired drivers.

One thing that cannot be denied however is that the stories are not new having been around for decades and have been reported by such diverse witnesses as on duty policemen, doctors doing their rounds, farmers and of course tourists. The source of the following encounters includes websites, forums and journals. Our first story was posted on the 'Secret Scotland website,' and on reading it I was intrigued. In the report, its author recounted hearing a tale of a phantom car, which was often seen racing along the roads near Sligachan with its lights blazing at full beam. Having no first-hand experience of it himself he was nevertheless fascinated by the subject and on striking up a conversation with the owner of a nearby farmhouse he enquired if she had heard anything about the ghost car. On hearing this her eyes instantly lit up. Leaning towards him in a conspiratorial fashion she then began her story. She recounted that it was common knowledge that the cars appearances were mainly confined to the old coast road after Sligachan. She further stated that in recent times the sightings had dwindled possibly due to the road being less used. She then took him outside where she drew his attention to an old chest, stored in a nearby barn. It had at one point belonged to her father-in-law and had apparently been the property of a farmer, killed in a car crash at the bridge at Sligachan. Could his fateful journey have been the one that had been indelibly recorded on the roads of Skye?

To back up the hearsay there has however been many solid witness accounts. Take for example this one by local postman Neil McDiarmid who described an eerie encounter with the phantom car while delivering mail. To add a frisson to proceedings it took place during the night of the full moon. While doing his rounds, and without warning he felt a sudden chill creep over him and glancing towards the shore clearly saw an old Austin travelling at high speed, with its front light burning. As he drew nearer, he noted a faint glow from within and could see no one was driving. The car then veered to the right before vanishing. This encounter featured in 'A Gazetteer of Scottish ghosts,' by the late Peter Underwood.

In more recent times a Fortean Forum post explored possible reasons for the ghost cars many appearances. One theory described an incident in April 1959 when a local minister the Reverend Alick MacLean picked up some locals, offering them a lift to the ferry port at Kyleakin. Being a close-knit community it was not uncommon for islanders to help each other and so the lift was gratefully accepted. Whatever happened on their arrival is open to debate as reports vary, but it is thought the car ended up in the water. Some suggest the minister accelerated while boarding the ferry causing the car to break through the opposing barriers before plunging into the water. Another alluded to the fact that the car struck the jetty before entering the water. Either way it is thought that in the ensuing panic the minister escaped however his passengers were not so lucky. Weighed down by their heavy clothing they remained trapped and drowned.

A further article stated that after his subsequent break down he decided to leave the Free Church for the Church of

Scotland. Could this be the source of the story of the phantom car? Possibly not, as further investigation revealed reports going as far back as the 1940s, a full decade before the ferry incident.

Suffice to say there have been many other incidents including earlier examples such as one described by a lorry driver who claimed to have witnessed the car in broad daylight. In other incidents both a local doctor and a postman also noted seeing an old Austin with a single lamp at the front. The stories have continued ever since including another similar incident, recounted some years back when a letter appeared in the Aberdeen Press and Journal. The encounter took place between Kyleakin and Broadford. In the letter the reader responding to an article on the 'wee black car of Skye,' recounted his own personal experience. He also indicted his surprise at the notion that after 1962 the sightings had stopped. He stated, 'I together with a climbing companion saw it in the early 1970s. The situation was precisely as described in previous articles. We pulled into a passing place between Kyleakin and Broadford to let a black Ford pass which we saw approaching along a straight stretch of road. Our passing place was just before a small dip in the road and consequently for about 50 yards or less the view of the road was blocked from our vision. We saw the car approach and then disappear. It never appeared again. It was impossible for it to have reversed or moved off the road without us seeing it. In fact, we made a point of searching the side of the road. But nothing. I might add we knew nothing of the story.' Today, the stories persist but have lessened significantly over the years. Some argue that the reason is because of road upgrades perhaps proving that even ghost cars dislike change.

Still on Skye this spooky encounter involved a local police officer was forced to slam on the brakes because of something he saw by the road. Jumping from the car the officer then ran to investigate while his passenger, unaware of what had transpired, remained inside. After some minutes the driver reappeared looking visibly shaken and told his companion that he thought he had seen someone, with what appeared to be serious injuries, standing beside the road. Somewhat perturbed by the strange turn of events they continued their journey, the policemen eventually shrugging off the incident. It was noted that a few days after the incident the officer was shocked to be called back to the very same spot, which was now the scene of a fatal accident. It would appear his terrible vision pre-empted what was to come.

Now back on the mainland the theme of haunted cars or roads continues with some disturbing encounters. Take for example the following recorded by a Mrs Kirkland whose husband was stationed at Aultbea naval base on the west coast in 1945. In a newspaper article which surfaced some 47 years later, she described returning home for Christmas leave and being driven by a local, Roddy Mckenzie. As they headed towards Inverness, they witnessed a black vehicle with lights on at full beam speeding towards them on the approaching road. As the road had only single passing spaces, Roddy halted to allow the approaching car to pass. After waiting for what appeared to be an interminable age for the car to pass, they eventually crept forward to find only open moorland devoid of life. In the aftermath both front seat passengers were convinced they had seen the same thing.

In more recent times a report from the early 1990s described similar events, proving that the story of the phantom car is not running out of gas anytime soon. On that occasion two locals Ian Morrison and John McDiarmid saw a 'ghost car' while travelling through Glen Drynoch. It was around 3am and as in previous encounters the area offered no means of hiding. Once again twin headlights were reported heading towards them at speed. Doing the decent thing they waited for it to pass, their view blocked by a roadside garage. Again, after a prolonged wait they crept forward and once past the building were greeted by an empty expanse, afterwards concluding there had been nowhere for it to go.

My favourite phantom car story however involved a family travelling from Glasgow to visit their granny in Ardgay. The witness described how they undertook the journey around four times a year and on that occasion, they were accompanied by their pets, a cat and a dog. Part way through the journey they had not long passed Fort William when the witness, now dozing, was rudely awakened by the sound of their Jack Russell, who was growling. Startled, she looked from the window where she saw what she described as 'a lovely old car with lights on passing by.' At the same time the temperature within their vehicle plunged. Quickly glancing back, she saw nothing but an empty road. The dog then apparently curled up and fell back asleep, unlike the witness, I am certain.

On a more disturbing note, the following was again mentioned in the 'Secret Scotland' website. The story described to the author of the report involved a long-distance lorry driver named Jim. Cajoled into sharing his experience by his drinking companions at the local pub, he was at first reticent to recount his story but eventually caved in despite a bit of banter flying about. He went on to explain that while driving down the A83 between Inveraray and Lochgilphead at dusk he had passed the municipal dump on the outskirts of the village. Without warning a figure stepped out from the verge and passed under his truck. The shocked driver slammed on his brakes and leaping from his cab raced back down the road where he expected to be met with a grisly sight. His search revealed nothing. Fearing the worse he then tentatively got onto his knees and peered under the truck but found nothing. It was then he became aware of a feeling of being watched and glancing back witnessed the sight of a motionless figure standing further down the road. Clad in black, it was described as wearing what appeared to be a monk's habit. It remained motionless and not lingering to find out who or what it was he leapt aboard his cab before speeding off. An unpleasant journey by any standard and one which he was unlikely to forget.

But now we head to one of the most beautiful beaches in Scotland, Sandwood Bay. It's a captivating location with a unique atmosphere, described as magical, spiritual and at other times chilling. This remote beach, situated in northwest Scotland around five miles from Cape Wrath is relatively inaccessible and remains unspoiled. It has for decades been home to numerous sightings many of which involve a phantom sailor. Multiple witnesses claim to have seen him peering in the widow of a ruined cottage in which they have sheltered. The haunting is not confined to the beach however and several beachcombers on returning, home bearing small souvenirs such as driftwood and shells, got more than they bargained for. I have written about this area previously, but as further stories have come to the fore, I felt it was worth a revisit.

The most famous case came from 1950s Edinburgh and involved a visitor to the beach who after picking up an innocuous piece of wood suffered several poltergeist type activities on returning home. The wood taken from a ruined staircase within the derelict was nothing more than a keepsake, yet she claimed that as soon as she returned home, she was woken by the sound of loud footsteps within the property while ornaments and plates were seen to be thrown from shelfs. On one occasion she witnessed the figure of a tall weatherbeaten bearded man who stared at her for some moments before vanishing. A strong smell of tobacco was also noted appearing at different times. The scrap of wood was eventually locked away and with that the disturbance ended. Another incident saw a father and son gathering driftwood on the shoreline. Without warning their pony became agitated before a bearded man appeared who demanded that they stop taking what doesn't belong to them as it was his property. Obviously, an entitled ghost, but nevertheless they complied.

A further witness recounted that on visiting the area as a child a similar scenario unfolded when she picked up a small piece of wood. On arriving at the beach, they came across an old house which was assumed to be a bothy. Still glazed and with the roof in good order, they tentatively tried the door before entering. Inside the four visitors had a short rest. It was while there the children took their souvenir from the exposed rafters. Literally thumb nail sized, it was quickly secreted in an empty matchbox. Afterwards the young girl claimed she felt she was then followed by a presence and convinced it was her brother turned only to be greeted by thin air.

Now back at home the family prepared for school the next day and the daughter now settled in bed was taken by surprise when a small piece of wood landed on the covers. In panic she shouted for her mother claiming her brother Robert was annoying her. Somewhat perplexed the mother replied, stating that her brother was sitting with them. Bolting downstairs, she confronted her incredulous family who on opening the matchbox which had contained the fragment of wood, found it to be empty. Who or what had removed the piece of wood and thrown it on her bed remains a mystery?

Another visitor named Emma recently contributed the following tale to the 'Highland Paranormal' Facebook page stating that some years back she had camped at Sandwood Bay and was woken at around 2 am by the sound of footsteps walking around the tent. Listening in terror the footsteps continued to pace outside for some time before stopping. Suffice to say she did not believe they came from a human agency and at the crack of dawn left vowing to never camp there again. Another from the same thread described a further incident which was related to him by his late neighbour. Occurring in the 1950s it involved his late neighbour's husband who along with several companions became disorientated when a sea haar descended. Barely able to see they were alarmed by the sound of horses snorting and stamping on the ground all around them. Somewhat perturbed they fled towards the dunes while the sound of the horses became louder. After a short time, the mist cleared, and all was silent. Given their ordeal they then decided to head for home and in doing so encountered a local. On recounting their experience to him he laughed and said, 'so you have heard them, did you?' Before stating that there were no horses kept in the vicinity.

Now in the capital of the Highlands, Inverness, we pay a visit to BBC Scotland's Highland headquarters on Culduthel Road, where in the late 1970s, instead of broadcasting the news, they made the news. At the time the building had been refurbished for use as a studio and the subsequent disturbances appeared across several articles at the time. Soon after strange sights and sounds were witnessed. These included sightings of a lady dressed in grey, the sound of a woman's voice screaming (at the time recorded) and a plethora of disconcerting poltergeist activity. The figure of the woman for example was seen fully formed and described as looking like someone in mourning. Whether the scream was connected to her in any way is pure conjecture, but a member of the technical staff was shocked to hear it on a transmission tape during playback. On another occasion producer Alan Bates plainly heard someone outside the studio door and on quickly looking outside found nothing. Soon after another senior reporter stated that on one occasion, he entered the studio closing the door firmly behind him and on glancing back found it to be wide open.

During the refurbishment several workmen also reported strange goings on including two, who after an unsettling experience, left the building never to return. On that occasion one worker went to fetch beer from a local hotel, 'The Beaufort,' leaving his colleague onsite. Several minutes later the lone worker heard what he assumed to be his workmate clumping back up the stairs. Calling out to him, he instructed him to put the beer in one of the adjacent rooms, however he was perplexed to hear the footsteps continue through the door. Minutes later his workmate eventually returned and on hearing the story they both decided to vacate the premises, one assumes with the beer.

With staff feeling somewhat unsettled by events, the BBC bosses eventually sanctioned a visit by a Glaswegian medium, Daphne Plowman who on walking around corroborated the sightings including those of the grey lady and a woman in 'widow's weeds.' It was reported she then put the spiritual 'heid' on the ghosts by conducting a blessing.

Sticking with Inverness, this time the following comes from the former Macrae and Dick Garage, now sadly gone. The story first came to the public's attention in several newspapers from 1968. It made fascinating reading and today one wonders if the area is still a magnet for spirits, or did they move on after the building's demolition? Described as a former stable it was thought to have been haunted by a phantom horse, due to the sound of a large animal being heard but it is with the sightings of a mysterious dark figure the story begins.

One evening a 32-year-old Pump attendant named John Maclean was on the night shift manning the pumps. It was Boxing Day night and as expected it had been quiet, the last customer departing some twenty minutes previously. John now in the office had the radio on for company when his attention was drawn to the sound of a car horn going off. Looking outside he saw nothing only then realising the sound came from inside the garage. On investigating he noted that the sound was coming from a black MG Saloon and as he approached the noise ceased before he reached the car. Puzzled he retreated to the sanctity of the office only to hear it start up again. Once again it stopped before he reached it. Puzzled and a little anxious his nerves became further stretched as over the next hours the horn continued to start up at regular intervals. In exasperation he eventually lifted the bonnet and carried out a full investigation finding nothing that could account for it. Although concerned he later mentioned that at the time he hadn't believed in ghosts. Nevertheless, he found the experience unsettling which was further compounded by the fact that on entering his own car to head home, he found a tyre inexplicably flat. Was it bad timing or something more?

A few days later, on the thirtieth of December, another employee, this time 19-year-old Paul Gamer, had a frightening encounter. Interviewed afterwards by the Aberdeen Press and Journal the apparition made more of an effort by rewarding the startled witness with a full-blown appearance as he worked in the garage. On that occasion the young mechanic was shocked to see a figure clad in black which glided across the floor before vanishing halfway. It was, as he later discovered, the same figure which had been seen earlier by others. When interviewed he admitted that at the time he had been a little sceptical about the building being haunted but had an open mind afterwards. He stated that he felt it would have been impossible for anyone to have entered the garage as it had been securely locked.

Leaving Inverness and travelling south we reach Culloden moor, the site of the last battle fought on British soil. It was there the brave Jacobite army gallantly fought against overwhelming odds to no avail, and today there is without a doubt a residual heaviness in the air. It is a poignant experience for those who visit the battlefield, and it goes without saying that there have been numerous sightings of phantom clansmen. A couple of witnesses recently told their tales on social media, both of whom had experiences on the road near to the battle scene. Thomas Brown recently posted that back in the day several fellow workers played in a band and would often travel to gigs across the country. On this occasion they were playing in the north of Scotland and found themselves travelling back near the site of the battlefield. According to the testimony they saw a mist on the road ahead and as they approached it took on the shape of a woman. They ended up slamming on the brakes and in doing so the doors of the van opened depositing their equipment upon the road. In response to this another witness who used the road regularly described his experiences. On reaching the battlefield the witness mentioned passing a farmhouse on the left near a forested area. Well acquainted with the road he went on to say that on several occasions he had witnessed a man in old fashioned clothing crossing in front of him. Most recently, my wife, who was working near Culloden spoke to a local driver. His job involved taking visitors from nearby hotels to the battlefield and in doing so has heard several tales connected to the area. Recently, a family he took there, went for a walk with their children. Part way through the walk their daughter piped up, asking, who are all those men wearing kilts running about and screaming? You can imagine the reaction. Did she witness a timeslip? She knew nothing of the area being so young. Perhaps her experience adds weight to the argument that children can see a reality which most lose upon reaching adulthood!

And now to Elgin and a haunted cinema where around ten years ago staff in the Moray Playhouse claimed to have disturbed something during a refurbishment which apparently stirred up more than dust. Built in 1932 it was a relatively old building and being a cinema, no doubt built up an energy over the years, mostly good one would imagine. Nevertheless, Manager Martin Thomson claimed that when alone in the cinema people had described feelings of not being alone. Cavernous buildings can of course induce all kinds of feelings of unease however he described those feelings had stretched back many years. It was also thought that there was at least one former staff member who passed away on the premises.

Both workers and staff also described feelings of being followed, watched or of hearing disembodied voices. The witness further stated that in one of the most recent incidents a handbag was witnessed flying from a counter by itself. When asked if this was a new phenomenon, he cited several historic incidents of poltergeist activity. The clincher, as it always is, came with the sighting of what was assumed to be a patron entering the ladies' toilet and not coming out again. A subsequent check found them to be empty. To add to the unease certain members of staff described being freaked out by the feeling that there was someone walking closely behind them. In October 2024 the cinema hit the headlines again in an article proclaiming it to be Scotland's most haunted cinema. Whether it is or isn't is irrelevant but manager Steve Bieszke who was interviewed indicated that the phenomena is ongoing and now focused in the foyer area near cinema two and three. It was reported that objects were found to be frequently moved or strewn on the floor and on one occasion he plainly saw a shadowy figure walk by him causing him to run from the area. Recently he was opening, and when he inserted the key into the cupboard where the lights are housed, he described hearing a voice in his ear say, 'are you ready?' I suspect not.

BOTHY FRIGHTS!

Although we remain in the highlands, we now find ourselves in the country's most remote regions, where the common link is that all the witnesses were hill walkers and mountaineers. The following incidents took place in and around bothy's, typical rough steadings and 'But and Bens,' common dwelling houses prevalent to these remote areas. Today these humble shelters are frequently open to those weary after a long day's walking and are maintained by the Mountain Bothy Association. There is something intrinsically creepy about them. For those less inclined to enjoy the great outdoors imagine for a moment lying in a desolate unfurnished room, encased in your sleeping bag, miles from humanity, the silence deafening, each creak, and shuffle stirring the imagination to the point where your heart audibly thumps. You know what I mean! I suspect under those circumstances even the hardiest of travellers have had their moments. However, be warned as many contain much more than imagination. Regarding this I was lucky to speak to several avid mountaineers who provided me with some well-chosen tales, while others were readily available to read in periodicals and websites. Here is a selection of my favourites. Perhaps if you are walker yourself you may consider alternative sleeping arrangements upon reading these. In this first account a hillwalker undertaking a solo walk she described the route she took while heading towards the Tarf Hotel. Incidentally the Tarf Hotel as it has become known was originally the Feith Uaine bothy, Records show that since 1794 it was used as a place of refuge but after the renovation of 1806 it became the haunt of poachers eventually becoming the haunt of ghosts. Burnt, rebuilt and then repaired by the Duke of Atholl it was eventually renovated by the Mountain Bothy Association in the 1990s. Who knows what misdeeds took place within the confines of its walls but over the years it has acquired a reputation for being haunted, a place where strange unaccountable incidents have taken place. Anyhow while walking down towards the bothy the walker became convinced that someone was following behind her, but on looking back there was no one to be seen. The same unnerving feeling continued until she reached the bothy though when on arrival, she sensed there was now someone inside. Tentatively she looked through the window and called out but received no reply. Despite this she intrinsically knew there was someone or something horribly menacing inside. She simply could not open the door. In the same building but on a different occasion another walker arrived to find it already occupied. Feeling awkward as one does in these situations, she introduced herself to the small gathering already hunkered by the fire. They appeared to be in good spirits, but the late arrival perhaps feeling a little awkward opted to sit apart from the group, delving into her book. Soon after the gathering was alerted by the sound of an almighty crash as if a rock had been hurled at the walls. Gathering forces, they grabbed torches and on investigating found the area outside deserted. Another group of guests at the 'Tarf' described that while staying in around 2018, they sensed a feeling of immense dread. They had a few drinks which they readily admitted to, but not enough to dull their senses. After a while the group settled down for the night. Sometime later and freezing cold they woke to see what they thought was someone at the window. The company went outside to look but found nothing. On re-entering they were met with the same terrible sense of dread and again a very sleepless night was had by all.

I later discovered that another contributor had stayed in the same building. He later wrote, 'I also had a scary night and at around 5am I was wakened by what I thought was a large human sneeze which came from inside the bothy. I thought someone had entered while I was sleeping. I wasn't brave enough to look but instead lay for about ten minutes until I dozed off, but then I was awakened by the door opening and closing making a banging noise in the wind. I stayed awake until 3am and heard a noise like two heavy stones being thrown very loudly against the wooden walls above me. I stayed put and eventually got a couple hours sleep.' No future solo visits were planned.

The following was kindly passed on to me by seasoned hill walker Ian MacDonald who I communicated with recently and involved an incident which took place on Tuesday the thirteenth of March 1973, in the Coirenalairig bothy near Braemar. Choosing to spend one-night there he planned to return to Aberdeen the next day. While walking in the gloaming with the river below him he described making his way towards his destination. After some miles he then reached a precarious looking bridge, which he crossed on his hands and knees, above the Baddoch river. Safely on the other side, and after a few hundred yards, he reached the house. It was semi derelict, with one half caved in, while the other was watertight, and on entering he could feel his boots crunch across the plaster which now littered the floor. Striking a light, he discovered the interior contained only the barest of furniture and so quickly fetching some water from the nearby river to make coffee, he settled in for the night. It was while lying there that he first became aware of a succession of strange noises from above. They were short bumping sounds punctuated by louder thumps as if things were being thrown onto the floorboards. Initially assuming that perhaps others were sharing the abode, he wondered why they remained upstairs. After some time, and with curiosity now getting the better of him he decided to investigate and gingerly ascended the staircase. It was in a state of semi collapse and after some careful navigation he entered a roofless room. Playing his torch across the desolation he noted several collapsed beams lying on the floor among other detritus.

Perplexed he returned downstairs and after arranging the frame of the dilapidated bed settled back down for the night, though around half an hour later he was again alerted by the same noises. Now lying awake in a state of alarm, he listened intently, though was convinced no-one could have gained access unless they had used the stair. Soon after the thumping continued, this time sounding as if someone was dropping a heavy weight, and it was at this point he seriously debated whether to leave. Despite his alarm, the warmth of his bed soon caused him to drift off though his rest was short-lived after he was awoken by an exceptionally loud crash.

Springing from his bed, convinced that part of the structure had collapsed, he listened intently but there was now only deathly silence. Afterwards he passed a very restless night, no doubt glad when the morning light made its appearance.

Sometime later he met a fellow walker who described a similar incident, in which several witnesses were kept awake by the sound of rubbish being blown around on the room above them. On investigating they found several pieces of litter lying on the floor which they bagged before taking downstairs. It was sometime later, just as they were dropping off to sleep, that the sound of what they assumed was tin can, could be heard rattling above them. Deciding to look, they crept upstairs only to find a random can in the middle of the floor. They were convinced it had appeared out of nowhere.

Now in Perth and Kinross we arrive at Glen Feal Bothy, which was the setting of an encounter, described as a vampire attack. Recounted in 1920, it is likely an apocryphal tale, though the testimony of the witnesses, two poachers, was assumed at the time to be real. Breaking into the bothy by means of a window the men decided to shelter for the night and as the door remained firmly locked, the window remained their only means of exit. After a spell, one deciding to fetch water, climbed out before heading towards a nearby stream while the other busied himself preparing a fire. On returning, he then climbed back through the window, whereupon the misfortunate poacher was seized by the leg from within the bothy and brutally savaged. His screams attracted his companion who quickly ran to his aid but whatever had torn his leg had vanished as quickly as it had arrived. It was noted that the following cursory search of their surroundings revealed nothing, but their own footprints. It was also reported that the man bore the scars for the rest of his life. Could he have just caught his leg on broken glass and panicked? It's possible. But what is slightly more intriguing is that while searching outside the men claimed to have witnessed white lights, white objects and faint blue lights in the sky? Could this have been one of the earliest UFO sightings ever recorded? In the aftermath of the incident locals gossiped about the bothy's supposed reputation and no one dared venture there, which was perhaps the reason for the story in the first place.

Although reputed to be haunted there has been very little recorded about the Loch Ossian Youth Hostel so for now the only the following applies, which was posted on a hillwalking forum. In the thread, the author, described meeting a young Australian couple, after a long day's walking. Glad of the company the three walkers then spent a pleasant evening socialising before calling it a night. On the following morning, the author again met one of the Australians, though this time he appeared ill at ease. When pressed on the matter he stated that during the previous night, he had felt very cold and so had decided to sleep in the living/dining room area which was warmer. In the middle of the night, he described being tapped on the shoulder and on waking received a terrible shock after seeing a woman's face floating above him. For now, I haven't been able to find anything further to corroborate the story.

Ben Alder last inhabited in 1918 is another infamous bothy well known among the walking fraternity for being somewhat creepy. There are several historic stories attached to the building which on the face of it seem a little fanciful including that of a stranded woman who became trapped in the cottage due to bad weather and in doing so was driven mad by hunger. According to the story she eventually devoured her own child. Other tales tell of a lonely inhabitant who ended their life in despair, their wrathful spirit now earthbound. Both have all the ingredients of a classic ghost story though both have since been debunked, the former a story made up to discourage unwanted travellers by a family living there in the 1930s. Soon after it was found that the supposed suicide was also very much alive passing away at the ripe old age of 83. The adage of never letting a good story get in the way of the truth, was never truer in this instance.

Despite this, more credible accounts do occasionally surface and several that persist included those of walkers hearing unexplained knockings and the sound of music being played on old instruments. Perhaps one of the most believable tales was supplied by the late Syd Scroggie. Despite being blinded in the war he continued to enjoy the great outdoors and was one of the most well-respected characters in the hill walking fraternity. On one occasion Syd and a companion staying over at the Ben Alder described hearing a succession of tapping sounds and footsteps before a packet of biscuits was thrown from the nearby mantelpiece.

He later said that while at Ben Alder he was awakened at around 2am by 'the sound of loud old-fashioned music playing in the room next door. 'I could hear shuffling, like someone having a party with dancing and jumping around. The room turned out to be empty. I'll never return.'

A more alarming tale next, which first appeared in the Scotsman newspaper of the fourteenth of October 1941 and concerned an experience witnessed by Frank S Smythe, the famed mountaineer. His ghost encounter purported to be true featured a timeslip in which the viewer usually witnesses a historic re-enactment of the past. These types of hauntings are fascinating due to their rarity and the detail provided suggests the witness was very much part of the unfolding drama. The location of his encounter was the Morvich to Loch Duich Road and took place on a bright sunny day which makes it even more unusual. In the article he was noted as saying that while walking he began to experience an apprehensive feeling. The feeling grew as his journey progressed until in the distance, he saw twenty or so ragged figures approaching. Observing from his vantage point he noted the group consisted of men, woman and children who by their demeanour looked exhausted. Suddenly and without warning a horde of what he assumed to be clansmen sprang from their hiding places and rushed headlong towards the travellers who they slaughtered indiscriminately. In the aftermath both the slain and their attackers vanished in a blink of an eye leaving the valley still once more. He later described having had a backward glance into a bloodstained page of Scottish History. What dreadful deed from the past he had witnessed remains unsubstantiated.

Taking a jaunt into the nearby Cairngorms, I was told of the following by a reliable witness concerning a legendary creature thought to haunt the nearby hills, the 'Fahm.' A mythical creature, its sudden appearance proved something of surprise for holidaymaker and former work colleague Mike Goonan who described the exact location of the sighting as Northwest of Braemer in Glen Lui, at Creag Bhalg. It was there while he and his family prepared to undertake a circular hike to Glen Quoich, that events unfolded.

Mike takes up the story. 'I was standing admiring the view at our campsite, basically waiting for the family to get ready. I was looking at one of the tops of Creag Bhalg when I noticed what appeared to be a large animal at the top of the peak. I got my binoculars out and in doing so got the surprise of my life. In the distance I saw what appeared to be a very large badger except with no markings. It was low to the ground with long greyish hair and immense paws. It moved in what I can only describe as a floundering motion and was moving at a quick pace. I called my family over and we watched it for around ten minutes before it went over the hill. It had large paws and seemed to throw up dust as it moved. I have heard of many strange stories about the area but only one refence to a creature like this. After thinking about it I realised that the description certainly suited what I had seen. The animal was very large much bigger than anything that should exist in the British Isles. It was noticeable without using the binoculars and I could see the dust rising as it moved. The children however seemed unimpressed remarking it's just a giant badger, so what! Afterwards I kept thinking what if we run into it on our walk.'

The Famh, is Gaelic for the word mole and seeing it was described as a portent of death though thankfully in this case the legend was unfounded. Poet James Hogg referred to the same creature in his work, 'The Queen's Wake.' In it he wrote, 'Oft had that seer at the break of morn/beheld the Famh glide o'er the fell.' Subsequently mentioned in another publication, entitled, 'The Shepherds Calendar' it contained an account from witness, Mr McQueen. In the book he described a similar looking beast, an 'evil and ugly monster, its head is twice the size of its body and if crossed before sunup will result in an untimely death.'

In 'Adventures of a Midnight Mountaineer,' which is another online blog. The following was described as taking place in the northwest highlands at the Bendronaig Bothy near Loch Monar. Managed by the Attadale estate, the bothy, at least at the time of writing, was in good order though contained nothing more than a few scraps of furniture and a fireplace. On that occasion, the author bedding down for the night described how he could not get comfortable and felt restless. At around four in the morning, he found himself awake; his eyes drawn to the fireplace. There he clearly saw two figures, the male wearing typical Victorian clothes, a deerstalker, tweed jacket and plus fours while the woman wore a buttoned dress and shawl. Listening, he could hear their soft dialogue and noted that they appeared to be discussing land reform. At that moment a bright light then flashed before his eyes which coincided with an agonising bout of cramp. Rising from his bed to relieve the pain, he noted that the two figures had vanished. He pondered afterwards if they were mere hallucinations or something more tangible. Creeped out in any case he left the bothy to continue his journey no doubt glad to be out of it.

Most of those incidents however pale in comparison to the following which reached a much wider audience after being featured on the BBC podcast, 'Uncanny.' Presented by Danny Robins. It is, I have to say, a full-on encounter and the witness Phil MacNeill, was interviewed in recent times at length about his experience. What makes it unique though is the phenomena allegedly continued after he had arrived back home. Later I will cover the second part of the story but for now this is what occurred at the onset. In 1973, Phil who was a young man of eighteen, decided to sleepover at the Luibeilt lodge near Fort William while hiking with a friend. On arriving at round 9pm they described that the temperatures within the building as being colder than outside and according to his testimony there was a peculiar feel to the place that did not seem right. To add to their unease, it was also apparent that someone had just recently vacated the premises. There was, as he later described, a table set for Christmas. Looking around they also found that the building was without electricity. Despite their misgivings they decided to settle in for the night. Soon after they became aware of footsteps walking on the floor above and the sound of furniture being moved.

Lying below, gripped with an icy fear they listened to what sounded like a frame bed being assembled and a boulder being rolled across the floor, both of which had commenced upon their candle being extinguished. Despite this they eventually drifted off only to be awakened at around 4am. This time there was something within their room and it was then he described all hell breaking loose. According to his testimony objects then began to fly around the room by themselves, books were thrown from a nearby shelf and their candle was flung into the air. To add to their horror the sound of footsteps then slowly descended the staircase stopping directly outside their door. Phil grabbing an ice axe raised it above his head and pulled the door open to reveal…nothing! Slamming the door shut they then heard the same footsteps ascend the staircase to the upper level. After a few moments indecision they quickly scrambled through the living room window and fled into the night. Glancing back, they noted that the pair of olive-green curtains, which had been open upon their arrival were now closed.

Returning in 1975 in the company of friends, Jimmy and David, he found the building in a poorer condition than before. On entering, it was recorded that the words, 'this house is haunted, this house is evil,' had been scrawled upon a wall, which begs the question, who wrote it and why?

Interestingly in the Aberdeen Weekly News 1890 and the Northern Chronicle of April 1890 it was noted that a former resident, John McAlpine who was a 40-year-old deerstalker/gamekeeper, hung himself nearby. On reading the article it stated that his wife noticing nothing untoward at breakfast had later become concerned when he failed to return home. On looking in the barn she had found the unfortunate man hanging from the crossbeam. The article concluded by saying, 'he was to have left his present position at first Whitsunday.' Researcher Gavin Jamieson, who should be congratulated, for posting his findings online has quite possibly solved the mystery, though there is more to come. But for now, we are again in the Cairngorms, Rothiemurchus Forest to be precise.

Described as one of the last great wildernesses it is the kind of place one can happily get lost in, idling away the hours while communing with nature. The area also has an interesting history and includes a local legend of alleged cursed stones, under which lies a great clan chief. Lumbered with the unappealing moniker of 'bucktooth' he was described as a savage warrior and his unquiet spirit is said to challenge passers-by to a duel. Those who agree gain his respect but for those who blanche at the prospect, their fate is to wander the forest paths eternally. I must admit I felt a little like that the last time I visited there however this was down to my poor map reading skills.

Another cautionary tale regarding the stones, states that those who dare displace them will have great misfortune. It is said that in the not-too-distant past someone foolhardy enough to do this, had come to an unfortunate end. Probably an old wife's tale but personally I don't like to tempt fate and so would leave them well alone. There is however one more story from the area that is more disturbing being featured in Affleck Gray's seminal, 'The Big Grey Man of Ben MacDhui.' In this fascinating book the author gathered numerous tales concerning this alleged frightening apparition. But first bizarre incident from the 1920s which was related to him by witness, Joan Grant. In the incident she recounted having to flee from the forest in terror due to encountering an invisible entity which instilled such horror in her, that she literally ran for her life. Herself, the author of several books, she later wrote about the incident in, 'Time Out of Mind.' The events are as follows. In 1928 Joan and her husband had spent part of the day walking towards the Cairngorms with the intention of returning to Aviemore by evening. While walking a sudden and illogical fear descended on her which she described thus, 'I was seized with such terror that I turned and in panic fled back along the path. Leslie ran after me imploring me to tell him what was wrong. I could only spare enough breath to tell him to run faster, faster. Something utterly malign, four legged, and yet obscenely human, invisible and yet solid enough to allow me to hear the pounding of hooves was trying to reach me.'

After around half a mile she burst through what she described as an invisible barrier only then feeling safe. She was by her own admission a psychic, but the question remains, what was it? Was it a genius Loci, the spirit or guardian of an area, or did some hideous incident in the past leave an indelible stain on the ether? What is certain is that in the aftermath of the encounter several reports describing similar incidents surfaced. There are stories of a similar ilk which have been reported across Britain, and I have in my time spoken to several witness who have recounted similar experiences but that's for another time. Lonely places can of course play tricks on the mind when alone but to visualise a four-legged pursuer akin to something H P Lovecraft would have written, takes it to a different level.

Scotland's most haunted mountain, Ben MacDhui has been written about in several books and acquired a reputation some hundred years ago for numerous sightings of a giant ghostly figure. I refer to of course, the big grey man, who is said to have pursued unwary travellers. Today of course the 'ghost' is thought to be nothing more than the Brocken Spectre, a rare but natural phenomenon. But is it possible there might also be something otherworldly going on? Those who described lonely encounters on the mountains foreboding peaks and on the desolate Lairig Ghru pass appeared convinced.

Take for example Miss Wendy Wood's 1941 encounter in which she described fleeing in terror from what was assumed to be a supernatural entity. On entering the pass, a light snow lay on the ground and though still daytime the sun was noticeably low in the sky. It was then she heard a booming male voice which, though indistinguishable at first, made her pause and listen. The voice she assumed had spoken Gaelic and it appeared to emanate from below her feet. Assuming someone had been buried in the snow, she then began frantically searching, only stopping when she became aware of the sound of heavy footsteps now following her. She later said the stride of her pursuer had not matched her own as she ran from the mountain. the mist making it impossible to see who or what her pursuer was.

Two years later acclaimed nature photographer Alexander Tewnion had an equally bizarre encounter which again took place in similar conditions after a dense mist descended unexpectedly. As he headed down the Coire Ethaca pass the wind which had picked up caused the mist to swirl around him. It was a desolate place, and ahead the hulking shadows of the crags loomed and receded as the mist flowed and eddied. It was then a large shadow quickly advanced toward him. Drawing his revolver, he fired three shots into the approaching shape which to his horror did nothing to slow it down. Taking the only option open to him he ran, stumbling across the boulder strewn hillside till he reached Glen Derry. He commented wryly afterwards that it had been the quickest descent he had ever undertaken. There are of course many other stories of a similar ilk but as they have been covered elsewhere, we move on to a little-known gem from the past. This time our destination is the shore of Loch Linnhe.

Reported in the Dundee Evening Telegraph of October 1938, the witness described the occasion of a gathering of British cyclists who had encamped at the village of Salen on the Isle of Mull. It had been a tough day by all accounts and as the group sat resting by a roaring fire, courtesy of the local hostel, one young teacher from Port Glasgow asked if the group would care to hear a ghost story. Sensibly they said yes, and he regaled them with the following which took place some five years prior at Loch Linnhe.

He stated that at the time he and four others all accountants from Glasgow had been on a cycling trip and during the day had covered many miles. By evening they had reached Appin and looking around for a suitable place to camp, chose a nearby grassy knoll. After pitching their tent, they cooked supper and while eating, Sandy, our storyteller, began to feel a sense of unease. He glanced surreptitiously at his companions convinced they were feeling the same. No one felt inclined to speak, so after brewing some tea they decided to call it a day. Now inside the tent the same ominous feeling began to slowly increase. It was described as evil and the narrator found it impossible to sleep, ending up tossing and turning for hours. He said later, 'I know too that not one other man in the tent was asleep, they were all going through the same thing as myself.'

At around half past four in the morning he whispered to his nearest companion to find out if he was asleep. He wasn't and sitting upright admitted he hadn't slept a wink either due to the malignant feeling. On hearing their whispers, the remainder of the group also rose, where it transpired, they too were embarrassed to have acknowledged their fear. Despite the early hour the decision was made to leave and after a quick cup of tea they packed and left. Riding a little faster than usual they quickly put some distance between them and the campsite. Further on they passed a stone breaker heading to work who enquired as to their early departure. Stopping briefly, they exchanged some pleasantries and in doing so described what had transpired. The local's expression changed before stating. 'Little wonder ye didnae sleep, hae ye heard o' the famous Appin murder? That wee hollow was the very spot where the tyrant Colin Campbell of Glenure was shot dead by a Stewart clansman.' On finishing his tale, the assembled audience reluctantly rose from the sanctity of the fire and headed to bed no doubt to face their own restless night.

Now back to another haunted bothy where the following story featured in my original book the 'Haunted North' some sixteen years ago. This one concerns the infamous Gelder Bothy. It has been described as a place of disquiet and mystery, set high on a wind-swept plateau on route to Lochnagar. Perhaps not the most accessible of places it is still a haven for walkers being the only shelter around, but would you choose to sleep there? Set in the Balmoral estate the Gelder Bothy was originally the royal stables for Queen Victoria when staying in the adjacent lodge and in the late 1870s was much used by the Royal Family. Rarely written about its reputation is well known among walkers who have borne witness to strange and frightening experiences.

I first became aware of the Gelder when in conversation with my colleague Thane who with two companions had spent the day walking in the area before arriving at the bothy. Upon entering they discovered that there were four wooden cot beds in the room, two on one side with another two on the opposite side. The single room had a table and some benches in it but very little else in the way of furniture and of course no electricity.

After catching up on the day's events it made sense to have an early night and so soon after they settled down. After some time, and unaware of how long he had been sleeping, he suddenly found himself awake. It was pitch black and as he lay there the terrifying sound of groaning could be heard coming from the centre of the room. He later described being too scared to call out to his friends who were sleeping on the opposite side of the room, so instead lay rigid with fear. The groaning sound, he surmised, went on for around 20 minutes before it stopped abruptly. In the morning, he asked his friends if they had heard anything during the night. One stated that he had, and it had sounded like it had come from inside the room. But what was it? The question continued to prey on their mind so when they returned home, they felt obliged to contact their friend's wife to ask if he usually made strange noises in his sleep. The answer was no.

My research uncovered further reports concerning faces being seen at the window, and mysterious noises keeping visitors awake so to find out more I asked around. I was pleased to receive a prompt reply from another climber who wrote: 'A mutual friend of ours, Mike, who is unfortunately now dead, once told me, that he and two pals spent a night in the Gelder in winter (this was in the days before the bunks were installed and had only planks nailed onto the rafters with a ladder for access.) He said that they were awakened by continuous hammering on the door and could not understand why the person didn't just enter as the latch was on the outside of the door. When Mike climbed down the ladder to open the door, the noise stopped. He opened the door to find no one there. But the strange thing about this was that a lot of snow had fallen that evening and there were no footprints on the doorstep. I knew Mike very well and he was not the type to make up stuff like that'.

Afterwards I spoke to Thane about my findings and was interested to learn there was a rumour that someone had died in a storm near the Gelder; though no one was quite sure when this had taken place. Needing verification, I contacted another seasoned climber, his reply arrived later the same day, containing a startling revelation. It read: 'It is certainly true. A walker coming down from Lochnagar in very bad weather tried to enter the Gelder stable, but found it was locked. He did in fact die on the doorstep. I think it was around 1948. Apparently when the King George V1 heard about it he told the Balmoral estate factor that the stable should always remain unlocked. Thereafter the stable was used at weekends by climbers and then became known as the Gelder Bothy. I have also been fascinated by the tales associated with the place and have made a point of staying there alone on several occasions out of curiosity, but had no strange experiences, but there are some people who claim they have.

Before we leave the highlands, we pay a visit to Applecross, a peninsula in Wester Ross surrounded by impressive lochs, Kishorn and Torridon. An isolated village not so long ago it was accessed by the notorious, 'Pass of the Cattle,' possibly Britain's most terrifying road. In the early 1990s Martin Rickard was employed as a team leader with the Venture Trust, which gave troubled young offenders an alternative to custody. It did not sit well with some locals and of course periodically the centre hit the headlines for all the wrong reasons. The building Hartfield House, an old hunting lodge has undergone several renovations, including the one which was in progress on the day Martin arrived to take up his post. On arrival it was plain to see there was still work to be done and so home for Martin and his family, was one of the nearby outbuildings. They were rustic and did not have bathroom facilities which meant the family were obliged to use those within the main building. The male facilities were deemed out of the question as they were regularly used for the builders working on the project, so the family used the female shower room instead. He recalled how slippery the tiles were and so was careful when he took his three daughters across so they could wash before bed. On one occasion while tucking his middle daughter into bed, she asked, 'who was that screaming in the shower?' Somewhat perturbed Martin played it down though it did occasionally nag at his mind. Soon after he went to visit an ex-member of staff who lived nearby to discuss some forthcoming activities and to seek advice. After chatting, and on the point of leaving, he asked if the building had any history attached to it. A throwaway question which elicited a strange response from the ex-workers wife, who turned pale and walked from the room. Martin left feeling somewhat ill at ease, and it was only after a second meeting that the truth came out, when he was told former staff had also heard strange noises from the same area. Where were the noises heard from, he asked, the boot room came the reply, which was now the lady's shower room. It was there that several staff members, all female, had heard what they thought to be shouting and screaming on occasion. He was told that at other times the sound of furniture being moved or falling over was also heard, though on investigation nothing untoward was found. This occurred on several occasions and was reported during morning briefings which were a regular feature of the job.

He told me, that given the nature of the client group, one staff member would be obliged sleep over in the main building, and it was noted that several reported waking in the middle of the night convinced there was fire, due to an overpowering smell of smoke. On one occasion, one worker even went looking for the source of the fire, questioning why the alarm hadn't kicked in. In another frightening incident one of the young people taking part in a review became agitated due to what she perceived to be smoke in the room.

The worker then claimed that the girl then 'freaked out,' after seeing the face of a woman looking in at her from outside. Scarily the meeting had taken place on the first floor.

Sometime later when visiting Skye, Richard's wife and daughters were visiting an art show in Broadford. The pictures had been pinned upon free-standing hessian backed boards and while viewing the work the mother noticed her daughter standing behind one of them. Enquiring what she was up to, the child replied she had been collecting coloured drawing pins. It was then that her mum noticed several articles pertaining to the area still pinned on the reverse side, and one caught her eye. On reading, it alluded to the fact there had been a murder in Hartfield lodge in the past, the victims being the wife and brother of a local gamekeeper. Thought to have begun an affair, they were soon discovered and in a fit of rage, the cuckold blasted them with his shotgun.

Soon after the family moved on but around five years later, Richard now working in a freelance capacity, decided to go back to help run the program. Now staying in the village, he described that over time he got to know the new staff members. Soon after a familiar pattern emerged when during one briefing a female on duty described being woken in the middle of the night convinced there was smoke in the room. Some things never change or so it seems, and as the witness and I are keen to find out more, I have reached out to local historians in the hope they can uncover more evidence.

Banff and Buchan

Moving east we reach Banff and Buchan which sits north of Aberdeen and is probably best known for its coastal villages and flat rural farmland. Prominent haunted locations include several castles and stately homes which we will look at soon. The first story however is one connected to a haunted road. I must admit, I do like a haunted road story and the following did not disappoint. Told to me by a former member of the band Orpheus, the occurrence took place around fifty years ago which involved a hair-raising encounter while returning to Aberdeen after a gig. This is what I was told. 'We had played at the Kelder bar in Banff and were returning home. There were four of us in the van, me and our lead guitarist who was driving and another two guys in the back with our equipment. There was hardly any traffic that late at night and we came to a long stretch of road which went downhill. There was a drystone dyke and a barbed wire fence and an open field behind it. On the driver's side there was also a dyke and behind it a steep hill with a forest on top. Ahead of us my eye caught a movement coming out of the trees. It was a figure, and it was running down the hill towards the road in an ungainly fashion. It appeared to be human shaped. When it reached the fence, I thought how was it going to get over? It came right through and onto the verge. The whole time I had said nothing to the driver until to my horror it stumbled onto the road, where I could clearly make out it looked human though it seemed to have a bag or something over its head which went down to its waist. It then stumbled right into our path before the driver slammed on the brakes and shouted out 'what the fuck was that.' We must have hit it but there was no collision, and we went right through it. I asked the driver to hand over the torch and I got out and checked under the van and even along the dyke. There was nothing. The rest of the guys who had been sleeping had woken up and began complaining how cold it was. On finding nothing we headed off.'

A week or so later they played the same venue and naturally told people about their experience and were surprised to hear several other similar tales. Who or what had happened on that desolate road remains unexplained. He then stated that he would have loved to have investigated the area but today it would be impossible, the exact location lost in the mists of time. He finished by saying that up until that day he had not believed in the supernatural.

Duff House in MacDuff is a beautiful Georgian house built for the Duff family who kept it as their home till 1906. Subsequently it was a hotel, a sanitorium for nutritional disorders and by World War two a prisoner of war camp as well as home to various allied regiments. By 1950 the building was alarmingly threatened with demolition, eventually saved by Historic Scotland. It is an incredible structure, and it is shocking to think what may have befallen it had it not been rescued. I worked there on a project some years back researching the history of the building, particularly the life of those 'downstairs.' One of my tasks was to research the gardener's diaries and it became obvious by several later entries that the diarist was asked to leave his employment, for having a dalliance with the owner's daughter, racy stuff. It is of course meant to be haunted and there have been numerous sightings of its most famous incumbent the Green Lady. She is thought to be the spirit of the unhappy Lady Dorothea, who according to tradition, attempted to shoot her husband the 2nd Earl in the library. There are of course worse places to be shot. Speaking of ghosts, I recently spoke to one witness who wished to remain anonymous, who described an encounter with the Green Lady. 'When I was about fifteen, I went to the Fife Lodge disco with my friend and afterwards decided to have a walk to Duff House with two guys. I remember that while we were there, we were walking on a gravel path when we saw this green shape of a person with smoky edges around her. This was above Duff House. My friend and I acknowledged this to each other and then we heard the loud sound of gravel and noticed the guys had run off. We had all seen the same thing. None of us had heard of the Green Lady prior to this.' On a recent Facebook thread on the Banff area one contributor Pauline Robertson described that many years ago when the house was derelict, her and her friends would often go to explore the building. In all those visits, she did not see any sign of ghosts, however the same could not be said for her aunt. This is what she wrote. 'My aunt told me that she was at the house once, when it was late in the evening, and she said there was lady walking towards her. My aunt was so frightened when she stepped back her leg went through a hole in the floorboards, and she twisted her ankle. When she got out, she never went back there again.' Happily, though, she did enjoy sharing her brush with the Green Lady and would happily talk about it during family gatherings.

A recent conversation with witness Sue Robertson elicited another story from the same location. I was told that while strolling in the woods she chanced upon the figure of a woman, walking hurriedly ahead of her. Having appeared out of nowhere just ahead of her, the witness was afforded a clear view. She described her as wearing a bonnet and crinoline dress, albeit one that was not particularly fashionable looking. She also carried a basket and appeared to be in a hurry. On nearing the house, the spirit then vanished. Was this the same figure that had been seen inside the building in previous reports? The question remains unanswered but is intriguing to think it might be.

Other spirits have, included, or so they suggest, the ghosts of a prisoner or prisoners of war, ironically killed by their own troops when the Luftwaffe bombed the house in 1940. Footsteps have also been heard, and staff have witnessed objects being moved whilst the spirit of a young boy, assumed to be a servant, has been seen on occasion. All par for the course and with such a long history its unsurprising that the spirits appear to be from varying ages. A recent report also proved that the activity is not necessarily confined to the building itself when one visitor had an unsettling experience while sitting in his car. On that occasion he described how the boot opened unexpectedly and then was slammed shut, but on exiting the car he found no one there. Figures have at times also been glimpsed in the grounds of the house including near the beautiful family mausoleum situated in woodland near to the property.

Heading to Banff, I recently posted a call out for ghost stories on 'The Real Macduff and Banff Community Group Facebook Page.' Typically, there was an abundance of potential leads however a few stood out more than the others. Regarding this, Sarah Murdoch, whose family home was at number six Strait Path, is first up, who told me that at the foot of her garden stood the Old Tolbooth Hotel, once used as a jail. The current structure replacing a much older one dates from around 1801, and it was there that legendary James Macpherson was held before his execution. Macpherson, a Scottish outlaw, thought of as a Robin Hood type character, was known to rob from the rich and give (at least some of) his takings to the poor. The illegitimate son of Scottish nobility his exploits attracted the ire of Duff of Braco (the local landowner) who eventually had him arrested on the charge of being a gypsy! According to the legend, and there are known to be several accounts, he was given a last-minute reprieve, but his persecutors knowing a rider was on his way had the town clock put forward by fifteen minutes ensuring he would be dead before they arrived. Being a gifted musician, it is said that on the night before his execution he composed a song, known as 'Macphersons rant' which he played upon a fiddle mere moments before his hanging. His spirit is said to haunt several properties in the vicinity potentially including the Old Tolbooth Hotel. Sarah went on to say that when she was young, she heard what she believed to be the sound of sawing coming from the hotel and on mentioning it to her mother, she approached the then owner and asked if he had been doing any work on the building only to be told, no!

The former owner of the hotel, Roy Robinson, then posting a reply on the same thread, described that in the cellar area of the building there were animal stalls, still in situ in the basement as well as an earth toilet. Regarding the ghost, he mentioned that loud footsteps were frequently heard from the upper floors when the rooms were empty and his dog, no doubt sensitive to the atmosphere, would refuse to accompany him there.

Another contributor to the thread, Marie Christian Dawes, also described several encounters, this time from the Plough Inn. Situated in nearby MacDuff the Plough has been investigated on several occasions by groups such as Highland Paranormal, who I was told uncovered evidence of at least three spirits. One, thought to be that of former proprietor 'old Jeanie,' is the most prolific, while the second and third, is an unnamed lady of the night and again James Macpherson. Regarding 'Jeanie.' A medium claimed that she was happy with the changes which had taken place since her tenure, but was quick to point out, that she had ran a tighter ship back then. You can't please everyone it seems, even those in the afterlife. Marie went on to say that there are several areas within the premises which are considered active, those being the pool area and the function hall, and several witnesses have seen shadow figures there. I was told there is also a tangible negative energy within the ladies' toilets, which have affected her dogs so much, they refuse to go into the area. Later the owner sent me across some footage captured on CCTV, which showed what appeared to be a dark translucent shape moving on the staircase. Could this be the restless spirit of Macpherson and if so, what is his connection to the building?

Heading out of town we now reach the Seafield Arms, in Whitehills. A coaching inn dating from the early part of the 1800s, it is said to be haunted and to find out more I contacted the owner, Dave. Speaking to him recently, he was more than happy to share his personal experiences, which began around 2013, after a refurbishment. He told me that soon after while sitting in the bar, he heard six almighty thumps coming from the empty lounge above, but on investigating found the room empty and still. Somewhat unnerved he headed back downstairs. Not long after another incident took place, this time while he was cleaning the lady's toilet. Not a particularly pleasant task, it nevertheless fell to him being the last person on duty and while in one of the cubicles he was startled by the sound of the hand dryers starting up. Leaving the cubicle, he discovered something had triggered the motion sensor and he was unable to switch them off.

On another day, while in the building with his colleague Tommy, another strange incident occurred. This time, while doing paperwork in the bar, he distinctly heard a woman laughing. He quickly called out for his colleague to come and listen but when he came through from the kitchen, the laughter had stopped. Tommy, perhaps thinking it was a prank, returned to the kitchen only to be called back moments later when the laughter started up again. Dave told me this pattern was repeated several times in quick succession. Later, the same female laughter was heard by cleaners Rachael and Elsie, but this time in the lady's toilet.

On occasion, guests would also report strange occurrences and in one instance a regular at the hotel had a particularly unsettling experience. Approaching the owner in the morning he was quoted as saying, 'is this fucking place haunted?' The owner alluded that it might be and then enquired what had happened. The guest no doubt keen to offload then told him that during the night he had gone to the bathroom and on returning found the wardrobe, which was large and heavy, had been pulled further into the room and then propped against the wall at a forty-five-degree angle. Afterwards he apparently barely slept a wink. Another guest, also had a similarly sleepless night, reporting that while visiting the bathroom during the night, someone or something had removed the door handle and placed the screws neatly on a shelf!

Lastly, an engineer called in to install a Sky dish had an interesting experience while working in the attic space. After some time, he reappeared and stated that he did not want to back into the loft due to a presence there. One might argue that much of what has been witnessed could be put down to recordings from the past, but when objects are moved that is an entirely different matter.

Speaking to witness Sue Robertson recently, she described several intriguing encounters from two locations in the town, Church Street and Braehead. Starting with Church Street she told me both her and her husband are in the process of renovating a property which they recently purchased, which has led to some surprising discoveries. Listed as an 18th century house when sold it was found to be considerably older upon the plaster being removed. Sue, a social historian, specialising in old buildings soon became convinced it was connected to the infirmary of the ancient Carmelite monastery which once stood there. She then stated that despite the renovations being sympathetic to the fabric of the building, it nevertheless appeared to incur the ire of its previous inhabitants. When an old downstairs bathroom was removed recently, and a new shower room installed, the couple found themselves unable to open the door one morning which remained obstinately shut despite their best efforts. Enlisting further help they literally had to shoulder it open and in doing so found that the room had been mysteriously wrecked during the night. She told me that in the aftermath of that event she then began to ask permission from the spirits before making further changes. This courtesy allowed the work to continue unimpeded. Still, despite this several ghosts have reportedly been seen by guests including two Victorian children, sitting together on the stairs. Another spirit, known to frequent the garden, was that of a medieval nun who has been seen on several occasions.

Thought to be part of the original infirmary garden it is by all accounts a tranquil place and one which previous incumbents might be loath to leave. This would appear to be true of the nun, who has been described as an elderly woman with a kindly face. Small of stature and wearing clothes which Sue told me would have been 14th century, she has been noted as carrying a basket in which she appears to be gathering things. Strangely she has also been observed in what has been described as a different level, reflecting the original depth of the garden. I was told during our conversation that sightings of this benevolent soul have been noted as occurring during periods of bright sunshine.

Given that the renovations are ongoing the couple are at present residing in another property, renting a 17th house in Braehead. Like Church Street it also appears to have stored some echoes from the past within its fabric, including the sound of horse's hooves across cobbles. This sound, always heard around 3am has been witnessed by not only the tenants themselves but guests who have all noted hearing the same thing while staying in the guest bedroom. Other phenomena have also included people hearing muted conversations. Despite this, I was told it is a pleasant house, and the atmosphere is non-threatening. On a final note, I was told that the current renovation will likely take time as they are keen to use material appropriate to the buildings age. It is for the spirits as much as the owners I suspect, which should make for a very happy home. On finishing I then asked Sue if she considered herself to be psychic, to which she replied no, but she believes that everyone has an ability to see, though most appear to lose it upon reaching adulthood. I could not agree more.

Now heading south, we reach Fraserburgh once one of the busiest fishing ports in the region and home to Kinnaird Head Lighthouse. The first of its kind built on mainland Scotland, it was purchased from the Fraser family in 1787, being converted from a sixteenth century castle. Robert Stevenson, a name synonymous with Scottish Lighthouse design then improved the building in 1824, building a tower within the existing keep which now houses the museum of Scottish lighthouses.

Kinnaird Head also has many stories and legends attached to it including phantom fisherfolk, old keepers and a phantom piper who allegedly haunts the nearby Wine Tower. The Wine Tower though cited as being built around 1570 by Sir Alexander Fraser is a bit of a mystery and stands around 50 yards from the museum on the edge of an outcrop of rock directly above a 30m long cave, known as Selches Hole. There is a legend surrounding the Wine Tower and it concerns Sir

Alexander Fraser's daughter Isobel who incurred the wrath of her father by having a dalliance with a piper of lowly stock. The enraged father forbade the union locking Isobel in her room. The piper was then taken to Selches Hole and chained up inside, where Fraser intended to dissuade him from continuing the romance. In the morning with Isobel at his side, Fraser approached the cave but unbeknownst to him it had flooded leaving the unfortunate piper dead. In despair Isobel fled from the terrible scene and climbing the Wine Tower threw herself to her death below. It has been said that during stormy nights the sound of piping has reportedly been heard coming from the cave. A great story, though like many of its kind it appears somewhat fanciful in the cold light of day. Not so fanciful however, are the sightings of figures in old fashioned clothing, spotted in and around the lighthouse, which I was told are relatively commonplace. A visit was long overdue and in doing so I had the good fortune to interview a former keeper.

During our conversation he told me of several incidents connected to the building and described how a few years ago, one of the guides had taken a party on a tour of the lighthouse. On reaching the top he noticed one woman turned and left the group. Slightly perplexed he continued with the presentation and on completing the tour went downstairs where he found the woman waiting for him. Once the other visitors had dispersed, she apologised for leaving so abruptly and hoped he did not think her rude. She went on to explain that while he was talking, she noticed a woman standing directly behind him wearing a dark shawl who was looking at her. The tour guide was a little taken aback noting that her description matched that of a fisherwoman.

He later added that the keeper's cottages used to house staff, and one employee's wife had often complained about the strange atmosphere in one of the back bedrooms and in the kitchen. His personal theory, he explained, was that objects hold memories and ties for people as much as building's.

Moving down the coast we reach Peterhead, and from it a tale recounted by author Stewart Lamont. It has always raised more questions than provided answers, but nevertheless it is thought by many to be true. The story goes that a driver working for the oil company Schlumberger, was driving on the Fraserburgh to Peterhead Road late one night. The distance between the two is around eighteen miles and during the journey the driver noticed the figure of a girl at the side of the road through the driving rain. He stopped and after offering her a lift passed on his jacket to keep her warm. Later he dropped her off outside her home and said he would come by and pick up the jacket tomorrow. Why he didn't take his jacket there and then is one of several inconsistencies within the story but nevertheless he duly returned the next day to pick up the coat. It was then the hitchhikers' distraught parents informed him that their daughter had been dead for two years, killed in a road accident at, you guessed it, the same spot. He insisted he had spoken to her on the previous night at which point her parents took him to her grave where they found his jacket lying upon it. Mr Lamont went on to claim that the story was well known locally and there had been a 'wall of silence,' around it. An associate, the Reverend James Miller later corroborated the tale, or at least the fact that Mr Lamont had been stone-walled while trying to uncover the truth. On reading it's difficult to say what I think about this. It adheres to the accepted tropes of a ghost story, perhaps too closely, but is even more intriguing given that the driver was apparently located and interviewed. The outcome? Well, it's still open to question. It's the type of story one would love to believe, and there have been several examples, including a very similar experience involving Telly Savalas, who I am sure needs no introduction. The author of course can only record what they have been told whether fact or fantasy and so this cannot be proven one way or another.

ABERDEENSHIRE

Now heading south, we head to Leith Hall where it has been suggested there are several ghosts, the most famous being past owner John Leith, who died after being shot in the head during a drunken brawl in Aberdeen's Castlegate. The fight took place just prior to Christmas in 1763 and the injured man once conveyed home, passed away three days later. Since then his ghost has been seen on several occasions and has been noted as having a bandage wrapped around its head. The most famous documented sighting was recorded by American author and psychic Elizabeth Byrd who spent time in Scotland researching for the historic novels she was most famous for. Occasionally accompanied by her close friend Hans Holzer, another prolific author who wrote extensively on the supernatural, they stayed in several haunted locations, recording their experiences for posterity.

It was noted that in 1969 Leith Hall had been split into several apartments while the rest of the building was used as a museum. Elizabeth Byrd was one of the tenants at the time and in her book, 'A Strange and Seeing Time,' she described several close encounters with the restless shade of John Leith. It was early one July morning when she had her first encounter and on waking the room was noted as being well-lit in the early morning sun. It was then that she felt a presence and on glancing towards the window, clearly saw the figure of a tall, bearded man wearing dark green breeches and a pale shirt, who had a grubby bandage upon his head. She screamed out in fright for him to go away only for the figure to take several steps back before disappearing through the mirror which stood nearby. Running downstairs to fetch the dog she returned to the room where she promptly fainted onto the bed. Sometime later her husband stated that he too had seen a bearded man standing by the fireplace. Soon after the authors mother came to stay but Elizabeth kept quiet about her encounter due to her advanced years. Her mother who had not long arrived, then heard what she described as the sound of a pistol shot being fired followed by a heavy dragging sound. This was then followed by the sound of footsteps which appeared to stagger along the hallway, ending with the sound of a body falling heavily against the door. Despite this she dozed off only to be awoken later by a repetition of the previous scenario.

Sometime later a family friend, also psychic, stayed at the property and on waking in the middle of the night sat up in bed convinced something was amiss. Peering into the darkness she heard cutlery scraping and the clink of crystal glasses as well as an aroma of cooking in the air. Murmuring voices could also be detected and occasional laughter. Later it came as no surprise to find the room she stayed in was once the dining room. The phenomena lasted around five minutes before ceasing altogether. Further phenomena from the property have included guests feeling as if they were being suffocated, the sound of children playing and sightings of figures in military uniform, no surprise considering the properties usage over the years including that of a military hospital.

Moving on, though still in Aberdeenshire I was told this personal story concerning a property in Easterton of Auchleuchries, around five miles north of the town of Ellon. The owner who described herself as a both a scientist and an agnostic conceded that the incidents which took place some years back were difficult to explain. On one occasion for instance, she plainly heard a male voice say her name while alone in the house while on another she heard what she took to be a cat jumping onto the pool table. She further told me that one evening her ex-husband, who at the time had been speaking to his girlfriend on the computer (thus the ex-husband she said) began to choke uncontrollably. He later claimed that while talking to her a shadowy figure appeared on camera which put its arm around his neck and began to strangle him, a fact his girlfriend later corroborated. Convinced it was of paranormal origin he then confided in his then mother-in-law who generously appeared with holy water. I was told that after it had been sprinkled throughout the house there were no further incidents.

The witness told me that she later sold the house in 2014 to an elderly man who passed away before it was purchased by an ex-colleague. As far as the witness was aware nothing of note happened, though while renovating, the new owners found a bible with a child's sailor suit wrapped around it in the cavity of one of the walls. She further stated that one of the locals used to jokingly call the house the Amityville horror house, though she never asked them to explain why. Possibly this was just a brief haunting in response to the real-life drama playing out.

The Northern Frights of Old Aberdeen

On the 12th of August 1971 Aberdeen Press and Journal or the pea n' ham as its affectionately known, ran an article featuring Deeford, a substantial Victorian villa used as a Church of Scotland hostel situated on the city's Riverside Drive. The article was accompanied by a photo of William Russell, then superintendent of the building, seen cheerfully gardening in front of the ominous looking building. An allegedly haunted house, it had been at one time the property of a local minister but since then had undergone several changes. Used at the time as a hostel for apprentices from the country it consisted of thirteen rooms and was by all accounts a very happy place. I remember as a kid going for a walk one evening with my mum and dad and in doing so, we passed the very building. Perhaps they had decided to walk there specifically for a closer look but anyhow I remember one of them saying, 'that's the haunted house,' I am not sure if I really appreciated what a haunted house was, but I distinctly remember that in the misty gloom of that evening it did not look inviting. Over the years I often pondered about the building and my interest was rekindled upon reading Norman Adam's seminal Aberdeen ghost book, 'The Haunted Neuk.' I then visited the newspaper archives where I chanced upon the original articles and read their contents voraciously. You may have heard the story before, you might not have, but either way it is a suitable start to our odyssey through my home city of Aberdeen.

I discovered that the phenomena witnessed within the building had by all accounts been ongoing for many years and the phenomena ran the gamut of what you would expect. It was said that frequently doors would crash shut of their own accord while glasses would be found smashed and cushions scattered on the floor. My natural scepticism came to the fore however, on discovering it was used at the time as a hostel for young boys. Accidents will happen I concluded, though on reading further I became more convinced as to the veracity of the stories, after all the Russell family had been custodians for around thirty years and witnessed many strange things none of which appeared to faze him. He had by his own words accepted the situation and learned to live with it. She was after all reported to be a friendly ghost.

The ghost he said was believed to have been the earth-bound spirit of a former occupant, a minister's daughter, who had given birth to an illegitimate child. It is alleged that the shame of which prompted her to take her own life in a second-floor bedroom. Some quick research indicated that there had indeed been a minister registered as living there which at least gave some credence to the story. But as for the rest, well that was never resolved.

Reading on, the most common phenomena noted was that of phantom footsteps frequently heard on the stairs and corridors, the loud staccato clicking alerting the family to her ghostly presence. On investigation they would abruptly stop. It was known that they would occur at various times both day and night. Mr. Russell's daughter Aileen, eventually refused to stay in the house alone after hearing footsteps coming from her mother's bedroom. On investigation she found the corridor empty and her mum still fast asleep in bed, for her that was the last straw.

They did on occasion also hear smashing glass yet on investigation found everything undisturbed. Sometimes and quite unnervingly rooms were suddenly plunged into darkness when lights were suddenly switched off and when interviewed the caretaker stated that the house had recently been rewired and new plugs installed. This you would assume ruled out the most obvious explanation. To back this up he mentioned a former tenant who had witnessed the same phenomena when the home was gaslit. Playfulness is one thing but there were on occasion incidents that were more alarming but what prompted this they could not say. Take for example, the day they found they could not enter the living room because a large armchair had been set against the doorknob. Was she just being playful? Perhaps, but nevertheless it took considerable effort for the family to gain entry and on doing so found cushions scattered across the floor.

Of course, being a hostel, it wasn't just the family who witnessed these occurrences and in fact the ghost was described as most active when in the company of children. One young resident recalled that while he was in the bathroom, the door he had just snibbed seconds before then swung open. Another young lad while laying ill in bed heard footsteps outside his room and assuming it was one of the Russell's called out for a glass of water. When he heard no response, he clambered out to get his own drink only to be met with an empty corridor. Mrs Russell indicated his illness miraculously vanished soon after, refusing to stay upstairs alone.

One long time worker Gladys Cox who was later interviewed, stated that both herself and her colleague had been working in the kitchen when they heard a woman's voice humming a tune directly behind them. A search revealed they were the only occupants in the building at the time. When the Russell's were on holiday it was Mrs Cox along with her husband who were tasked with looking after the building. One evening while in the living room they were alerted by knocking at the door and called out to see who it was but got no response. I suspect they rued the day they volunteered to housesit. The ghost became known as Mary and during the Russell's long tenure she was described as a friendly ghost. Mr Russell had of course done his own investigating and indicated Mary had been around long before his tenure as after speaking to former residents she was seen as far back as the 1940s. During that period similar stories had been recorded and in one incident a former resident saw Mary in the flesh as it were, when he saw her reflected in the mirror behind him. Momentarily he thought it might have been his wife, but discovered she had not been in the room at the time

By the mid-70s however Deeford had been renovated, ceasing to be a hostel, and it was around this time that Mary made her last appearances. A further article around twenty years later made no reference to the ghost itself but rather focused on Mr Russell, then retired, who met with former boarders from the hostel at the Burnett Arms, Kemnay. Ninety-six former apprentices turned up from all corners of the world to swap stories and reminisce and I wonder if the subject of their conversation turned to Mary?

Next stop, literally, is the King Street bus depot in Aberdeen. It has undergone many changes in its long history from army barracks to tram depot and in more recent times as headquarters for Aberdeen Corporation Transport before becoming First Bus. The building has featured in several books over the years, and I had the privilege of visiting the HQ on several occasions chatting to staff and hearing first hand of their experiences. It is fair to say it is one of the best known and most intriguing ghost stories to come from the region. On my visit I remember looking around the old tram sheds, the infamous south turret and military hospital, sadly most of which has gone. Though the building has changed one thing is consistent and that is the enduring story of its ghost, Captain Beaton. I covered this extensively in my previous book, 'Aberdeen's Haunted Heritage,' but I wanted to recap for those unfamiliar with the story. The spirit thought to haunt the building is that of a soldier who on receiving news of his impending return to the trenches of WW1, took his own life. This allegedly happened in the south turret and while visiting there some years ago it still contained a frayed rope hanging from its cross beam. During recent renovations however I was told that some buffoon had thrown it out. Unforgivable, but such is the fate of buildings during refurbishments. The rope thought to be the one from which Beaton hung himself was a macabre artefact indeed. It is without doubt a tragic story, if true. To add to the mystery the officer who died there may not have been called Beaton as there are no records in the Gordon Highlander's Museum to support this. Notwithstanding the lack of physical evidence there have been numerous sightings of a soldier, or soldiers over the past hundred years. Witnesses have included bus drivers, cleaners, former residents and other administrative staff especially from the 1960s onwards. Accounts such as an employee being knocked over while cleaning a bus or the driver who saw a kilted man reflected in a window were par for the course. On another occasion I have it on good authority that the unexpected sighting of a soldier in full battle dress was so terrifying that the witness wet himself. One of my personal favourites though involved a night watchman in the not-too-distant past who was working alone on Christmas Eve. Depressing as that must have been he was obliged to visit various outbuildings throughout the site. It was no doubt cold, and the cavernous transport sheds must have been unappealing as they stood silent in the dark. Leaving the main administration block I was told he then crossed the yard and entered the tram shed. Ahead lay several pits in which mechanics worked from and at the far end sat a vintage bus, beautifully repaired. Further on lay a large wooden door, heavily padlocked and the only means of entry to the now derelict military hospital once used by recuperating soldiers during the Great War. It was latterly used to store spares parts, most useless due to their age, and was home to pigeons both dead and alive. As he approached, he distinctly heard the voices of two men arguing and assuming a radio had been left on in one of the pits went to turn it off. Finding nothing he realised that the voices were coming from within the hospital. Approaching the padlocked door, he heard from within the sound of a heated argument. After some moments he ran. Wouldn't you have done the same? These are just the tip of the iceberg and sightings have even taken place out with its confines, including one young girl who on travelling with her mother by taxi, witnessed a soldier walk across King Street before vanishing.

Occasional others surface and I feel it's my duty to air each one as it's such a fascinating subject, and the latest nod to this great building comes from Brian Sellers. He described to me that during the sixties he was gainfully employed by ACT, Aberdeen Corporation Transport, who ran the bus network. As a ticket collector, they would work alongside a driver. His driver, I was told was called 'spooky Winton,' so called because of his obsession with the occult. By all accounts a clever and well-read man he habitually carried a small Ouija board which he would whip out at every opportunity conducting ad hoc seances using a nip glass. I would have loved to have met this guy.

This is what Brian described. 'One afternoon whilst in the bus canteen in Marischal Street, Bill, Mr. Winton gathered all the crew around and began a session. He asked me as usual to put my finger on the glass and then asked if there was anybody there. I was getting a bit fed up with it and therefore made the glass shake and moved it to yes. Bill became more excited and asked if there was a message for anyone. Looking up I saw Rosie the canteen lady and so swiftly moved the glass to yes and then spelt out Rosie. What is the message to Rosie asked Bill and I randomly spelled out "history repeats itself" after which I moved the glass off the board. As one would imagine everyone walked away mumbling and laughing and saying, "that was a load of shite." Bill thought it was true and that I had a special gift. I thought no more about it until I met Rosie on Queen Street some two weeks later and I asked if she had been on holiday. Rosie replied no, and that after she went home that night (after the seance) her husband took a second heart attack and died. I felt terrible and the question is, did something make me spell out what I did or was it just coincidence? We had another session one night at the King Street Garage as Bill was trying to contact a Gordon Highlander who was supposed to haunt the depot but that occasion nothing happened.'

It appeared that Mr. Winton may have tried on other occasions as a now retired former driver stated he witnessed a similar seance in which the name 'Corporal Beaton,' was noted. Could this be the answer and is the unfortunate soldiers rank the stumbling block to his identity? Only time will tell. It is safe to say however that the phenomena continued up to the renovations with several workers having uncanny experiences including one being pushed on the stairs by something rushing by and another having a brick pulled from his hand that fell to the ground slowly before bouncing, which he later described as impossible.

Now to Maberly Street best known for being the location of Richards Textile Mills. A sprawling collection of listed buildings, quite beautiful in fact, it now lies in terrible disrepair no doubt earmarked for demolition. Staying in the top floor flat of number 42 as a young boy, Graham Taylor described how he would often lie in bed and watch the shadows cast from the larger buildings across the way. When his grandmother sadly died his grandfather moved in with the family and shared his room, sleeping diagonally across from him. One night he awoke unexpectedly and looking across to where his grandfather lay, saw a figure standing by the side of his bed. It looked down at his grandfather and when it turned, he saw that it was his grandmother, she then smiled at him before disappearing. He stated later that he didn't mind that as it was someone, he knew but described having to walk through 'people' in the lobby to get to the communal toilet, outside on the stairs which was more frightening. He later described them as slow-moving shadow beings who never spoke or made a sound. He went on to say that as he got older, he would sometimes sense an overpowering smell of lilies in the house and it was quite common for him to see the spirits of those who passed on, before being told of the fact. It was in a sense normal to him and not particularly frightening unlike a visit to his father in law's home, Crochdane or 'slaughter of the Danes,' in Cruden Bay. It was while there he had a much more unpleasant experience after seeing a solid figure standing at the end of his wife's bed, there being only single beds in the room. Initially thinking it was his wife he began to speak to her but was shocked to see the figure slowly dissolve from top to bottom. This was accompanied by a feeling of threat which he had never felt before. He told me that afterwards he never went into the room again and could not even look through the door if it was open.

Now on Constitution Street, where a former nurse told me about her grandmother who lived at number 64 and witnessed an apparition there in the early 1900s. On the night in question, her granny woke and became aware of an overpowering smell of tobacco. Rising slightly from her pillow she observed an elderly man with white hair sitting by the fire. He appeared to be staring into the embers which were still glowing. The man gave off an aura of contentment and was seen smoking a pipe. He wore a white collar, and it was then she realised she was looking at the figure of a priest. The apparition then slowly faded. A great story made even better on discovering the building was the former home of Priest Gordon one of the founders of Blairs College, revered in Aberdeen for his good work. Upon his death they say half of the city turned out to pay their respects before he was interred in the Snow Kirk.

Speaking of which this amusing story was featured in a newspaper article some 140 years back which I came across recently. In the article it alluded to the fact that the ghost who allegedly haunts the Snow Kirk was none other than the late Priest Gordon. Why they thought it was him was uncertain, however there is a legend that alluded to the fact that the last person buried there was obliged to hang around until a new incumbent arrived. It was said that soon after the burial of Charles Gordon, his spirit began to haunt the kirk, though selfishly only his voice was heard. The voice, according to the report, spoke in either broad Scots or Latin. Perhaps it was true then, as the bishop himself had on occasion urged Gordon to speak properly as befitting a man of his standing, and to stop using the Aberdeen vernacular. A servant girl from a nearby manse was the first to claim to have heard his voice, a fact corroborated by her beau who was with her at the time, however others in the company questioned whether a priest, dead or otherwise would swear so prolifically. Considering this several volunteers keen to get to the bottom of the mystery then secreted themselves amongst the remains of the derelict Snow Kirk in the hope of hearing the same. Soon after, they were not disappointed when the ghost appeared. Disappointingly however the spirit turned out to be no more than a callow youth, the third part of a love triangle with a courting couple. Quickly seized by angry locals, he admitted under questioning that due to jealousy he had tried to scare off the other lad. In court he denied trying to imitate the priest's, 'ghostie,' rather claiming he was 'scared enough lying among the graves in the dark without doing anything to anger or rouse their occupants.' It was said during proceedings that apparently the guilty party's rich vocabulary had been mistaken for the 'Roman tongue.' I am sure he was delighted when no charge was brought against him. Though tales about the haunted snow kirk persist there is little evidence to support this. If you should care to visit, the graveyard is situated near the Powis Gates in Old Aberdeen discreetly tucked away in a car park, an ignoble last resting place for some of the city's most famous sons.

Moving onto the High Street the spires of King's College now come into view. As with the Chanonry it has numerous buildings vying for one's attention: the Powis Gates leading to the Powis estate and directly in front, the tomb of Bishop Elphinstone. It was on this spot that a passer-by allegedly witnessed a ghostly duel several years back. Requesting his name be omitted for personal reasons, however he nevertheless was adamant that what he saw one evening was genuinely paranormal. Returning home through the stillness of the High Street, the usually bustling streets were bereft of students being out of term-time. It was approximately 11pm and though getting dark the sky had enough light left to illuminate the surrounding area. In the gathering dusk he noticed movement on the grass directly to his right and glanced over. He was shocked to see two men in what he described as 'musketeer type clothing' engaged in combat.

Whirling and parrying, they appeared relatively solid though he noticed that there was a certain 'wispiness' to their forms. Thinking initially, it was either a prank or a re-enactment, he stood for some seconds before realising that when their swords met there was no sound. With the spell broken he now ran from the scene. He stated that he did not feel scared as such but was unsure of what would have happened had they noticed him.

Now through Powis Gates we reach Powis House which I wrote about previously in Aberdeen's Haunted Heritage. It is tempting to go over old ground as this building is still one of the most interesting, I have ever covered, with some very interesting first-hand accounts. Tales of a spirit named Annie had been around for decades and certainly many cleaners and centre users claimed to have seen her. Without sounding too dramatic I have it on good authority that several either quit their positions or literally would not leave their own homes, as such was the case when a group of teenagers saw her floating apparition some twenty odd years ago. Another interesting tale involved a group of young musicians whose session was interrupted by a crashing sound outside the studio and on investigating they found a fire extinguisher outside the door with its nozzle now broken. It had been securely held there in a bracket some minutes before which was perplexing as someone would have had to have lifted if off, before dropping it. This would have been impossible given the only people within the building were those in the practice room. A former caretaker was also noted as seeing a phantom monk in the basement and staff members have cited seeing a dark-haired woman. I visited several times in the past and found it to be a genuinely creepy building particularly in the basement and attic. I also interviewed several people connected to the building one of whom left her job as a cleaner after seeing something that frightened the life out of her in the attic. Sometime later visiting the same spot I also felt genuinely unnerved which is something that doesn't happen too often. In my experience there have only been handful of buildings that I felt were either genuinely eerie or offered up a broad range of well documented experiences, the top two being the First Bus depot and Powis House. I cannot rate it highly enough, so I was delighted to be contacted a few months ago with several new anecdotes the latter of which is genuinely unsettling.

The following was passed onto me by witness Pauline, who described that when she was younger, she had been told that the ghost that was supposed to haunt the building was that of a servant who had worked for the Leslie's. It was thought she had subsequently hung herself from the middle staircase due to some undisclosed scandal, though it has never been verified, and her ghost subsequently named Annie. Before moving from the area in 1992, Paula spent much of her time at the centre as did her mum who worked there. It was described as a second home. She told me that her first experience happened when she was about primary five or six after she bunked off school with her classmate Lisa. Not knowing what to do they decided to go to the community centre where they spent some time messing about in the conference room. This room is situated on the first floor at the top of the stairs alongside several offices Without warning they then heard voices downstairs, which began heading up. In panic her friend Lisa then ran upstairs to the top of the building where she hid in the empty caretaker's flat. Pauline refusing point blank to follow as she hated the place was forced to hide behind a chair.

Seconds later her mum walked with two acquaintances, Davina and Dorothy. On finding her daughter she was furious of course and demanded to know who the girl upstairs was. Pauline explained it was Lisa, but I didn't realise that she had already run back downstairs and had been caught. So, who was the third person that could plainly be heard upstairs? In the aftermath Pauline was grounded but remained adamant there was a third unknown party in the building that day.

She further elaborated with the following: 'I used to get a bad feeling in the top flat that was not an asthmatic thing. I would be lying if at the time I had put it down to the paranormal, but I had been in that community centre almost every day in one way or another. I was only in the top part about three times and felt the same way every time and I just avoided it from then on. It was as if my chest was tightening and like someone was holding my mouth and I couldn't get breath. The only other time I felt like that was when I was in the Tolbooth Museum. I had been many times with my children but on this day that same feeling overcame me, so I just abandoned my kids upstairs which was out of character for me, but I just needed to get out. When I got myself together, I reluctantly went back in to let a staff member know I had left my kids upstairs. They wanted to know what happened and when I told the staff member, she said that several people had similar experiences which they believed was caused by a spirit. I am sure this is what happened at Powis Community Centre. Anyhow one night me and my mate Mark decided to stay all night at the centre, so just before closing time we hid in the bathroom till all the lights went out. After ten minutes we snuck out. It must have been summertime as when we got to the kitchen, I don't recall it being dark. We messed around for a while, played some pool and tried to make a cake, not realising we needed flour and eggs to do so. A mess is about the only thing we managed to make. We then mucked around in the room we called the disco room where we found a packet of biscuits in the cupboard. As it was beginning to get dark, we decided to go upstairs to eat them, where light from the lamppost was shining in one of the rooms.

Mark then had the idea of going into the basement because we could put the lights on with no one seeing us. In the basement we ended up playing with some musical equipment and I remember Mark pretending to play the drums. I don't know how long we were down there but as we sat finishing the biscuits we then heard someone coming down the basement stairs. We both looked at each other in pure shock, you should have seen the expression on our faces. We went to hide and could hear every step coming down and although we couldn't see who it was, I visualised it was a man. I then heard what I thought was a chain with keys on it jangling and a sound as if he was out of puff, like he had just walked up ten flights of stairs. When it reached the bottom, all was quiet, but we knew someone was there, so we sat tight. It felt like forever. Eventually we went out to investigate but couldn't see anything. As we were trying to figure out what the hell had just happened, the drum behind us gave a massive bang. We then fled out of the room and straight through the exit door that led outside setting the alarm went off. I had never known the alarm to go off before despite the door being opened on many occasions. The next day my mum was raging as she was both cleaner and cook and had to clean up the mess. I felt like a criminal mastermind but never told anyone as the janitor got called in from home.' Like this story, I am certain there are others out there and hope to hear them in the future.

And now back to town and a story from the former Millets store at the east end of Union Street. While working there, former employee, Kelly, told me that in the mid-90s she had several creepy encounters. The manager (possibly winding up her young staff) would regale them with spooky stories and often told them about the ghost who was supposed to haunt the building. The staff took it with a pinch of salt though no one particularly liked going into the stock room. It was noted that things would often randomly fall off shelves or be found strewn on the floor and an inexplicable pungent smell of cigar smoke could be detected.

Sometime later Kelly was doing a mock 'interview' with the manager for a school project, and as part of this was taken for a tour of the building. This is what happened. 'We went to the basement and the atmosphere felt a little uneasy, without warning the temperature began to drop. At that point we had been taking photographs and the conversation had turned to the subject of ghosts. At that precise moment an overpowering smell of cigar smoke filled the space, and we bolted. Upon developing the film there was a strange flamelike figure on the image which stood next to my boss. It really frightened her and after a short time she handed her notice in.' During our conversation she stated that unfortunately the photo is at present lost as it was tucked away years ago.

Heading east we reach the Castlegate area, the most historic part of the city and no stranger to paranormal sightings. Buildings reputed to be haunted include the Tolbooth, Marischal Court, Marischal College, Victoria Court and the Town House to name but a few which I have previously covered. Always on the lookout for something new, I was passed on the following story from an ex-resident of the area now living in Edinburgh, who shared a rented property at the end of Union Street while at university. Sitting in front of historic Shiprow the building had been modernised, and contained none of the Victorian features one would expect of a property of its age. It was while living there she described what she thought was the outline of a friendly child waving at her, and though initially freaked out she put it down to a dream. Or was it? This is what she told me: 'It was an attic flat, internally it was modern, and my bedroom was small with a Velux window. The child was sitting on my desk, and it was like an outline. I had a wall of photographs above the desk which I could see through it. I thought she would have been about two or three. I remember it felt friendly, but I put on my light and television as I was scared. My flatmates however didn't experience anything. However, in the week running up to it I could hear what sounded like drawers being opened and shut in the room to my left when there was no one in. After the sighting, the noises stopped altogether. Fast forward and I start researching my family tree. Turns out my great grandparents lived back-to-back with this building. I was told my grandfather was the youngest of four boys. Upon more research I discovered he had three other siblings who all died at that address, two infant girls and a toddler boy. I think boys had longer hair back then. Coincidence? Perhaps, but had I not experienced this, I wouldn't have looked for them.'

Still in the immediate area, the next story was related to me by former cleaner Chris who worked for Aberdeen City Council. The sightings took place in the Town House, and I had long heard rumours about it being haunted so was delighted to hear at last someone backing up what I had heard. Notable for its grand interior staircase, the building was completed in 1865 and partially covers the old Tolbooth Prison which is now incorporated into it. Full of rich architectural gems, the entrance hall contains a large statue of Queen Victoria which has over the years moved to several locations, no doubt leaving her unamused. It is a cavernous building, and one would imagine due to its age is obliged to have a few ghosts.

This is what the witness explained, 'a year ago I was an early morning cleaner for the council starting off in St Nicholas House, where each cleaner had a whole floor to themselves, it was a bit of a workload to get through. Anyway if someone from the Town House was off for whatever reason then occasionally we would be asked to go over and cover for them and a lot of long standing cleaners would flatly refuse, let's just say there were whispers of it being haunted, For whatever reason (I kidded myself I was good at my job) I was eventually transferred to the old part of the Town House. To be honest my initial reactions were, why doesn't anyone want to work there. The workload was far less, the cleaning areas allocated being much smaller, though I soon found out why people didn't want to work there. You entered in the morning through the new part of the building up to the first floor and along the tunnel that runs above Concert Court (a cobbled lane that separates both the old and new buildings). I would go left along the corridor and downstairs to the cleaning cupboard which would take me to the ground floor at the bottom of the stairs. On the left there was a door that would take you out to Concert Court and directly across was the door to the Society of Advocates. To the right was an open plan office and at the end a passage which led to the toilets and a small kitchen. Straight on led to another larger office and to Broad Street, and further on two more which led to the vestibule and Union Street.'

He continued, 'Now the door at Concert Court used to shake violently but I would just put this down to the wind or a passing bin lorry. What was unnerving and hard to describe unless you had felt something similar, was that in that first office, you'd often get the overpowering sensation of being watched. It emanated from the passageway to the point you didn't want to turn your back to it. I really cannot describe this too much without sounding like I am over exaggerating. It literally messed you up. I even shouted for it to go away. One morning while I was busy hoovering in the second office, I just got this feeling and looking up saw what could best be described as a shadow figure strolling down the centre of the office. I briefly saw it and just stood there stunned in a, "did I just see that" moment before I legged it out of the there.

Now I am not saying I categorically saw a ghost, but I did report if afterwards. My supervisor eventually confessed there had been other stories, but she downplayed them and as expected my tale was spread amongst the other cleaners. I spoke about it with a few of them and some were unfazed or indifferent while others were of the, "it's not the dead you should be afraid," variety. Some of them told me stories including one of a cleaner who opened the door to the stairway leading to the Minstrel's Gallery and saw a figure of a man standing there and the cleaner never returned (perhaps this was the person rumoured to have quit their job). What was interesting was that a few council workers having heard of my experience approached me at the end of my shift to talk about it. One said that apparently in the same office they had seen the figure of a man sitting facing the passageway while another said that most workers in that office would not work alone or late. I got moved to the office above soon after which was not as atmospheric but given the cleaning cupboards right next to the stair leading down, I did once or twice hear the door shaking violently and what sounded like a shouting voice, but that must have been the wind eh?'

Another council building conveniently situated opposite the Town House, was St Ncholas House the former HQ of Aberdeen City Council. Never a bonnie building it dwarfed its neighbours in what was once a beautiful street and after its demolition some years back it took with it, its only ghost story. Described as a modern looking spirit, the incident was duly reported and for a short time staff were somewhat anxious at the prospect of meeting her in the lift. The witnesses, both female council employees who had never met until that occasion, described seeing a dark-haired woman enter the lift ahead of them. She was completely solid and so they had assumed she was a fellow worker. On opening the door to join her both were taken aback to find the lift empty. One was quoted as saying, 'We were both very spooked by it and were holding on to each other. I had never even seen the other woman before. I asked the other woman if she had seen the figure go into the lift and she said yes.' A council spokesperson later said that they had never heard of a ghost haunting St Nicholas House, but they had heard rumours of a ghost in the Town House. The Reverend Angus Haddow chairman of the Scottish Fellowship of the Scottish Psychical and Spiritual Studies said: 'If this ghost walked into a lift, she is presumably a modern apparition who is accustomed to using a lift.' Previously there had been a sighting of a woman supposedly floating through the similarly named St. Nicholas church yard, though the only connection appears to be that they both just manifested once.

Almost next door, but now hidden in a tangle of questionable new architecture sits the lovely Provost Skenes House. A 1545 town house it is one of the last survivors of the Guestrow which was decimated in the slum clearances of the last century. Town planners like Sir Patrick Geddes from Edinburgh, faced similar issues, however he chose to argue for 'conservative surgery,' rather than demolition which the city still benefits from today. It was while working there that I had the opportunity to interview several colleagues about their experiences and though I have already written about those in previous publications I wanted to include a few here for the uninitiated. The house known as Cumberland House has had a turbulent history including being taken over by the 'Butcher Cumberland,' whilst heading to Culloden. It was at varying points also tenements, a 'doss house,' and of course home to one of Aberdeen's wealthiest merchants, Provost Skene. Sightings of apparitions were for a time commonplace however in recent years the building underwent a series of unsympathetic changes. Did the spirits show their displeasure during this process or flee in disgust, I cannot say, but either way I can sympathise. Some fifteen years ago however, that was a different story.

In the first scenario a lone visitor approached the reception, asking if there was an event being held upstairs, and if so when would it finish? The attendant then asked which room she was referring to, to which the tourist replied, the painted gallery. This beautiful room, one of the best preserved in Scotland, attracted at the time many visitors and academics and she had travelled some distance specifically to see it. Perplexed the museum assistant then asked what she meant by an event. The woman then explained that on reaching the door to the gallery she found she could only open it a few inches because of the crowd inside. She then described them as wearing old fashioned clothing. On hearing this the attendant quickly took her upstairs where the room was found to be empty. Perplexed, the visitor was then assured she was the only person in the building so far. Interestingly the room was thought to have been used as a place of worship.

Sometime later another visitor had a similar experience while touring the house, where upon entering a small dressing room she encountered a ghost. At the time, the room, notable for its beautifully painted wood panels contained nothing but a single chaise longue and it came as quite a shock to see an elderly woman sitting upon it. Dressed in black with a crinoline bonnet upon her head the spirit remained completely unaware of the visitor's presence. Rushing downstairs in fright the subsequent investigation again found nothing. Perhaps my favourite though is the following, which was recounted to me by attendant Dorothy, who having worked there for many years had a particularly memorable experience whilst locking up. Now at closing time and in the process of switching off lights she heard the rustling sound of silk approaching along the corridor. Much to Dorothy's shock a woman in a voluminous dress then stepped into the room who she later described as looking surprised, blinking once, before vanishing. Dorothy later told me that after the initial shock she quickly locked the premises before leaving. What I have described is only the tip of the iceberg and I remain convinced it was, and hopefully still is, one of Scotland's most haunted buildings.

Heading back up Union Street we arrive at the former TSB Bank on Union Terrace where the following took place. Dawn, who having worked at the branch for many years described to me several instances of paranormal activity within the building that was witnessed by colleagues. The building, at least externally, may seem a little austere but inside behind the public area lies a beautiful example of late Victorian banking architecture complete with wood-lined boardrooms. The building also has five floors and a basement, the perfect place to get lost in. This is what I was told. 'I worked at TSB on Union Terrace; it had five levels and had been added to over the years. Now nothing happened till changes started on level one, to make a private business lounge. Walls were knocked down in the process. Our cleaner, an older woman called Carol, kept seeing people and hearing noises, it got to the point where she was so freaked out, she handed in her notice and left. We were then banned from talking about the ghost. The next incident of note happened was when we had our lift maintenance. It was a company from Newcastle who did the repairs as it broke quite often. I was in the tearoom at the top of the building eating lunch when the lift man came in white as a sheet. He was shaking and said he didn't believe in ghosts, but had I heard anything about the building? I quietly told him about the cleaner and he told me that while he was in the loft area something caught his eye, and he saw a tall man wearing a top hat and a black coat. He was terrified.'

Later several further uncanny incidents unfolded including one involving a co-worker who had to stay back on a Saturday as the fire alarm was playing up. While there she took the lift to the tearoom and was in the process of making tea when the lift started up before travelling down to the basement. Apparently, this would only be possible if someone in the basement had pressed the button there. Being the only one in the fully locked building she declined to investigate, perhaps the sensible choice. Dawn described the building as having a creepy atmosphere at times a sentiment echoed by other former employees. Today it lies derelict waiting to welcome new owners who I suspect may find they are not the only ones residing there.

While speaking recently to Kieran Begg, podcaster for 'Eerie Earth,' and a long-term researcher of the paranormal, he kindly passed on some interesting stories, the first of which being from his home city, Aberdeen. I should point out that he is firmly on the fence when it comes to the paranormal and maintains a healthy scepticism though his long-term interest was probably fostered at an early age by encounters like these. I was told that while at school he would occasionally 'bunk off,' with his best friend, preferring to hang out and play video games. At the time his friend lived in St Swithin Street, a Victorian tree-lined thoroughfare built from the city's grey granite. The story he now relates in his own words.

'On the day in question, we had decided to skip class in the afternoon, naughty I know but it was sports and anyone who knows me, knows I do not play sports. So that would have made the day a Wednesday. We had decided at lunch time to go to my friend's house. His name was Chris and lived in a very large house in the west end area of the city. His father was the co-founder of an oil company and in the nineties and early noughties that meant you had a lot of money. His house used to be an old folk's home and was a four story, six-bedroom, four-bathroom mansion, I suppose you would call it. I never saw it as that though, nor did I ever see his family as being millionaires (which they were) Unfortunately, his grandfather had passed away, only recently so it was still raw for the family and his Mum and Dad had ventured down to England for the week to help sort things out. So, there was no one in house, no one to catch us skipping school.

We entered through the front door, and just to be sure he yelled "Hello!" but got no response. We went into the kitchen and turned on the oven to the desired temperature and waited for the oven to heat up. While it was heating up, Chris wanted to take his pet rat, Dr Dre, out of his cage. So, we went up to his bedroom, in the converted attic. It was essentially a flat, it had two bedrooms, an office, a kitchen, and a bathroom. I was always very jealous of this space. We took the rat down to the smallest bathroom in the house (which was still a reasonable size) and let it run around the floor. I was standing next to the door, with my back against the wall and my hands in my pockets. Next to me was the pull string for the light in the bathroom. This room was between two bedrooms so had no windows, so when the lights were off it got very dark in there. When he was finished letting the rat have free roam in the bathroom, he put him back in his cage and brought the hoover in from the corridor and started to clear up the sawdust, not wanting the evidence of our truancy to be left behind. He flicked the switch on when suddenly the room was plunged into darkness.

Chris yelled at me as he was hoovering to turn the light back on. I obliged thinking that I must have turned the light off with my shoulder. I then decided I was being more of a hindrance than a help so stood outside of the bathroom in the hallway, watching as he finished clearing the mess. Suddenly the light went out again with a loud click. He turned to me ready to shout colourful profanities my way, when he realised, I was standing at the top of the stairs, a good twelve feet away from the light. Chris stood, glued to the spot, the hose of the hoover in his hand, his eyes were wide, and his jaw slack. He then threw down the hose and bolted from the room, nearly knocking me over and leapt down the stairs. I followed in hot pursuit bursting into the kitchen where the door clattered against the wall leaving an indent in the plaster. Downstairs the sound of the hoover could still be heard above us. We discussed what happened and tried to come up with an explanation, but we could not quite reach one. Then as we were talking, we noticed something, something was different, the house was quiet. The hoover had turned off.

After a while we decided to go and investigate and so we slowly crept up the stairs. We reached the top of the stairs and the hoover was still where we left it, but it wasn't running. We concluded that we must have imagined it, we must have turned the hoover off, and the sound of it was just still playing in our minds. That was the only explanation.

We shrugged it off and Chris finished off hoovering the bathroom. When the same thing happened, the light clicked on and off and again we bolted, this time we were certain that we had left the hoover on as we could hear it running. We decided we had to investigate it, to find out why this was happening, but this time Chris decided to take a large, bladed kitchen knife. I said something along the lines of "What the hell is a knife going to do against a ghost?" he replied with a shrug of the shoulders and said, "it might not be a ghost." At this, I grabbed a knife too. Then we discovered why it was silent, the hoover had been unplugged from the wall, the plug sitting neatly next to the hoover, the wire had been wrapped up and neatly placed on top the cylindrical bodice of the hoover. We started shouting around the house for his brother, whom we thought may have come back from school and was messing with us, knowing we were skiving from class. No response. We then checked every single room of the house, but we got no response. We started down the stairs, but when we got to the half landing, from the corridor which was now at our head height, we heard footsteps charging towards us, muffled on the carpet but definite and loud. We threw the knives on the ground, bolted down the stairs taking two at a time and bursting through the kitchen door, bolted out into the garden.

Looking back, I could clearly see in the kitchen window, his mum had a bunch of Lilie's she had received from friends for the loss of her father-in-law, but behind the flowers I could see an old woman, her hair was pure white, and crazy like Albert Einstein. She wore a baby blue nightie and seemed to be tending to the flowers, which were moving as she touched them. We could not see any features on her pale face. Without stealing my vision away, I asked Chris if he was seeing what I could see, a very numb nod confirmed my suspicions. We quickly bolted through the back door of the garden and charged along the lane at the back of the house, leaving the horrors within.

Chris returned home later that day when he knew his brother would be home and he told me later that the atmosphere in the house had totally changed and was peaceful and normal. It took me a few weeks before I could pluck the courage to return to his home.' A terrifying incident but there was more to follow as he later explained.

'Two weeks later I went back to his house for a catch up. On that night there was another guy there, his name was Craig. We were sitting watching music videos on MTV. A few weeks prior the family had sadly lost their pet which was an Old English Sheep Dog and as they were sitting, Craig turned to us and said "Christian, do you have a dog?" His eyes instantly began to well up and after taking a deep breath replied, "no, she died a few weeks ago, why?" Craig then replied, "I have just seen a dog run up the stairs!" Kieran then asked him what kind of dog he saw. "I don't know, it was big and fluffy."

Still in the granite city, this creepy tale was told to me some years back and having previously worked in the Sunnybank area of the city as a tutor I knew the location very well. Sitting within the nearby community garden is the 'Gibberie Wallie,' or Gingerbread Well. The last time I was there, it looked a little forlorn, having been graffitied upon, but back in the 1940s it was a little different and was surrounded by trees. The following was described to me by a former local Edith Mustard who I had the pleasure of working with in several community groups over many years. During one conversation she told me the following which occurred when she was a young girl. This is what she said.

'I remember taking Jim (her younger sibling) out in his pram and we went down to look at the "Witches House." This was an old ruin, like a shack that sat behind the well and was surrounded by trees. Years before an old woman had lived there and I suppose she was teased and thought of as a witch.

The local kids were scared and used to dare each other to go there. Even though the house was gone we were still all wary. So, as I said we were near the house when a tall figure stepped out from behind a nearby tree. His face was indescribable and not human and to this day I have never forgotten it. He had this moonlike face and this huge split mouth, very thin and narrow and incredibly wide. He put his finger up to his lips and went shhhhhh! Like it was telling me to be quiet. It then stepped back and was gone. Well, I never moved so fast in my life. I was terrified. Even today I can't explain what it was, but it was unnatural.' A terrifying encounter which she told me is still fresh in her mind today despite the passage of time.

Our next tale took place in 1995 and as is often the case came to light through a series of coincidences. I already featured this story in a previous book however it is quite exceptional. In January 2008 I was taking photographs of the remains on an old hotel on Carmelite Street Aberdeen when I got chatting to the site manager Ian. During our conversation he related to me an incident that happened to some of his friends in the early 1990s at the Torry Battery. This incident involved multiple apparitions. At the time we were unable to complete the interview, so I returned a few days later and as we sat in the Portacabin that doubled as their office/canteen, I began by asking him to recount the story. He spoke in detail about the incident and on finding out that I was a serious researcher admitted that he had in fact been present himself that night. I assured him that I was taking his story seriously and mentioned a prior tale from the same location in which a biker named Sandra had gone there one evening with three friends. As they were hanging around having a cigarette two young girls entered by the main gate and walked right past them. After some time, the girls did not reappear and as there was only one entry/exit point to the walled Battery the four friends went to have a look. The girls had vanished. In panic they fled off on their bikes, convinced the two pale looking girls had been ghosts. Later stopping in the Duthie Park they chained their bikes and went for walk only to be alerted minutes later by the sound of an engine revving. Running back, they found one of the bikes on its side with the chain randomly snapped in half. They then quickly sped from the park convinced something supernatural had just occurred. This was the tale I recounted though I had not mentioned the witness's name. While I was telling him the story, the only other worker in the bothy, a young lad, immediately spoke up and asked if the lady I was referring to was called Sandra. I confirmed it was and he explained that she was his closest friend's grandmother. Some might call that co-incidence but if so, that is one hell of an example. He then told me he was aware of the 'motor bike incident' having heard the story first-hand before. Ian then began to describe his experience, and I have been given permission to repeat it in full.

'It was in the summer of 1995, and I was an apprentice at the time. We used to meet down at the breakwater near the mouth of the harbour and stay out playing football and having parties. On this night there were three of us heading towards the breakwater, myself and my two mates, Kevin Porter and Alan Black. It was a perfect night in the height of summer, no breeze and still hot. It was starting to turn dark and as we were running late someone suggested cutting through the Battery. We were walking through the Battery when out of the corner of my eye I noticed Alan looking at something. We were stopped in our tracks by the sight of a group of people wearing old-fashioned clothing, like out of the television programme 'Foyle's War.' There were women wearing long dresses, just standing there, and a soldier standing nearby wearing army greens and a cap. There were others wearing flat caps. We were rooted to the spot and though I suppose it only lasted seconds, time seemed to stand still. It was surreal and though not exactly frightening. The air was perfectly calm, and I felt at peace. The strangest thing was that there were also children playing, and one wee boy wearing what looked like plus fours and of Asian appearance was running along with a hoop which he was directing with a stick. Like an old-fashioned toy. The only noise I could hear was the sound of the hoop rattling on the ground and the stick hitting it. We looked at each other and bolted across the Battery over the other side and ran all the way to where our mates were. When we arrived, we were breathless, and my friends looked pale. We told the rest of them what had happened, and they laughed and thought we were winding them up. After some persuasion they agreed to come back with us and so they did. Between us running to our mates and returning must have only taken around ten minutes but when we got there the place was deserted. There was no sign of life not even a crisp packet on the ground, silence. My mates continued to dispute what we saw claiming that it must have been someone making a film. They did not believe us, but we knew it wasn't a film set as there were no cars or vans about, nowhere for anyone to go. There is no way they could have cleared the place out in the ten minutes it took us to return. The experience has stuck with me and though it felt more surreal than frightening, we were alarmed to an extent.'

It goes without saying that both military personnel and civilians used the battery in the past, so the descriptions provided are very accurate. Perhaps what was witnessed will never again be repeated, maybe it was the right combination of time and the elements that opened this window to the past. If that is the case, I suggest that Ian was very lucky indeed. The Battery which was built in 1865 in response to a potential attack by the French during the Napoleonic Wars was a barracks for many years, and in peace time provide basic housing for homeless families. Greyhope Road Trust now operates a wildlife watching centre from the Battery which has helped elevate what was in recent times, a forlorn area.

But before we go, the following was recently described to me by local Brian Battensby and if nothing proves you can't keep a good ghost down, well certainly not in the vicinity of the Battery.

On that occasion, while visiting with a friend to take photographs around the harbour mouth and the battery, they later parted company with Brian heading off towards the old jetty downhill from the Battery. He said: 'I was there for around ten minutes or so when an oldish man appeared who was wearing what I would have described as a Crombie type coat though it could have been from the 1800s.' He went on to say that he had not heard nor noticed the man until he stood beside him. The man then proceeded to talk and in doing so began to mention the ferry timetables and how different they were on Sundays. Afterwards he moved on to the subject of trains and began chatting about Kittybrewster Station, which of course is long gone. Somewhat perplexed, Brian listened as the man continued his discourse describing a factory Brian had never heard of and of gathering berries to sell in Torry. All the while Brian remained somewhat bemused. He told me later. 'What went through my head as he was speaking was, are you real?'

Even stranger was that during the conversation a family with a lurcher type dog walked past. The dog apparently gave the old man a wide berth and instead ran over to see Brian. He indicated to me that the family appeared to be unaware of the other man's presence and carried on by. He finished by saying: 'The old man then said goodbye and started walking back towards Torry while I went the opposite way back to the car park at the Battery. On looking back, I couldn't see him. I can't remember the ferries at Torry, nor can I remember the station at Kittybrewster. I remember the buildings but not as a working railway.'

To the north of the city is the suburb of Bridge of Don, most of which is relatively new. However, when you first cross the bridge and turn left, there are several streets where the buildings are akin to those in Old Aberdeen. There, set back from the road, are several beautiful Georgian structures and quaint cottages including Glover House. Thomas Glover known as the Scottish Samurai who was responsible for modernising the Japanese Navy, providing ship building and trade opportunities. Nearby sits another impressive property, Bridgefield House, former home of Laura Mahady who told me the following.

'I lived in Bridgefield House, Balgownie Road between 2006 and 2019. The house was built around 1764 and comes with some history commensurate with its age. When we first moved in there was something about the guest bedroom and the drawing room on the first floor. I said nothing about my feelings, but my three teenage children quickly expressed the same opinions. On a few occasions when I was downstairs for example, I heard a woman's footsteps coming from the drawing room going along the hall and down the stairs, not only did I hear them there but also while tidying in the guest bedroom. I have never had experiences like this in any of the other houses I have lived in despite them being old, and my dogs responded accordingly. One night I woke to find a small very plump middle-aged woman standing in the bedroom. She had a long pale blue dress on and a long white apron and a little cloth cap that tied under her chin, covering tight curly hair. After a while she vanished.'

Soon after, sightings of people became more prolific particularly in the bedroom and her daughter who had rooms in the basement also complained of visitations in the night. Her husband a chemical engineer continued to deny the house was haunted despite mounting evidence until one night when he was shaken from his sleep by a man. After that there were no more sightings which begs the question did these former residents just want to prove their existence? She went on to say.

'I am an academic who worked at the University, and I was eventually moved to an open plan office at Foresterhill Hospital. The bound copy of my thesis vanished from my workstation, and I looked everywhere for it. I then turned the house upside down. Six weeks later I came home one evening and there was my thesis sitting on top of a pile of books in the living room. There were other incidents including internal doors being inexplicably shut and a strange feeling of claustrophobia or feeling tapped. The woman I saw was a stranger to me. I had a strong feeling that in some way she was connected to the house. She wore a big white apron, so I assumed she was possibly a cook.'

In the 1940s the council bought the lower part of the garden to allow them to put Balgownie Road in and it was further noted that by the 1940s the house was being used to help rehabilitate officers who had been injured in the war. With its age and multiple uses it is not unthinkable that some of those same spirits may be present today.

Crossing back over the bridge we head back along King Street to Old Aberdeen and the Spital. The Spital an ancient thoroughfare named after a medieval leper hospital has its fair share of ghost stories. One of my favourites was first brought to my attention by author Norman Adams in Aberdeen's first proper ghost book, The Haunted Neuk. The story has been mentioned in several subsequent publications since and concerned the Argo family, who lived in the Spital. During the initial interview, Mr Argo described a series of events which took place in 1966 when living at a property there with his wife and four children. At the time, the building was known to have been rebuilt and next door to it was an old bakery from which the owner plied his trade. All very handy, however his assistant soon made it clear he was unhappy when working alone. Mr Argo was no doubt surprised to hear of his employee's reticence particularly given his excuse, that the building was haunted. Whether Mr Argo believed him or not at first is a moot point for soon after he had his own unforgettable experience.

It was while sleeping in the living room one night that John Argo woke with a start. Staring ahead he clearly saw a man materialise from a wall cupboard before entering the room. The figure then proceeded to walk across the room before fading. The image however stayed firmly planted in his mind and he later described him as being a man of short, round stature, wearing a gaberdine coat wrapped tightly around his waist with string. Strangely he was also leading a black and white dog, He was not wispy, smoky or see through as is often reported, but solid, like a real person. His sleeping wife remained unaware. After a conversation with a neighbour in which he described the apparition, he was told that it would have been Mr Alexander, a former resident who had lived next door. The phenomena slowly faded as time progressed however a mere two doors up other spooky occurrences took place some years later with the appearance of a woman wearing 19th century garb. On this occasion she made a grand entrance, stepping down from the ceiling as if traversing stairs which would have existed at the time. The building at one point was thought to have been connected to a house of correction.

Still in the Spital, the following was passed onto me recently by Jeanette Craig who lived at number 90 from 1986 to 2009. The flat situated just outside St Peters' Cemetery and while living there she described an outbreak of poltergeist activity that lasted for years. Others in the communal area had also claimed to have seen what appeared to be Victorian figures. This is what she said: 'On moving in, my daughter who was thirteen at the time opted for the smaller bedroom as she felt freaked out by the vibe in the one overlooking the graveyard. The activity was centred around the kitchen and my bedroom. We were wakened in the night by the pots, which were in the cupboards, banging and clanging which would then appear on the worktop. I also began to feel a presence which was constantly behind me. As a child I used to sleep with my right foot hanging out over the bed and I was, on at least four occasions, woken by my foot being pulled by very cold hands. When I told my partner, at the time, he did not believe me, so we swapped sides. He quickly swapped back as he thought he felt something. There were many other incidents over the years. For example, my daughter's cat would not go past the middle landing and would sit staring at something, before it would back up on itself and run in a typical, scaredy cat fashion. I learned to live with these strange happenings. At other times door handles would move and I would get the sensation of someone blowing in my ear and the pet dog would howl and get upset. Later, my partner left, and my children grew up and moved on, so I was living alone.'

By this point the phenomena showed no signs of letting up and often the kettle would go on by itself, the toilet flushed by its own and on several occasions tiny glass shards appeared on the bed. Alarmingly she also woke on one occasion struggling for breath as the duvet had been tucked around the back of her head. She told me that she had felt like she was being held there. Distressed by the incident she then undertook some research on the area where she discovered there had been a leper colony situated on nearby Nelson Street. She further read about a potential secret tunnel which ran under the Spital, once use for transporting bodies. As a prison officer at the time, she discussed the strange happenings with a visiting minister, who regularly attended the prison. He suggested she try sitting in the area with the most activity and open the window. He then instructed her to light a candle and in doing so speak to the entity in a calming voice and ask it to leave.

She later said that during the process she was terrified, unsure what would happen, and half expecting to hear a whoosh! as the trapped spirit made its way out of the window, but there was nothing. She then sat for 10 minutes reassuring whatever it was that it was time to go, before being asked to be left in peace. After blowing out the candle she then retired for the night and had the most peaceful sleep she had for a long time. The next six years of her tenancy passed without incident.

She added: 'I remember visiting a psychic in her home at North Anderson Drive, maybe a year after taking up residence. I was sceptical but was there to support my friend. The psychic was very wary of me and walked around me twice moving her hands around and then asked if I had a twin sister. I said no. She then said I'm sorry I can't give you a reading as you have a bad spirit with you!'

I do like haunted hotels, they're almost on par with theatres as hot beds, no pun intended, of spookiness. This story comes from Marie Middleton who in the early eighties was a live-in chef at the Station Hotel. I know the building well and at one point it was pretty much the place where anybody who was anybody would stay. In the 80s it was also a decent venue for gigs and hosted some great bands while in more recent times it catered for oil workers who after imbibing copious beers would pour themselves onto the nearby trains, heading south to meet their dutiful wives. The enforced pleasure of their company undoubtedly ruining everyone's journey.

Marie stated: 'The staff rooms were on the 5th floor and opposite my one was a door that covered up an old staircase. I don't know where it originated from, but it was sealed off as I recall. Sometimes, usually when I was on an early start at 5.30 am, I would hear heavy footsteps coming up the stairs before the door would bang open and somebody would start banging on my door, shouting "get up, get up." When I went to look there was never anyone there and the stair door was always closed. I only opened my door a couple of times until I was told by another staff member that it was the ghost of an old guy who was hammering on the door who was supposed to be looking for someone. They always laughed it off, but to me it was as scary as anything I have ever encountered in my life.

Nearby in the Green, stands the Old Kings Highway. It's a great traditional pub and commensurate with its age has several ghosts. The encounters have been ongoing for years and I was passed on the following stories from customers and ex-employees. The first contributor is Chris who described the following while in the pub at around 3pm on a quiet Saturday afternoon. On visiting the bathroom, he felt three distinct tugs at his trouser leg above the right knee as he stood at the urinal. Perturbed he quickly washed his hands and headed back to the bar where the landlady noticing his expression asked if he was ok. He said he was but explained what had happened. She looked taken aback and asked if he was winding her up. When he said no, she then told him that a few years earlier a paranormal group held a vigil one night and the most common phenomena reported was that people had felt their trouser legs being tugged.

Another witness stated. 'One Thursday night I was sitting there having a few beers with a mate who had been offshore. We started talking about the weird things that had being going on such as voices being heard in the cellar which made certain workers unwilling to go down there. There were also the mysterious pools of water from no obvious source which were noted to have appeared on the dancefloor overnight. Then as we were talking there was this almighty bang, a huge noise like someone had whacked a 2x4 piece of wood across the bar at which point everybody jumped. I'm sitting at the bar looking down towards the quiz machine when I see a bottle of Britvic orange juice fly off the shelf. I start telling the landlady Tracy to watch her feet on the glass, as I assumed it had smashed on landing. The bottle however was still completely intact and was standing on the floor behind the staff.'

Another former employee, Grant, who worked there in the 90s described that on one particularly hot day he had gone upstairs to the bathroom and on leaving encountered what could only be described as a freezing cold spot. Somewhat taken aback he then noticed out of the corner of his eye, a white shadow which he was convinced looked like a young girl. He later said that to this day he never went back into that toilet. Another regular, Keith, also described an unexplainable incident on being tapped on the shoulder while alone at the bar. On turning he saw no one and from what I gather this happened on several occasions. Who or what is haunting the bar remains a mystery with some claiming it could be an ancient entity, such as a monk while others are not so sure. Recently for example I saw a compelling image of a figure sitting at a table which was taken during a function. It was glowing and human shaped. Could this be the mysterious entity?

My favourite story however, which has been corroborated by multiple witnesses, took place while a group of friends were chatting. Interrupted by one of their mobile phones going off, the recipient then checked to see who was calling and the name came up as, 'The Old Kings Highway.' Strangely the pub phone was still on the receiver at the time, and no one had touched it. The group then sat with bated breath for several moments until the phone rang off. Everyone laughed and someone joked that it was the ghost who had made the call at which point the lights at the end of the bar began to flicker, all accompanied by a sudden drop in temperature. Having popped in for a drink in November this year I was pleased to hear that 'Stevie,' as the ghost has been christened, is still making his presence known. With one of the current owners stating that a few days prior he witnessed what he took to be a figure, seen through glass of an adjoining door.

Next up is the Kincorth housing estate which at first look is much like any other, but surprisingly it has a rich hidden past including its ownership by Arbroath Abbey. I am pleased to say is an area rife with paranormal activity. In the late 12th century King William, the Lion founded Arbroath Abbey and gifted it various pockets of land throughout the Northeast of Scotland. The Abbot of Arbroath was overseer of these lands and money raised by leasing areas to various parties went to the church. Many years before the current urban sprawl, crops were grown in its rolling fields, tended by the monks who lived and worshipped in the area. Current street names reflect this, some of the most notable being, Abbotswell Crescent, Arbroath Place, and of course 'The Abbot', a local hostelry.

Unsurprisingly, tales of hooded figures have already found their way into the public consciousness, an early example through Peter Moss's book 'Ghosts Over Britain,' in which he recounted the tale of a cloaked beckoning figure. This incident took place in 1970 when local resident Mrs Gladys Ewen was taking her usual route to work at Morningfield Hospital. It was a quarter to six on a cold winter's morning when she left her home to wait at the nearby bus stop and as she approached, was shocked to see a figure standing in a nearby patch of grass. The tall, cowled form then beckoned her towards him with an outstretched arm and hypnotized by the sight, she wandered towards it, fixated by its looming presence. When she was around six yards from the figure it began to evaporate and dissolved into a mist which drifted off. The hypnotic spell now broken she took off towards her bus stop. On arriving at work colleagues were shocked to see her distress though whether anyone believed her is a matter of conjecture. After the initial shock she fell back into her usual routine and mercifully never saw the figure again, however similar figures have been seen in nearby Kincorth Circle, causing another local resident to flee in terror. The witness, a former community worker told me that one evening she had a memorable encounter, one that she has never forgotten.

She explained: 'I have had a few strange experiences during my life particularly around the Kincorth area which I would say have been of a supernatural origin. Some have also occurred in my place of work. But on this occasion, it took place in nearby Kincorth Circle. On the evening in question, I was walking along the street towards my home. I remember it being a very cold crisp night. It was dark although the lights illuminated certain parts of the road, and you could clearly see your breath due to the cold. I was the only person about, and the streets seemed unusually quiet. As I passed a block of houses something moving caught my eye and I glanced in between them into the 'backie' area. I clearly saw a cloaked and hooded figure which appeared to have no feet. It was floating along in the space between the houses. I was startled and not knowing what it was I quickened my pace. When I came to the next break in the buildings the figure was there again keeping abreast with me. I began to run and again glancing towards the garden at the next break in the buildings I saw the figure moving faster and keeping up with me. I panicked and bolted as fast as I could. I did not bother to keep looking for the figure, and by the time I reached home my heart was thumping in my chest. I still maintain it was the figure of a monk and can never forget the fact it floated rather than walked.'

The Dundee Courier supplied the following gem from late last century in which another Aberdeen home appeared to be haunted, this time on Canal Street. It was noted that the ghostly goings on attracted a massive crowds of gawkers estimated to be between 500 and 1000 people. For those unfamiliar with the location, it lies near the current Mounthooly Roundabout at the foot of the Spital. The area today is barely recognisable however with only a preserved granite entrance attached to a newer build as a nod to the past. Old images however show the street contained several ancient and interesting dwellings which had they been preserved would have made a fine street. News of the ghostly visitant soon attracted the attention of locals who then decamped outside the property. It soon transpired that the owners had been visited nightly by a spirit, 'who had disturbed the nocturnal slumbers of the household, making the night hideous and filling the bosoms of the inmates with the utmost terror and alarm,' or so it was written.

It all began when the maid was woken on hearing the soft tread of steps heading upstairs closely followed by the sound of a heavy thud on a table. She of course roused the household who soon recoiled in horror at the visible presence of a lady in a silk dress who was seen gliding into the room of the unfortunate maid, who then had her bed clothes pulled from her. Her story was affirmed by another servant within the house and the owner's son who also witnessed the apparition. Vigils were kept and in doing so, 'extraordinary sights were seen at midnight such as furniture dancing and skipping about and more than one watcher being slapped on the face for their troubles.' And so, with each new report the stories became more outlandish, and the readers credulity sorely tested. One witness went on to claim that the ghost had appeared in varying forms, firstly without a head and secondly with a head albeit a very small one. This ghost was also described as clutching at its throat across which were a series of vivid red gashes, 'after the manner of Banquo's ghost as seen in provincial theatre.' Another account stated that the ghost had related a tale of woe as to its demise and its bones should they be discovered and given a Christian burial would free it from its earthbound torment, though rather unhelpfully it did not suggest where to look. The more outlandish the story the bigger the crowd and soon the street was swollen with humanity. Further reports indicated that visitors then had their hats helpfully plucked of their heads by the ghost who had now began to act as a spiritual doorman if you like. The story, as was suggested, was likely the product of wicked rumour mongering though at the time several ministers read passages from the bible just to be certain.

Another Aberdeen tale, of the more sinister kind, took place at 14 Watson Street in early 1976. It featured in several sober articles at the time which described a terrifying ghost encounter witnessed by resident Diane Samat. The story was first reported in the Press and Journal at the time, and it frightened the hell out of me as a kid.

It was a one-off incident but was so terrifying it was never to be forgotten. Diane and her husband Isa who was Malaysian had not been long married and on moving into their flat they settled down to married life. All was well until one night when an apparition, in no uncertain terms, showed its displeasure. Describing her ordeal to a reporter afterwards she stated that she was awoken by a malevolent feeling and looking towards her bedroom door saw a tall elderly woman standing there. This is what she said: 'I did not believe what I was seeing so closed my eyes and when I opened them, I found the figure standing over the bed.' She later described her as a tall, thin woman, who wore a yellow and grey dress with the sleeves rolled up, glowing within as if lit by an internal flame. Diane was then horrified to find that the woman's bony ice-cold fingers had now locked onto her throat and looking up she described seeing the elderly woman's face contorted in anger. During the ensuing drama her husband rather unhelpfully continued to sleep peacefully by her side. Desperate to scream she slowly felt herself being strangled and on the point of blacking out the figure then relinquished its grip. Diane later recalled grabbing the woman's wrists which she described as feeling like cold putty. Now able to shout out she witnessed the figure drift towards the door before melting away. Bruised, battered, and terrified she described the woman to her husband who knew who the culprit was instantly. It had been Mr. Samat's grandmother. Afterwards there was strangely no bruising found on Diane's throat, but her chest and neck was nevertheless painful to touch for some time. She also stated that she was unable to sleep with the light out for some weeks, The spirit thankfully never reappeared I suspect it was satisfied as it had set out to do what it intended, show her displeasure.

Still in Aberdeen and a story I first heard many years ago. Unearthed by the venerable Norman Adams, the building on Kingsgate is still there today. A nice example of Victorian architecture it is situated in the city's West End and was converted into flats in recent times being one of a row of similarly appointed villas. The renovations were sympathetic however and a grand communal entrance hall complete with antique cabinet greeted householders on arrival. It was however an experience that sounded so full-on I admired the owner's tenacity in staying despite the elegant surroundings. Hideous screams heard by multiple tenants, destructive poltergeist activity and full-bodied apparitions were all experienced by multiple witnesses including the owner of the property in question.

According to the account, Walter, a successful businessman had barely set foot in the door when the first indications of something being amiss had manifested. On that occasion he had invited a colleague along to see his new abode and she had accepted. Inside the elegance of the surroundings was somewhat marred by what she later said was a deathly smell in the bathroom. The new owner noticing this also was perplexed, there was no reason for the pungent odour, at least none he could see, so surmising it was the carpet, he had it changed. The smell remained however its nauseous odour appearing randomly at varying times. On another occasion whilst having a bath the volume of his music system went up unexpectedly. Afraid to upset the neighbours he bolted through to the living room but before he could reach the dial it had helpfully turned itself down which he plainly saw. As an aside it was noted he had been listening to the Carpenters, which I suspect rapidly went from easy listening to uneasy listening.

On another occasion while leaving the flat, he quickly returned to pick up his bank card and in doing so saw 'a solid woman,' polishing the oak dresser. She kept her back to him, but he had a clear view and later described her as having her hair in bun, wearing a long ankle-length dress, and was aged between 20 and 30. She vanished after several seconds. Sometime later a friend named Ross stayed over and was peacefully relaxing upon a camp bed in the lounge when they were alerted by the sound of a horrendous scream coming from the hallway. Quickly racing downstairs, they found nothing.

In a further incident he described witnessing a glass candlestick being literally chopped in half then sent flying across the floor. Was the ghost angry and why was it so destructive he pondered? Certainly, he had done nothing that he could think of unless the refurbishment was the catalyst. Bearing this in mind, a conversation with neighbours revealed that one had heard the very same scream some time before and that she too had found nothing on investigating. On speaking to a third neighbour, he was surprised to find that she too had experienced the occasional visit by 'Jane,' as she was named. During the conversation he was told that the spirit was prone to playing with her late cat's ping pong ball. Now kept as a memento inside a dish it was not uncommon to find it placed around the room randomly on her return. She would also make her presence known by banging on doors which on investigation would stop abruptly. It was as she described like a sound coming from a different time. Several noted citizens were known to have resided there in the past including a minister and it goes without saying that the figure that was witnessed in the hall dressed like a servant. Why she remained there is difficult to ascertain and even more so if she was responsible for the horrendous scream, what terrible scenario was being replayed? It became clear though that as the interview progressed the householders had become accepting of their uninvited guest and in doing so her anti-social activities ceased. Perhaps she herself was equally accepting of their presence? I often contemplated contacting the current tenants out of curiosity to ask if they too have had any unusual experiences, but some might consider that a little unfair, would you?

As a footnote and perhaps to prove the haunted pedigree of the area Walter confessed to having seen another spirit, though in that instance it was next door. It transpired that on entering his flat on several occasions he had noticed the figure of an elderly woman, who appeared to always be seated at the upstairs window of an adjoining property. Her appearances were so regular he began to feel mildly irked and thinking she was being nosey, began to close his curtains. Later when he made enquiries as to who she was, he was somewhat taken aback to be told that the property was empty though it was allegedly haunted by the spirit of an elderly woman.

Gordon Lane demolished some years back was given the soubriquet of 'Poltergeist Alley' from locals who remembered tales of an alleged haunting which took place there in 1920. Aberdeen Central Library has a great collection of digitised vintage newspapers which are an invaluable resource and within those are numerous references to this case. It became, at least for a short while known throughout Britain and has joined the pantheon of great poltergeist stories since. But was it a real phenomenon, or the product of superstition and fakery? its locale became something of a national phenomenon being reported in such diverse papers at the Glasgow Herald and The Yorkshire Post. Having trawled through numerous papers and with some new information, what's most surprising is that the main protagonist, young John Urquhart may have been responsible for the 'haunting,' all along!

In 1920 Gordon Lane was one of many indistinguishable down-at-heel backwaters in the city. The Urquhart family Johnny, mum, dad and siblings lived in the top floor of a whitewashed cottage entered by a forestair. An image from the time, shows the occupants solemnly standing on said stair. For some reason I found it reminiscent of an image of the fictional family of 'Rand Hobart,' who featured in 'Night of the Demon,' arguably the best British horror film ever made.

It was on January the 11th 1920 that the Urquharts and their neighbours were first alerted to something being amiss by a violent thumping on the floor which was reported to sound like a hammer and on investigation it was claimed that Johnny had levitated while lying in bed. The Grants, neighbours from across the way corroborated the story after hearing the same noise, which continued at periodic intervals. The bed was allegedly seen rising and falling hitting the boards and so somewhat concerned Mr Urquhart then drove to the central police office to seek help. Quite what they thought of his story as it was blurted out remains unknown however soon after six constables, a sergeant and an inspector arrived. A logical bunch, they first scrutinised the roof and walls but after finding nothing untoward investigated the derelict blacksmiths shop below the property but drew a blank.

The 'invalid boy' as he was described was then moved to the back bedroom where it was said the sound followed him. He was by all accounts a poorly child and so during the ensuing weeks was known to have been left alone for extended periods while the family, press, spiritualists and anxious locals held court in the room next door. Crowds of idlers soon gathered as the news spread adding to the circus, and then soon after several spiritualists arrived. This only added to the mystique and for some nights they held seances to find out who the ghost was. It was then revealed that the property below now derelict had been used by a blacksmith some 50 years previously who had mysteriously vanished from his home. A long and protracted search ended when it was revealed that the unfortunate man's remains had been found in a wood near Countesswells, clutching a poison bottle in his skeletal hand. Inside his jacket a loaded pistol was recovered, and it was obvious he had taken his own life. The mediums soon discounted him from the proceedings, despite his grisly end, and so for some time the rapping's continued. Later it was reported that a perplexing incident occurred when a model motor car with which John had been amusing himself was dismantled and left lying on a nearby table. It was noted that at the time it would have been around 11pm. Some hours later they were awoken by a tinkling sound and then loud banging and on investigation found the car lying on the floor and now intact. Later that night at two in the morning loud knocks described like 'those coming from a hammer' dragged the family from their slumber. The story of course was quickly picked up by the papers and ran for several weeks but slowly fizzled out as the public's appetite for it began to wane. The mediums who attended however continued their vigil until out of nowhere one announced that the spirit, a friendly one, had merely wished to impart a message to the Urquhart's. The assembly gathered in an anticipation and was told the spirit was that of Johnny's late grandfather, who reminded them to look after their grandmother. Though positive it was somewhat anti climatic and probably not the exciting conclusion those who had followed the story from the beginning had wished for.

In the aftermath of the haunting, he became known as 'Johnny Ghostie,' though many believed he had created the phenomena himself. The more charitable or gullible, depends on which way you see it, believed he had attracted a malicious energy due to his troubles. This they suggested was because of several tragedies which occurred in the vicinity, including a van man found dangling from the rafters of a stable in nearby Gordon Street and a near neighbour who took a razor to himself, small wonder the area had the reputation it had. Interestingly, in 1989 a former resident of the street E T Shepherd, who was sixteen at the time of the disturbances, wrote a letter to the Evening Express paper stating that her mother was called in by Mrs Urquhart at the onset of the problems. She recalled that nothing untoward ever happened while John was in the room with them. She went on to say that at one point he was even caught jumping on the bed and on being discovered shouted, 'there's your ghost.' She later said, 'there was no ghost,' and that 'he would rock in his chair, jump on the bed and was never seen outside.' Looking back now it would appear that perhaps John, due to his erratic behaviour was responsible for creating the phenomena but for him the story doesn't end there.

In a disturbing twist of fate Johnny's erratic behaviour continued into adulthood and in doing so took a more serious turn when he was caught for a series of assaults against minors. It was on the 18th of January 1923 that the Press and Journal reported that the then 16-year-old message boy of 1 Gordon Place had pled guilty to indecently assaulting several young girls whose ages had ranged between 6 and 8 in various locations including Springbank Terrace, Albury Road and a 10-year-old in the Queen's cinema. The furious relatives of one of the victims then arrived unceremoniously at his home and beat him severely. In the aftermath they were arrested and soon Mrs. Catherine Mann, Bernard Mann, labourer, Robert Mann, a motor mechanic and Jane Mann all of Kintore Place were in court. During the proceedings one witness a Mrs Grassick stated how she had been shocked to see the injured boy at her door sometime later with his face described as a 'terrible mess.' Mrs. Catherine Mann then described that on the day of the attack her son had headed to Johns to have words, though she tried to dissuade him. On arrival her son had entered the property and struck the lad while she had remained outside. The accused now under caution was asked if 'she wasn't afraid that her son would hurt the boy?' she replied, 'no but I'm feart at ghosts.' The son was found guilty and duly charged.

In his final argument Johns solicitor stated that he (John) did not quite realise the seriousness of the offences and had been punished enough after one of the parents had given him a severe thrashing. The judge then ruminating said that had he been younger he would have received a sound birching but as it was, he was fined five pounds, not exactly a fitting punishment.

Sometime later John again appeared in court. Now seventeen and a labourer, he faced five charges of fraud, selling fictitious bags of peat to various householders while collecting the money in advance. His father suggested borstal might be a good idea as he was beyond his control. Later in the proceedings however his father changed his tune and suggested another chance was needed as he had never been in trouble before. This argument was quickly shot down however as we have already seen, with the fiscal reminding the forgetful father how his son had 'committed a series of grave offences already.' He was committed to pay three pounds of which he had two weeks to find or alternatively spend twenty days in prison. I'm not sure which alternative he chose, but he certainly chose a rocky path.

Sticking with Aberdeen and as a companion piece to the Gordon Lane poltergeist, I was interested to come across a very similar story in which the centre of the activity was in Shuttle Lane. Now demolished the building can only be seen in a few faded photographs from the time, it was a poor working-class area. The article described the extraordinary scenes which unfolded when over 500 people assembled near the home of a local, Mr Lamont. Why? because he believed it to be haunted and had openly claimed for several weeks that both he and his wife had been subject to all manner supernatural occurrences. Like the Gordon Lane fiasco some 18 months earlier the public appetite for such stories had remained unabated and so on the first night a ghostly flash mob arrived. With the street now crowded with gawking idlers the police had their hands full trying to persuade them to leave. They did so reluctantly only to reassemble sometime later. A gaggle of mischievous younger people then took great delight in entering the lobby where they proceeded to tap and make knocking noises on the wall. The owner now in a rage then took matters into his own hands by turning a hose onto them much to the delight of the throng while, 'one of the women in the house damped the ardour of the crowd with sundry buckets of water.'

Two spiritualists who had been sent for then arrived and the crowd roared cordially in their approval. Another media circus had begun. Inside a séance was held which by all accounts bore no fruit and in the wee small hours they literally gave up the ghost. Afterwards deliberate footfalls and the peculiar creak of leather was heard. The report stated that number of theories were then put forward as to the cause, though ultimately it was thought the noises were probably caused by rats.

The former Aberdeen Students Union, Broad Street is our next destination. Once a great venue where thirsty students could recover from their hard toil, ahem, it has lain unused now for many years, but back in 1963 it hit the headlines due to an alleged haunting. The reported claimed that the ghost had manifested itself to show its displeasure at a group of students using its beloved building as a base for preparing for a student show. I have in my time been to a few students shows myself and believe me I would have shown my displeasure too had I not been so polite. During this time the committee room had been taken over and several sewing machines installed. The seven volunteers tasked with producing hundreds of dresses for the event, soon found themselves literally chained to the machines. It was an unenviable task not made better by the appearance of what was thought to be a ghost. Locked doors were soon frequently found unlocked, lights flicked on and off and electric sewing machines started up on their own. To add to the chaos dresses were described as constantly being found 'thrown,' from their hangers and in one incident a 'beautiful salmon pink creation,' was found with a hole bitten out of it. Was it just sabotage from a disgruntled student?

It could have been, but Lyn Stephen wardrobe mistress at the time described a list of incidents and to prove her point, drew the reporter's attention towards one of the machines which had conveniently started up. It then whirred away happily until switched off. Most of the occurrences however took place in the evening and at first they naturally suspected faulty machinery. Because of this one machine was returned to the shop, but a thorough check found nothing, the mechanic stating afterwards that it should have worked properly. Later, another conversely defied their efforts to start it and after being pronounced dead, started working again. Soon after the sighting of a 'red shadow,' was then seen through the glass panel of the communications door and typically, the ensuing search proved fruitless. In another incident the supervisor enquired if anyone was wandering about the Union building, which had been securely locked. after footsteps were heard plainly walking around. Those present were quickly accounted for causing the supervisor further discomfort as minutes earlier she had been disturbed by loud knocking at her door.

Now to the Kaimhill area of the city, where I met with a former cleaner, Mrs. Horne some years back. While chatting she told me about her experiences while working in the original Kaimhill Primary School. Though the school is still there, it was completely rebuilt after the older one was demolished around fifteen years ago. I worked there on occasion, and it was typical of its kind, a good sturdy building with wide corridors, gym hall and stone staircases. One area, described as the red corridor due to its garish colour, was thought to be haunted and staff members often described hearing footsteps following them while working there. In one incident a startled cleaner turned around to speak to her colleague who she assumed was walking behind her to find nothing.

During our interview she described how there was one area in the upper floor that they avoided, due to sightings of a veiled figure. The description she provided was indeed terrifying and on one occasion while ascending the stairs she glanced up and saw a veiled woman, staring down at her. To say she received a shock would have been an understatement and on talking to colleagues she was surprised to find others had seen her too. Who the woman had been in life remains a mystery and by all accounts her sightings went when the building was demolished, as nothing has been reported since. There is perhaps one clue though, at the end of the street still stands Kaimhill Crematorium and the figure was described as looking like someone in mourning.

As I mentioned in the introduction, I had toyed with the idea of grouping the stories under location, theatres, homes etc and was originally going to do a chapter on shops and so would have called the following, 'messages from beyond,' but it was not to be. Anyhow we are still in the granite city and the following was provided by my friend, Catriona Platten who at one point worked in Hammerton stores (a popular deli) on Great Western Road. The time of the incident was around 2014 however it had been a shop for about 100 years. As the manager part of her duties included cashing up for the night in the downstairs office, which was situated in a maze of storerooms, all very dark old and creepy. Here is what she said, 'So one night when I was cashing up it was around 7pm all the lights were off and only the streetlights outside were illuminating the shop. It was winter so it was dark and as I ran upstairs to get my coat and bag; I was suddenly aware of a figure standing near the counter of the shop. I thought it was a customer at first, but the door was locked. The figure was a dark shadow rather than a real human, but it was around the same height and shape of an adult, it faded away almost immediately. At first, I put it down to a trick of the light and me being in such a rush. A couple of weeks later, again rushing to leave I was then faced by two figures in the same area but this time it was an adult and a child. I called out but the figures, but both just faded away. Both sightings didn't frighten me, and I felt calm as if I was caught in a different time like watching a film of Hammerton's from the past. The third incident was a couple of months later but this time I did not feel calm at all in fact I nearly shat myself. I was sitting in the office doing some spread sheets when I heard heavy footsteps walking quickly across the ceiling which would be the shop. I thought it was the owner coming back to check on something but looking on the CCTV I saw nothing. I immediately called out and then had a good look around, but nobody was there. I didn't hang around too long but felt stupid afterwards for fleeing from the shop. I didn't tell any of my colleagues about it until one told me about her spooky experiences. It then turned out that many of us had seen and heard things we couldn't explain. A lot of people were quite scared of being downstairs but weirdly it generally felt calm.' I was later told that apparently stock would often be lying on the floor when the owner arrived in the morning.

Again, in Aberdeen this story is linked to a tragic accident near Stonehaven. The question however remains if it was just coincidence or a genuine paranormal occurrence? For the record my moneys on the latter. The story was kindly passed on to me by local man, Rob, who described the events which took place on January 1971. On returning from work at approximately 21.30 in the evening he was surprised to be called upon by his brother Raymond and wife Aileen. They had never visited at that time before, which Rob found slightly strange. While chatting he received further visitors this time in the shape of his aunt and cousin who lived opposite. They had witnessed the arrival of Ray and Aileen and thinking something was wrong had decided to pay a call. Rob said, 'shortly afterwards, a friend of Ray's, Larry Pacetti who had been out for a walk with his dog, saw the light on so popped in for a chat. I could not understand what was going on as no one had ever visited me at that time of night. Suddenly Larry's dog a collie began to howl uncontrollably. We all found this funny as the dog was old and very quiet and none of us could recall it doing that before. I then went to put on the kettle and at that moment Ray jumped up and said he had heard a noise in the back bedroom. We got up and searched but could find nothing untoward. Shortly after there was a knock at the door, this time it was a guy called Hamish Mackay a reporter for the Evening Express and Press and Journal, who was also a friend of my other brother Christopher. Hamish would often meet Chris at my house but never at that time of night. I told him that Chris, who played in a band called the Corvettes, was away at a gig at RAF Edzell (village near Laurencekirk). Hamish gave me a puzzled look and said, "oh so you didn't know then!" He then told me there had been a horrific accident on the road outside

Stonehaven and that Chris had been killed. I was in shock and remember walking into the living room, just saying 'Chris is dead.' I heard what I thought were people screaming and laughing but really, they were crying. Until that point none of us knew about the accident. I concluded that something supernatural had arranged for us all to be together that night.' Terrible news to receive under any circumstances and stretches credulity to think it was just coincidence. Perhaps a higher source was at work.

Lastly in Aberdeen, a story from Mitchell Greg who after recently submitting this to a forum, allowed me to use it. It took place in 1995 in the children's ward at Aberdeen Royal Infirmary where he was recovering after being knocked down by a car suffering a broken leg, arm and nose. While lying in bed at night he witnessed an astonishing sight. He stated: 'I saw a group of around ten ghosts in the children's ward in the middle of the night, women of all different ages who were all beautiful, dressed in white, in what looked like uniforms. They walked around the beds talking amongst themselves. They then came to my bed, and one of them told another I would be okay. They then all stood around another boy's bed who I think had been in a fire. His face was half-burned, and he had a clear plastic screen around him.' After falling asleep he woke in the morning and noticed the boy had gone. He then spoke to the nurse on duty and asked her who the other people were who had been standing around the boy's bed. She then stated that she had been the only one of duty and then ran off crying.

Moving out of the city we now reach the suburb and Maryculter House. A rural area it has some interesting locations including the above which is now a hotel.

Interestingly it has been suggested that the house was built on the location of a college for the Knights Templar a religious order formed to protect pilgrims visiting the Holy Land. The land surrounding the hotel was thought to have been granted to the order by William the Lion in 1187 and today there are still fragments of their buildings in situ. The house itself has undergone some major changes since I visited as a child and has been expanded upon. It is also thought to be haunted and sightings of a male figure for example has been reported within the premises. But its outside where the action lies, with the grounds thought to be haunted by a Green Lady. Honoured by having a campsite named after her, courtesy of the City of Aberdeen Boy Scouts Association, who purchased the land for their use in the 1930s. One can imagine the type of stories that have been told around the campfire ever since. Who the green lady was in life is debateable, but one legend claims that she may have been a lovelorn Saracen princess who travelled from the middle east to be with a knight she had fallen in love with. In typical Romeo and Juliet fashion it is said they ended their lives on realising their romance was doomed. All very fanciful and typical of countless other tales however a recent conversation with an ex-resident provided me with something much more tangible. His name is Chris Lothian, and this is his story.

'Even though it has been over 40 years now and I had a few pints, it's still crystal clear in my memory. As I remember, the night in question was practically pitch black, so it must have been during the winter months. I had been in town that night and took the last bus home back to Culter as there were no buses on the South Deeside Road at that time and I started to walk home (about two miles). I think it must have been between 11 and 12 o'clock as the Mill Inn pub was still open so I went in and had a few pints. Theres a path from the Mill Inn caravan site which cuts about 20 minutes off the journey, so I decided to take it partly because it was a clear night. The path led back through Templar's Park and was spooky (we had grown up with all the ghost stories and legends associated with Templars, the green lady etc.)

The actual route from Templars to Maryculter is across a hill with no path so being dark I couldn't see a thing and I stumbled rather than walked up it. As I got to the top of the hill something made me look to the left and that's when I saw her. The usual stories to do with Templars were to do with a Saracen maiden following a Templar back from the crusades but the one I saw was that of a middle-aged woman dressed as a nun in full regalia, the black habit with a white wimple framing her face. She was standing in front of the trunk of a tree and must have been around 5ft tall. This bit sounds highly unbelievable, but I swear its true, she had a beautiful, serene smile on her well-lined face and was surrounded by an aura of bright incandescent light. I was so shocked and scared that I just ran off down the hill and almost shredded myself on a barbed wire fence. I told the story to everyone when I got back down to the house, but they just laughed and said I was just pissed and so I kind of dismissed it, but I've never forgotten it and the image is as clear in my mind today as it was over 45 years ago. Anyway, that's my story. Because the normal story is about the Saracen maiden, I could never figure out what a nun had to do with it but a couple of months ago my sister's partner was telling me that some old gardener had shown him the remains of an old nunnery close to the seminary of Blairs College (a Catholic school near Maryculter) so it started to make more sense.'

A very interesting building but changed somewhat since back then. The grounds and graveyard at Templars remain atmospheric and one can only imagine what may still be attracted to the area to surprise the unwary.

DUNDEE AND ANGUS

Moving south we reach Dundee and its environs where the following stories took place. The first was originally reported by the Society for Psychical Research where it was brought to the public's attention. Thought to be a timeslip the witness may have stumbled across the aftermath of the Battle of Dun Nechtain fought between the Northumbrian King Ecgfrith and the Picts led by King Bridei Mac Bili, which took place on 20th May 685 AD at Dunnichen, Angus. Related by Dr James McHarg of Dundee to the SPR he described in detail events witnessed by the late Miss E F Smith of Lathan village, Dundee who recounted her experience to him. Astonishingly between the date of her experience, 1950 and the date of the battle, 1265 years had elapsed. Interviewed in 1971 by a clinical psychologist, the witness then in her seventies recorded her experience for posterity, taking them to the original battle site. This is what she described.

On 7th January while returning from a cocktail party her car skidded into a ditch leaving her with a walk of around eight miles to get home and for two of those miles, she was forced to carry her dog. It was now round 2am and while approaching some woodland, a route she normally took, an unaccountable nervousness came over her. Veering to the right she walked on but began to see torches in the distance. Walking on she then found herself witness to the sight of oddly dressed men lying sprawled across the grass. With nowhere to go and now amid the tableaux she continued her journey noting in detail the faces of the slain warriors. Others appeared to walk among them, stooping occasionally to turn them back on their fronts. Many held torches which she later described as being bright red, thought to have been fashioned from Scots Fir. It was exclusively visual and during her progress no sound or smells were detected. The men, she later recounted, wore what appeared to be long tights dark in colour at which on certain points there were rolls of material, these matched the description of Pictish warriors. It was later found that two years prior to her experience Dr F T Wainwright head of the department of history at Queen's College Dundee had produced a detailed paper on the battle. According to him Smith's descriptions proved to be accurate. Later some suggested she had somehow subconsciously seen his paper to which she answered, 'I had not seen it before I saw this. Someone gave it to me afterwards, to read, but I merely told him, I was one up on him.'

Next up a quick look at the haunting of Montrose aerodrome near Lunan Bay, a fascinating story which clocking in at over a hundred years old shows no sign of abating. The spirit who is thought to be most active is Desmond Arthur a pilot killed in 1913. The Royal Aero Club Accident Committee suggested in the aftermath that he was the victim of a crime however in 1916 a further report was alleged he was killed by his own recklessness. In the aftermath it was thought that Arthur, an honourable man in life, had endeavoured to communicate his displeasure by appearing before former colleagues at the base. Several sightings took place soon after, particularly in the officer's mess. The stories slowly filtered out into the public eye attracting none other than pioneering spiritualist Sir Oliver Lodge. The plane which was then examined post-crash was found to have had a badly glued spar which was assumed to be the cause of the accident and of course vindicated the airmen.

His first recorded appearance soon reached the ears of the press, and several articles were then written which were refreshingly earnest in their approach. One such report described how one evening in the Autmn of 1916 an airman who had been working late at the aerodrome saw a young officer wearing his flying kit walking ahead of him. It was too dark to see him clearly and the pilot did not recognise him but followed at distance. He observed that on reaching the door of the officer's mess the figure stopped momentarily before vanishing. Putting it down to fatigue the memory of his encounter slowly faded over the ensuing days that is until he saw him again. On the second occasion it was noted that the officer repeated the same pattern and vanished at the doorstep of the mess. Despite seeing the same apparition on five occasions he never once repeated the story for fear of losing his commission accurately summarising that the brass would have no doubt accused him of some mental malady.

Another officer later woke in the semi dark and saw a figure some feet from his bed and on leaning forward for a better look, found he was staring at an empty space. Later, again in the old mess, two officers were awakened simultaneously by a feeling of oppression and sensing that they were not alone struck a match which revealed nothing. Similar events were now happening with greater frequency prompting feelings of distinct unease amongst the men and these reports continued up until its closure.

Today, despite the passage of time the young airman is still thought to haunt the aerodrome. Though now a museum, the buildings are used for a variety of purposes and more contemporary reports have alluded to the sound of footsteps being heard walking around when there no one is there. Perhaps the maligned spirit of the late airman refuses to leave despite being exonerated.

And now to Glamis Castle, one of Scotland's most famously haunted buildings whose stories include that of the infamous Monster of Glamis. Apparently, the deformed son of the laird kept locked in a secret room, its legendary status is oft quoted. Undoubtedly a legend it nevertheless is an enduring story. Another equally famous tale tells of a bargain between a former resident and the devil who on cursing him was doomed to play cards for all eternity. Known as Earl Beardie, his story appeared to be another example of Scottish mythology, that is until a recent conversation in which Emma recounted a personal experience. On hearing it is possibly one of the only examples of its kind. This is what she said.

'I was a young girl of eight in 1993 and had gone on a school trip to Glamis castle, I was paired up with a new girl and we were at the back of the line. We weren't paying attention and dawdling behind so got separated from the group. On passing a room we saw two men sitting inside playing cards. We stood there mesmerised. When the teacher came back and found us, she was annoyed and asked why we hadn't paid attention. We told her why, but she just got angrier thinking we were lying. We couldn't understand why she didn't believe us. When we were picked up after school, we told our parents what had happened and explained what we saw. The men were sitting down hunched over with their elbows on their knees and cards in their hands, one of them I remember was a lot clearer than the other and had long dark hair and a long beard to his collar bone. I remember the body being like a shadow, they never looked up. I don't remember any feelings or smells at the time. We were just watching two shadow men. It was very real to me.

The teacher must have told my mum because she didn't believe me neither. I could never understand how my story was so unbelievable. To me it wasn't as if we had seen a centaur running around. So forward to 2018 and my mum phoned me and told me to switch on the TV because there was a program on about Glamis. The documentary was on ghosts of Glamis Castle, and it was then she discovered the story about Earl Beardie, supposedly consigned to purgatory, forced to play cards with the devil for all eternity. Afterwards I phoned my mum and said, 'now do you believe me!' Although some might argue it's a case of false memory the witness was clear in what she described and made for a compelling experience.

On reaching Dundee, the following appeared in the Dundee courier of 1949. In it the following story was submitted by a Perth reader who at the time worked as a nurse in what was described as a 'big fever hospital' in the city. The ghost or at least the main ghost was thought to have been that of a priest and typically the wards were abound with tales, some no doubt embellished to scare the young nurses. One of the earliest reports concerned a maid who having witnessed the ghost standing on a nearby balcony had been genuinely terrified by his appearance. Footsteps were also heard frequently pacing outside the ward though no one was ever seen waiting there on investigation. Staff were naturally anxious, particularly when working nights and it was policy at the time for those on that rota to work a two-month shift, which was highly unpopular. Soon after our main witness was given the dreaded night rota and on the first night of her shift, she was extremely anxious, spending much of the night listening out for any sounds that might be deemed out of the ordinary. She later described that night as 'unending.' It was at around twelve, while doing her rounds that she found one four-year-old girl wide awake. Afterward she said: 'She looked steadily past me towards the big old-fashioned fireplace. When asked if she would like to get some sleep the girl replied in the negative saying that she liked watching the lady. She then went on to say that the lady goes when the nurses come in but appears again when they go back.' The nurse initially laughed this off assuming it was a dream and when this was suggested to the youngster, the young patient replied claiming that the lady looked just like one in a picture at her Sunday school, and that she sits at the fire every night. The nurse, now more than a little rattled then heard footsteps outside and looking from the window was horrified to see a figure slowly approaching the building. She could plainly see he wore a white collar. Now beside herself she then realised that whoever it was, was heading to the ward. She felt a scream rising in her throat as the door handle turned, before her nocturnal visitor entered the room. Much to her relief a kindly voice then enquired if she knew the whereabouts of ward 15, as there was a poor man dying there who needed the services of a priest!

Another tale from Dundee which I felt compelled to include was another case of mass hysteria. The year was 1883 and the location Blackness Quarry, where the neighbourhood was in a state of alarm due to the appearance of a black spectre. Not just a run of the mill black spectre but one described as being of herculean proportions, wearing a topcoat or cape from heel to nape, completing his ensemble with a slouch hat. First witnessed by children, adults muttered their disapproval putting it down to the 'havers of bairns,' but when the children refused to play outside locals grew nervous. Soon after sightings of the same figure were then witnessed by several adults, described it as gliding noiselessly. As news spread the 'Dundee Courier,' was soon on the trail, and reporters set about trying to contact locals. Things however didn't get off to a good start when they inadvertently insulted the entire neighbourhood, describing it as 'a dreary and gruesome region especially at night.' We all know places like this!

A local woman then claimed to have been followed home by the ghost, who had demanded spirits of an earthlier kind from her 'New Year bottle.' So much for sharing. She quickly fled, her screams attracting the attention of nearby residents. The ghost it would seem was not all it was cracked up to be. Later an ex-policeman saw the ghost standing in a nearby lane and plucking up the courage to confront him seized a poker, demanding to know his business. The spectre then fled splashing through the mire into a nearby quarry.

Several days later a local resident no doubt inspired by the ex-policeman's grit took it upon herself to do the same.

Grabbing a poker, she confronted the ghost only to find it was an innocent gentleman going about his business. A rag tag mob quickly gathered who intervened saving the man from a potential beating. The former policeman who witnessed the debacle said afterwards, that the ghost 'would have made two of him,' adding insult to almost injury. Like all stories of its ilk, boredom and hysteria played their part and sightings of the black spectre quickly evaporated.

Obviously, a vagrant of some description he no doubt left the area for a quieter life, though further appearances were noted as late as the 1920's. Given the timescale however, if it was the same man, he really would have had to have been a ghost. A vigil was reportedly held, and some hours later a cold and disappointed crowd gave up the ghost, literally, and went home. So much for mass hysteria, but the world of the supernatural is littered with such stories and one wonders if some hardier varieties that survive today grew from the same seed?

And now something more tangible and more terrifying also from Dundee. In 1974, Orcadian Shirley Brown arrived in the city to study nursing. Gail Bruce a fellow trainee became her flatmate, and they took up residence in a tenement in Morgan Street. Over a year had passed since they had moved into their flat, so it came as quite a surprise when out of the blue a series of inexplicable and frankly terrifying events unfolded. It all began early one morning when Gail unable to sleep became aware of someone walking around in the bathroom. After some time, curiosity got the better of her and she peered out but there was no one there and the front door was still securely locked. Puzzled she then climbed back into bed before noticing the figure of an elderly woman leaning over her flatmate, a figure that she described as oozing a feeling of evil. She noted that the woman appeared to be whispering something in her flatmate's ear, though she could not make out the words. Moments later the figure then vanished. Later that day on returning from work she divulged what had happened to her flatmate who was shocked on hearing the news.

Sometime later a second incident occurred, again while Shirley was in bed. In this instance she became aware of the sound of footsteps which appeared to come from the kitchen. Assuming it was her friend she then tapped on the wall to get her attention. Hearing no reply, the silence was then shattered by a terrifying volley of battering and clawing sounds, which she later described as being so frantic, she feared they would come through the wall. Her frightened flatmate then appeared from a different part of the flat and quickly joined her in bed where they both cowered until the noise abated. The girls, now out of their wits with fear grabbed a few belongings and quickly left the flat. It was on their way out however when they realised, they had left their keys behind and so momentarily returning, they quickly switched on the living room light which then exploded in a blue flash. It was later noted that the Dundee Royal Lunatic Asylum once stood upon the site.

It's tempting to think that a recording from the past was responsible but typically we always hope for an answer to what is potentially unanswerable. However, in Geoff Holders, 'Poltergeist over Scotland,' the author uncovered a very interesting piece of historical evidence connected to area. On the 30th of January 1933 three elderly sisters were noted as being found dead at their home on Morgan Street. Emily,

Martha and Jesse Miller, all victims of a gas poisoning were found in bed, in a chair and in front of the stove respectively. Could this terrible accident have been the catalyst for the phenomena? The truth of the matter is we don't know and as far as I am aware the phenomena which occurred in 1974 did not extend to the tenants that followed in their footsteps. Whatever it was appeared angry and malicious, though upon checking the kitchen wall they found it to be unscathed despite the ferocious pummelling.

PERTH AND KINROSS

The Perth and Kinross area has a great haunted pedigree and the stories from the area are fascinating. Discounting the more obvious castles and stately homes there is also a plethora of pubs and haunted hotels some of which are featured in the next few pages courtesy of 'Perth Auld Bairns' and other contributors from one of the most beautiful areas of Scotland.

Ali Pibworth is first up, and she told me the following which took place in Perth. 'My granny used to manage The Steeple now the Half a Tanner, back in the 1960s and my grandad would go to check the kegs in the cellar for her. He always had his dog with him. His dog was very loyal and would never leave his side but would never go into the cellar of the pub with him no matter how much he tried to persuade it. Equally there were strange things that would often happen across the road at what is now the Venue, where the cellar is very creepy. Across town there's the Station Hotel and when I worked there the duty manager would stay in one of the rooms on the top floor. The top floor was narrow and dark and low ceilinged and was probably originally the staff quarters. One of the managers swore when he had gone up there to do a night round before retiring for bed, he saw a presence in the corridor. He described it as being like a dark swarm of bees. He did not complete his rounds and did not go to bed that night. Downstairs in the reception area, the front desk and office had a store cupboard which ran along the left side of them. It had formerly been the original entrance from the station and sometimes you would hear footsteps walking along when there was no one there. There were also a few times late at night when I was doing night shift reports in the back office, when I could have sworn, someone had come to the front desk and tinged the bell. When I went to investigate there was no one there.'

But now for something truly terrifying where our next stop is Rosslyn House a former workhouse. Built in 1861 and situated on the Glasgow Road, Perth it housed inmates, uncharitably described as lunatics and paupers. The H-shaped building was designed to segregate the men, woman and children who live there, the latter more commonly housed on the outer edges of the wings. Described at the time as having all mod cons, inmates were allowed one bath a week which might make it sound appealing, but it was not. A foreboding looking building, inmates were expected to work hard for their keep and any privileges were hard-earned, by 1917 however many had been transferred to other institutions such as the Breadalbane Poorhouse. Renamed Bertha house in the 1930s, the building then went through multiple changes becoming a care home, nursing home and latterly offices for the social work department, it was eventually converted into luxury flats in 2001, and this is where our story begins.

I first read about the building on the Auld Perth Bairns Facebook page, then in an article in the Evening Telegraph in which a former tenant related her experiences while living there. It proved a popular thread, and many contributors were quick to chip in with their anecdotal accounts. It was interesting to hear that some stories also stretched further back than its current usage.

One account from that period was from a former handyman who at the time looked after the building. He reported witnessing lifts operating by themselves. He later claimed it would have been impossible for them to do so and on more than one occasion saw the lift doors open in front of him despite it containing no one. Quite intriguing, however in more recent times a former resident described how she broke her tenancy halfway through a six-month lease after being terrified by an invisible presence. Harassed by the sound of footsteps, she became convinced that someone was somehow gaining entry to her flat and moving her belongings. Contacting the agent, she enquired if a duplicate key been inadvertently handed out, but the answer was no. This did little to assure her and she would often hear doors opening and closing which on investigation revealed nothing. It was also intensely cold in certain areas which was inexplicable. Things reached breaking point one night while lying in bed. Outside she could hear footsteps creeping along the corridor which got progressively louder until abruptly stopping outside her room. Lying with bated breath, too afraid to move, she eventually plucked up the courage to dress and fled from the building where she spent the remainder of the night at her parents. In the morning, she persuaded a friend to accompany her back and once there collected her belongings before leaving for good.

Keen to know more about the building's origins and particularly the experiences of other tenants, she was vindicated by the level of feedback on her post. Take for example another former occupant who claimed to have heard a child bouncing a ball on the corridor when there was no one there, or the woman who returned home to find her pillows had mysteriously been placed at the end of the bed! Sightings of shadowy figures were also noted as was the sound of voices.

All the grist to the mill but several accounts topped them all, the first happening to an unwitting visitor to the flats named Shanna. Employed as a care worker she had taken on a colleagues shift and in doing so was assigned a client visit to Rosslyn house. She had at the time never been inside the building and in the aftermath of that first visit vowed never to return. While there her client had asked if she could fetch something from the cupboard and as she went to retrieve the item described the lightbulbs in every room exploding as she walked by. Somewhat taken aback by this turn of events she grabbed a brush and began sweeping the glass and it was while bending over, she felt a hand on her shoulder. Glancing back, expecting to see her client, she saw nothing. It was then she noted a wet handprint was present on her uniform. In shock she quickly headed downstairs and in doing so felt something then rush by her. The client later stated that light bulbs popped frequently though they appeared nonplussed, unlike Shanna who suffered a series of nightmares in the aftermath.

The second account was related to me by a former resident Kate who lived in the block for five years and in that time described many strange and frightening occurrences. Living on the left-hand side of the building on the first floor she noted phenomena such as hearing children's voices and hearing unexplained footsteps. She later described seeing a ghostly apparition which appeared, 'coming down from the ceiling,' and packed her bags after, 'a very bad sleepless night.'

Terrifying indeed, but a recent conversation with former tenant, Paula provided perhaps the most disturbing account to date and is further evidence of the former occupants' refusal to leave. This what she said: 'We moved into Rosslyn House and since the very first day there would be knocking in the hallway. The first time I heard it I went to open the door but there was no one there, no packages, no one heading to the exit. The walls are extremely thick, and it isn't possible to hear knocking from the other side of the neighbour's wall. A few days later my husband heard the knocking and again went to the door, no one was there. My parents were visiting and alerted me that someone was knocking at the door, by which point we realised it was likely that no one was there, but we checked anyway. While in my bed one morning, my husband was sleeping in my oldest daughter's room, and I heard knocking on the wall about three or four times. I then sent him a text, and being annoyed asked: "Why are you letting her knock, the baby is still sleeping?" He replied that he wasn't knocking and that she was asleep too. Our flat is in what used to be the girl's dormitory and when we moved in, we would have electronic toys going off in the living room by themselves. When my daughter was three years old, she began to ask us, who was in the hallway? She would sometimes point and say, "who's that?" Usually pointing to the hallway but sometimes to other rooms.

Once I was playing with her in her room. I was sitting on the floor, and she had made a trail of foam blocks leading out of her room into the hallway and was happily bouncing from block to block in and out of the room. She then turned to her left, looked, then turned back and said, "Oh there's a man standing in the hallway," then continued playing. I was just frozen trying to absorb what had happened, it was like a movie. On another occasion she pointed to an elephant painting we have on the wall in the living room and said, "there's the elephant and there's the boy!", to which I replied, "what boy?" this being the first time I had engaged in any conversation when she said things like this. She then said, "the boy there" and pointed. I asked her what his name was, and she said verbatim, "I don't know, he doesn't talk he always has his mouth closed like this," and she proceeded to shut her lips tight to show me, which stunned me. About six months later she asked one day. "where's the boy that was in my house, he's gone?" I then asked, "what boy?" and she said, "the boy who is not real."

On another occasion I was in my bedroom alone where I have a vase of fake flowers, quite long in length. There were no windows open, no draughts coming in, but I could hear something moving against the wall so I turned and could see one of the stems moving up and down. It was brushing on the wall. Then there was nothing for months until one night while we were watching TV on the couch. Outside the room we heard the very distinct sound of a letterbox opening which was startling given the time of night. I sat thinking what could possibly mimic the sound of a letter box opening. It's a very distinct sound but at first, we didn't check. Around 15 minutes later it opened again, and I sent my husband to check but there was nothing there.'

Judging by the volume of comments the story attracted it is obvious the memory of living there still induces shudders in both former tenants and workers. Its grim history serves as a reminder of the conditions the poor had to endure, and it is little wonder those fragments from the past are imprinted there. Typically, though, many others were undisturbed during their tenure and appeared puzzled by some of the comments, which suggests as always, the more sensitive tenants were prone to experiencing the supernatural.

Once a school, the Tulloch institute on Tulloch Terrace, Perth, is now a club boasting of over 1000 members, and is regarded by many as being very haunted. There has been a lot of evidence gathered over the years to justify their fears, and it boasts several ghosts befitting a building of its age. One is thought to be an old headmaster who still roams the halls. He has been described as wearing a cape and mortar board and is seen walking with his hands clasped behind his back. The second spirit is that of a young girl who has been named Mary, who may or may not have been a former pupil. It is said she was murdered on the premises, though I have found no evidence to support this. Of course that doesn't mean it didn't happen. Regardless of how Mary met her end she is a permanent fixture in the building and members of 40 years standing have grown older while she remains young. The stories first came to light some years back when several long-serving staff members were interviewed for the local paper. People love reading about ghost stories and the feature proved popular. Since then, the stories have resurfaced on various platforms, and I was fortunate to speak to several witnesses who recounted experiences ranging from seeing shadowy figures to outbreaks of unpleasant poltergeist activity. It was also noted that it was not unusual for glasses to be found mysteriously broken when the club was opened the next day. Several clocks were also found lying on the floor despite being securely attached. Initially the idea of the building being haunted was seen as a bit of a joke but as the phenomena increased so did the concern of the patrons.

Head steward at the time, Bill Lindsay and colleague Jimmy Craigon who had been at the club for many years had several experiences to boast of. Most were thought of as low key, until one evening when barmaid Shirley McKay was in. Arriving a little early for her shift she decided to have a drink. Around the same time Bill was in the cellar changing a barrel when he caught a glimpse of something behind him. Turning quickly, he a saw a woman walking away. Assuming it was Shirley he quickly retreated upstairs to ask why she had been down there but found her seated in the bar. The puzzled men then had the nerve-wracking task of checking the cellar but found it empty. It was noted in the aftermath that Shirley would often wear long dresses like the apparition was seen in.

Chairman Hugh Reid, another witness, eventually refused to go into the building alone at night after the apparition's erratic behaviour made him anxious. Take the following for example which occurred late one evening while staff were sitting in the lounge. Without warning Hugh then jumped from his seat claiming he had just seen someone walk down the hall. They quickly checked the area but found nothing. Afterwards Hugh described never feeling the same about the building again. Poltergeist activity increased, and bottles, glasses and mugs were quite literally described as flying off shelves at certain times, as if they had been thrown. It became something of a bind to clear up and on another occasion, a member of staff described how he was almost brained by a thrown object which flew past his head. He stated: 'A mug that had been sitting behind the optics hit the bar and landed on the floor and to do that it had to come off the shelf and travel three to four feet through the air.' I recently spoke to one of the unlucky recipients on that night, Jimmy Craigon, who elaborated on the story. During our conversation he described that on arriving the next day after the mug incident he found a clock lying smashed to pieces on the lounge floor, which had been securely attached to a bracket. It had stopped at 1.50 am. On another occasion the destructive spirit smashed a glass bowl to smithereens though strangely the tumbler contained within remained unscathed. Secretary John Ramsay saw the aftermath and was quoted as saying, 'the bowl had sat in the office for years but when I went in on Wednesday morning it was smashed. There was glass on the chairs, in amongst the files, everywhere but the tumbler was sitting there without as much as a scratch. I just thought everyone was having me on before this happened, but now I do believe in ghosts.'

Most recently I spoke with several long-time staff members one of whom was Tanya. She had several personal experiences on the premises including witnessing cigars being strewn across the bar floor, which was most perplexing given that they sat upon a deep shelf, making it impossible for them to have fallen off by themselves. On another occasion she described an even stranger experience while sitting in the cellar area, between the main bar and function room. While in the process of closing for the evening she heard music coming from the latter and feeling distinctly uneasy phoned her mum, who she asked to keep talking while she locked up. She later stated that over the years several psychics had visited the premises and noted the presence of a young girl who liked to make herself known. Speaking to the ex-treasurer Jock Ramsay recently, he also described a strange incident. On that occasion he had been counting staff wages but did not have room in his office to set the money out as needed, so decided to decamp to the manager's office. Once there he quickly counted out the cash but realising it was short returned to his own office to double check. On opening the door, which had been locked, he was shocked to find the whole office had been turned upside down, with furniture upended and broken glass strewn everywhere. He told me during our conversation, that neither him nor his colleagues could account for what they found given he was the only keyholder. On a final note, Jimmy finished off by saying that once the papers got hold of the story the whole thing became farcical when they insisted on visiting at Halloween but as far as he was concerned these were genuine incidents. Perhaps the occurrences were connected to the buildings previous use as a school, he surmised.

While working in the 'Bothy,' a pub formerly known as 'Matthew Gloag Whisky Bond' on Kinnoull Street, employee Laura described what happened when it first opened after a massive renovation. She stated: 'One quiet afternoon I was working alone in the wee bar when the cellar door behind the bar opened by itself, then by the time it would take you to walk to the big heavy central doors, the external doors opened by themselves too. Ali Pibworth them commented. 'I was the piano player at the venue for years and around the anniversary of the second year of it opening, and the initial renovations, people started getting locked in the lady's loo. Doors would not open on the cubicles although there was nothing wrong with them. Then one night something came through the wall, the back wall of the wine cupboard downstairs from the tunnels behind it. Nothing was taken just the plasterboard punched in a human shaped hole through from the other side. I stopped going downstairs myself after that.'

Our next location is Perth Academy. Haunted schools are among my favourite type of buildings and many of the following were described to me by Michael, the former Janitor. Take for example the following when a cleaner who was working next to the English department saw a teacher walk past in the corridor and disappear into one of the rooms. Surprised that a teacher would be in that area after hours the cleaner then followed her to ask what the problem was but found there was no one there. The corridor was also empty. Afterwards the cleaner described the teacher to Michael and several colleagues who were told she wore an old-fashioned gown. Months later when they were short staffed, the same cleaner was then asked to work in the Head teacher's office. While there she noticed a photograph on the wall dating from the 1930s and on closer inspection was dumfounded to see the same teacher in the picture. One of Michael's colleagues, Fiona, later corroborated the story by describing the following: 'She (the cleaner) had never been in the head teacher's office till that night and had never seen the image before. She said it was the hair that was so spooky.'

One another occasion Fiona described an incident while walking along the English department corridor. Without warning a young lad ran past her and along the hall before entering one of the classrooms. Thinking the pupil was lost she quickly followed but when she looked in the room was empty. She then entered and shut the door behind her before checking the room thoroughly. It was later suggested that the sighting of the young boy may have been linked to a young pupil who collapsed, and I assume died, outside the classroom some years prior.

On another occasion a male cleaner working overnight at the academy was cleaning the corridors in the English department when he was witnessed running down the stairs screaming and who then refused to go back upstairs to put his machine away. Who or what he saw remains a mystery as I was told that he never came back to work. It was also common for doors in the English department to open and close of their own accord and for lights to go back on or off by their own accord. One janitor remembered having to go upstairs one evening multiple times to switch the lights back off, eventually giving up and leaving them on.

Michael finished by saying, 'I remember an incident in the assembly corridor when I had just finished setting up for the exams on the Friday, I hadn't finished so went back on Sunday to finish off. I went up the stairs by the main foyer but could not walk along the top corridor. Every time I tried to walk along, I became cold and the hair on my neck stood up. I ended up going a different route. I have been back and forth a thousand times since and have never felt the same thing again.' Ending on a lighter note Michael then told me that on one occasion he was given a row by some of the teachers for telling spooky stories to the seniors his accounts finding their way into the school mag.

'City Stores' in Perth is our next venue, when several years ago an outbreak of unexplained phenomena took place. Not confined to the shop alone it spread into several flats above and adjacent to the premises. On one occasion for example the owner described hearing someone cough loudly in his ear one day. Soon after, Hugh Mailer, who owned a nearby camera shop described how one of his employees witnessed the apparition of a short-bent figure which appeared on a CCTV camera. Upon calling in a psychic, who knew nothing of the sighting, they described the presence of a hunched old man. Not to be outdone, several tenants from nearby flats then reported a spate of poltergeist activity such as drawers opening and shutting on their own accord. After an investigation, negative earth energy caused by an underground stream was put forward as the cause of the disturbances. Soon after a nearby shop owner then claimed that on entering their premises one morning, they found the shelves in disarray with hairspray, varying products and clothes scattered upon the floor. A fan in the vacant shop next door was also apparently found to be running despite there being no electricity. An investigation captured unexplained noises in the premises which were quite startling however, and as is often the case, the evidence went astray. In the aftermath of an investigation, it was thought that at the back of the shop there was at one point an old burial ground. Whether this had any bearing on events is open to conjecture. There have been no further reports in recent times, at least that I'm aware of, but theoretically they could still be occurring. Interestingly, a previous tenant around some 40 years prior to the reports, described the very same phenomena, with her hairdressing business being plagued by something which moved objects and left her materials in disarray.

Next, we visit another haunted pub, this time 'The Royal George.' It was there Averil McGillivray's dad used to work as a night porter and she described how one evening he had such a bad scare at work that afterwards he began to take his dog for company. The fact was corroborated by another witness, Lynn, who briefly worked at the same venue one summer and remembered how news got around that the night porter had 'encounters.' Averil went on to say that multiple witnesses had reported seeing someone standing at the top of the stairs opposite reception.' She further stated, 'My poor dad was a big man, but this happened on so many occasions he was terrified, he was certain it was a woman as he could often smell rose perfume too.'

Still in Perth, I spoke to Gordean Finlay who told me the following: 'I worked in the Twa Tams in the early 2000s One night after lone working I was mopping the floors, one of the last jobs of the evening. I locked up and set the alarm, but the security system indicated there was someone in the building. As you can imagine this was scary for a lone lass, so I entered the building and rechecked everything top to bottom but found no one there. As I walked out to reset the alarm, I noticed wet footprints going all the way across the floor but in the opposite direction of mine, and they were also a lot bigger than my size fives. I felt I was not alone, and it wasn't human. During all the time worked there it gave off strange vibes, there were noises and a feeling of not being alone.'

A phantom monk allegedly haunted another place of work, this time a factory on Whitefriars Street, home to 'Taygame' where sightings of a monk were sufficiently newsworthy to make the papers around thirty years ago. Despite being a relatively new building it was built near the location of an ancient Monastery. Destroyed in the 16th century its subsequent excavation in the 1980s revealed several skeletons including one set apart from the others stuffed inside a drainage ditch. Soon after completion full-bodied apparition(s) of a monk or monks duly appeared causing two workers to flee the premises vowing never to return. This was corroborated by the then director Ian Thomson who stated, 'The women who ran out were absolutely petrified and refused to go back, even to collect their handbags.' One of the workers Julie Robertson quoted afterwards: 'You felt like you were being watched, then there was one night when I saw a white face and that was it.' Other workers including office staff also claiming to have seen same figure described it as wearing a habit, one butcher also complained of feeling a ghostly hand firmly press his shoulder. At the end of the interview, it was stated that the director though showing a certain degree of sympathy had thus far refused to have an exorcism. The reason for his reticence, was, as he claimed later, due to him not being religious. But what about his staff?

No going further back in time we are now in Perthshire where I found the following first published on the 29th of April in the Sunday Post 1945. In the reader's letters was a description of an encounter with the spirit of a monk on Kinnoull Hill, Perthshire. Famed for its beautiful walks the area has for years, allegedly been the location of a phantom monk. The witnesses who submitted the letter, a Mr and Mrs Fairweather from Cumberland, were holidaymakers, and it proved a trip unlikely to be forgotten. This what she wrote, 'My husband and I holidayed in Perth last summer, on our last evening at about 10 o' clock we set out to climb Kinnoull Hill. It was a beautiful evening, but we lost our way and decided that by the time we reached the top it would be too dark to see any scenery, so we stumbled down and nearly reached the foot. Then just below us on the edge of the road, on the way to the monastery, we saw a figure all in white.'

She went on to describe how it was clad in the robes of a monk, its face obscured by a hood. Drifting weightlessly, the pair stood mesmerised as the monk floated by them and headed towards a seat where it momentarily halted. The pair then slid down the hill to get a better look but at the last moment the witness's nerve broke and she fled in terror. Glancing back, she described seeing the ghost glide up the hill before it disappeared. Later a friend said they must have mistaken the figure for that of a white deer, but the witnesses were adamant that it had been a monk, drifting literally five yards in front of them. She later stated when it initially appeared her husband challenged it by saying, 'If that's someone trying to be funny, I'll show him I can be funny too,' but it remained unaware and never hesitated in its journey. Certain it was no human being she saw, further enquiries revealed that others had seen the same figure.

Still in the region the next story comes from the village of Kirkmichael and took place in 2015 at 'The Log Cabin Hotel,' formerly known as, 'The Pine Lodge' and 'Edelweiss Lodge' respectively. Emma a former employee, though now a family historian described that quite often while working there the hotel hosted large events such as weddings and birthdays. It could get extremely busy and one occasion while working behind the bar, the thirsty clientele polished of their supply of vodka. Being in the middle of nowhere, Emma and her colleague were then asked by the supervisor if they would be willing to 'sell,' their own personal bottles to the hotel. Knowing they would be reimbursed later they both agreed, with Emma heading off to get the bottle from her room. While returning along the corridor, she described being grabbed on the arm quite forcefully and dragged back as if someone was wanting her attention. She lashed out in fright and quickly headed back to the bar where for the rest of the shift she pushed the incident to the back of her mind.

It had been a hectic shift, and later back in her room she quickly drifted off to sleep. Just then the kettle began to boil and so staggering out of bed she switched it off. Soon after the same thing happened just as she began to doze off. Frustrated and a little angry she then pulled the plug from the wall suspecting it to be the result of some kind of fault. Again, at the point of sleep the kettle boiled for a third time. Out of frustration rather than fear she then sat up in bed and asked whatever it was to stop doing it. Afterwards she told her boss, who having heard similar reports from other staff members then invited a clairvoyant to visit. Staff had been explicitly told not to divulge any information so on her arrival she knew nothing of the phenomena. During her walk around she eventually arrived at Emma's room.

Emma then stated: 'There was myself, the medium and my boss and the medium announced "it's something to do with the kettle." Afterwards I am working and Maggie who was the supervisor there at the time and she asked me what I thought of the medium's findings. I said I was not too impressed. Maggie then asked me if I believed in such things, and I said I did, but needed stronger proof. At that moment all the lights switched off and the power went out before starting up again. It did this twice. Maggie then said is that enough proof and of course it was.' Emma later told me that on another occasion she clearly saw a shadowy figure that appeared to be male standing in the corner of one of the rooms before vanishing.

Next up is a tale from Thomas Brown who kindly allowed me to use the following which he first posted on the Haunted

Perthshire Facebook page and took place in a former mill in the village of Luncarty. On reading further I discovered that Thomas and several other contributors including a Mr Patton, had at various points worked there. Their reminiscences were of great interest particularly given the mills long-standing reputation for being haunted. It had by all accounts several potential ghosts, one of which was described as a man often seen standing at one of the machines. Colin Patton who worked around the same time as Thomas wrote recently. 'I worked there too and covered all sorts of shifts night and day. I worked in nearly every department at one point and there were numerous stories throughout the works and in the village of Luncarty. My one experience was on a nightshift where I saw someone or something walking around inside the main office. This was approximately 3am and the office was locked up and closed. The night watchman was standing chatting with me at the time. I pointed out what I had seen, and he just shrugged and said this was a normal occurrence, he was used to seeing many unexplainable things around the works. Over the years I heard many similar experiences from those that worked there.'

Thomas, employed for nineteen years at the works then described cycling to work every day, where he operated a machine that burnt the hair off the fabric. He also described working at night and how the crew consisting of around six men were usually confined to certain areas within the factory. This could sometimes change though and on occasion he was sent to other parts of the building. It was by all accounts a creepy building, large and foreboding with much of it deserted.

One day his usual workmate was off sick, so Thomas was joined by a new man, and as they worked, they struck up a conversation. As they chatted his new colleague told him how he once used to work nightshift but requested to be moved to day shift. Thomas was curious and asked him why? He then explained to him that the factory was supposed to have a ghost and although Thomas had never heard about this, the man appeared sincere. He explained that at varying times he had to pass the area where Thomas now worked and that on one occasion, he had seen the apparition of a man standing at the machine at around two o'clock in the morning. Terrified, he realised the figure was neither that of the nightwatchman nor any other worker. Unfortunately, there was no conclusion to the story other than the mill was eventually demolished leaving nothing more than the lade and of course the memories of those who worked there, whether their experiences involved ghosts or not.

Again, mentioned in the 'Haunted Perthshire' Facebook page, the following took place around the spring of 2010, and described an incident on the A823 near Auchterarder. The contributor who along with a colleague had been sent to retrieve broken-down police training vehicle, getting more than they bargained for in the process. She stated afterwards that it was such a terrifying experience she can remember it clearly to this day. On arriving at the scene of the incident they quickly hooked a broken-down Land Drover to their vehicle and headed back along the Dunfermline to Auchterarder road. Keeping at a steady 40mph due to the winding road and heavy load, they eventually reached a stretch of road approximately 2 miles from the A9. On their right they noticed a slight slope approximately 10ft high with straggling trees while on their left sat a stone dyke. Behind it the ground dipped downwards offering a clear view. Without warning a dark shadow appeared ahead on their right-hand side which then went onto the road around 20ft in front of them before disappearing down the slope to the left. It was clearly visible to both and in shock the driver slammed on the brakes. The shadow was described as semi-translucent and was human sized but without apparent limbs and undulating. She said later: 'There was an awful feeling from it.'

'Bankfoot,' another village in Perthshire, is home to the 'Bankfoot Inn,' an ancient allegedly haunted hostelry. Its ghosts are said to include that of an old woman, a little girl and 'the thing.' Who or what 'the thing,' is, has remained frustratingly vague, as no one seems to want to impart the all-important information. Perhaps it's a gimmick, but nevertheless there are enough stories within its walls to keep those interested guessing. At the time, owners Peter and Judith Jones were just some of the several witnesses to their nocturnal ramblings one even making an appearance at Halloween, which was apt. The phenomena had been prolonged and, in some instances, bizarre. Take for instance the occasion when Mrs Jones was ironing and part way through the laborious task went to make tea. She described that on returning to the room the ironing had been finished off, and neatly folded. A considerate ghost, and one that would be welcome in most homes. Head chef Robbie Richardson also reported numerous incidents including one occasion when he went to answer the phone while carrying a food order only for it to combust in his hand. There were of course no naked flames anywhere near the paper to have done this. He later reported that on entering the kitchen a rack of utensils appeared to be swaying and moving by their own accord. Momentarily fascinated he stepped forward to get a closer look and on touching them found they were unnaturally hot despite the area being cold. On a third occasion, while approaching the building, he became aware of a white clad figure of a woman watching from the window who slowly faded from view.

Perhaps you may assume that such sightings would put customers off, far from it, in fact 'Barbara' as one of the ghosts is known appears to be a bit of a draw. One couple for example described seeing a white floating apparition to staff and returned a week later in the hope to catch a further glimpse. Whether she obliged or not remains a mystery, but I admire their tenacity.

Now for another haunted hostelry, this time the Royal Hotel in Dunkeld which featured in an article some ten years ago. It was purchased in more recent times by the Melville Group to add to their existing portfolio and consequently the ghostly tales associated with the venue have since been played down. Such was the spooky goings on at the time however that a medium named Linda McCann was called in to provide answers. The most haunted areas, according to reports were thought to be on the third floor and in one instance a film director who was booked into room 306, refused to stay because of a feeling of dread. A second guest and a cleaner also mentioned similar feelings in the room. After the investigation, the Menzies, who at the time owned the hotel were told there were several unquiet spirits in residence.

The medium cited room 306 as having a very negative feeling attached to it though she was not told anything of its history in advance. It was later revealed that someone was supposed to have hung themselves in the room. While touring the area the medium then sensed a heavy smell of smoke which again proved accurate, as there had been a fire in the same area in the early 20th century. Other spirits were noted as including a pregnant lady forlornly waiting for her husband to return from the war, a black cat and a man wearing an eye patch. A veritable motley crew. She then picked up in one of the rooms a rather serious meeting taking place at a round table. It was a room of importance she stated which was later corroborated, the space being one of the oldest Masonic rooms in Scotland. In room 201 a male energy was also thought to be present as was the spirit of two young lads. What connection they might have had is unclear but as a coaching inn many would have passed through its doors on a nightly basis.

Still in the countryside here is a vintage tale which took place some ninety years ago. According to reports at the time, the ghost of a young child thought to be around five was witnessed by several farmworkers, near Longforgan, in an area known as the Carse of Gowrie. The workers all tenants on a local farm, were interviewed at length by the local press and described several unsettling encounters in and around an ancient well, which they speculated may have been the source of her demise. The witnesses predominantly based in the cottar houses, were at first loathe to acknowledge what they were witnessing but after some coaxing several described seeing a young girl with flaxen hair. First witnessed in an area between a ruined abbey and the well, her appearances were reported both in the evening and early in the morning when the men left for work, though the latter being the most frequent. The well was used frequently by the local children tasked with fetching water and it was while one was doing this chore that the little ghost appeared. Visibly upset upon reaching home, the child was quizzed by her mother before she stated, 'I have just passed that wee bairn.' The poor child was then described as taking around an hour to recover from the initial shock. One of the worker's wives later claimed that her husband had laughed at her on mentioning the ghost, however he later admitted that he too had seen the apparition on the very first morning he had started work at the farm.

Soon after, another woman from the same farm was given a severe shock when she saw the same girl running along the fence in the early morning. News spread and soon The Dundee Courier was on the case reporting that on the 24th of April 1930 at around 11 o' clock one of the tenants, a young man, was found collapsed after answering the front door. When recovered he later said that upon opening the door he was met with the sight of a young girl.

Assuming that the sightings might be a portent of some impending tragedy a palpable sense of unease now blanketed the community culminating in one memorable creepy encounter. On that occasion, the witness described how she was almost terrified out of her wits when the girl paid her a visit. This is what she said. 'On Hogmanay I was standing at the door at about elven o' clock at night looking at the lights in Dundee when I was terrified to see a little white-haired girl come up the path towards me. I went in and shut the door. She is just a little thing about five years of age, just like a girl who has come to an untimely end.' And so, with that, the story also came to an untimely end. A further article later claimed that a girl who died at the age of seven in Dundee Royal Infirmary some three years before the first sighting, apparently lived in one of the cottages. Could she have been the mysterious ghost girl?

Our next stop is in the village of Comrie near the beautiful town of Crieff. This house unlike some of the previous locations is a bona fide ancient structure which was once upon a time used as a gaol. Given its pedigree it is no surprise it is haunted and not just one ghost, but by multiple spirits including two girls. The following was kindly told to me by the homeowner, Andrew, who has had to contend with some hair-raising incidents. He described the following.

'My house is situated just outside Comrie on the Crieff side. It sits on a big rock about half a mile outside the village. There are two houses there and both have had some activity, but I will just talk about my house now. My house is a converted stable block with part of the original building, which had two feet thick walls and bars on the windows. A local historian told me once there was an article about it in the Scots Magazine a long time ago. It supposedly used to be a stopover prison before they were taken to Crieff and hung the next day. At first any activity that happened around the house only occurred when we were doing alterations. My father fitting kitchen units for example left the room to get something and when he returned all his tools were lined up in a row. A few days later he was still at the units when the door opened. Thinking it was my mum he began a conversation not lifting his head away from the job, (because he could feel a female presence) and when no one answered he noticed there was no one there. I had been living there since I was 7 but moved to Crieff. Years later I returned to the house when my child was three. My child's bedroom was next to ours and one evening we were woken up by banging on the wall, quite vigorous banging coming from our child's bedroom. Thinking there was something wrong we got up to see and found her sound asleep. On another night while were lying in bed we heard someone opening our front door, walking up the stairs and coming to our bedroom door before knocking. I was forced to check it out but there was no one there. Most recently I was woken by the sound of two girls having a conversation outside my bedroom door, I could not make out what they were saying but I heard the names Susan and Sally mentioned, and it sounded like they were jangling keys.

These occurrences weren't just connected to my house though as my parents who stay in a but and ben about 300 yards away have also had experiences. My dad for example has been woken on several occasions and found a girl standing at the foot of the bed and saw a group of people who appeared to be eating in the living room. On another occasion he witnessed the apparition of an elderly lady sitting in a rocking chair in their sun lounge. No one knows for sure why the area has so many sightings, but one theory is it sits on a lay line.' Another story from the same village was also passed on to me by the same witness, below is what he told me.

'This story was told to me by one of my customers. Apparently, this area was a stronghold for the Roman Empire with camps in Comrie and ten miles away in a village called Braco. In this area there is an undocumented story about a lost Roman legion whose demise was at the hands of the Picts, and in a field a few miles west sits a stone which has an inscription in Latin upon it alluding to the fact that 1000 men died there. There is also a 'Lix Toll junction' on the A85. I wonder if 'lix' roman numerals? Anyhow my customer who used to stay on the west side of the village of Comrie told me that one night while she was sitting in her living room a Roman legion walked through her house! They kept on marching in the direction of a camp road where they were supposed to have been billeted. It was one of those stories that you hear, and think, is this for real? But knowing the person was of sound mind, when I spoke to her, I knew she was telling the truth.' Outlandish as it might seem, there are several similar stories from the area.

Now in Crieff itself, an arresting story about a haunted police station, which I heard, is being developed into a hostel. Whether that would be conducive to a good night's sleep is debateable, and to add a further frisson to the situation, the cells will be the bedrooms. Built around 1900, the four-story building was used by the Perthshire County Constabulary. Situated on King Street, it had enough room to accommodate three police families whose wives would often take a measure of responsibility in their husband's job. The story most often repeated is that the wife of a Sergeant died there under tragic circumstances, though how she passed remains a mystery. By 1964 the Gow family were now resident, consisting of Sergeant Johnny Gow, his wife and daughter. One evening whilst walking along the narrow path which led to his house the sergeant distinctly felt someone brush past him and though perplexed, he shrugged it off. Sometime later however they were given a fright when woken by their pet Corgi who had been clearly frightened by something. Listening, they then heard the clump of footsteps headings upstairs towards the bedroom. No doubt anxious Mr Gow investigated but found nothing. The footsteps were later noted as being heard on around eight different occasions either at midnight or between two and three in the morning. Sometimes the sound of rustling paper could also be heard coming from the bookcase as if someone was looking for something. Things culminated one morning when their daughter described being woken in the middle of the night by a woman in her room. She was tall and dressed in a silky black dress and carried a tray of glasses, which the child distinctly heard making a tinkling sound. To her surprise, the woman then vanished through the wall. It is not known if anything further occurred but as far as I am aware, no further accounts, at least not written ones, exist. In later years the building was changed internally and after becoming open plan, functioned as an office and in doing so, perhaps the unfortunate spirit moved on. In more modern times little has been reported, apart from the odd noise, though officers on duty have put it down to natural causes, or was it?

Taymouth Castle near Kenmore is our final stop in Perth and Kinross. Once home to the Marquis of Breadalbane it has had a long and varied past, used for both a hotel and summer school before becoming abandoned in 1982. A category A listed building there are many superlatives to describe it, but both house and gardens are outstanding examples of their kind, being thought of as one of the finest residences in the country. Although still at risk and badly deteriorated, its present owners are now in the process of undertaking a massive restoration project, before its new lease of life as a hotel. This story however dates from the 1940s when still in use, although the owners were away at the time. Because of this a local caretaker, Willie Wright, was employed to make daily checks on the sprawling property which had within its walls an astonishing 101 bedrooms and 18 bathrooms. On one evening as he was doing his rounds, he was horrified to see a white ghostly shape rise from the shadows in one of the rooms. Hurriedly switching on the light, he was somewhat relieved to come face to face with a sleepy looking stranger wrapped in a dust sheet. Wullie, by now irate, demanded to know what was going on. As it transpired, the sheepish guest had been hiking all day and after coming across what he assumed to be an empty building had taken it upon himself to bed down for the night. He later claimed that the caretakers' footsteps had woken him in fright, though his 'fright' no doubt increased further when the local constabulary was called. After a brief interview in which his particulars were taken down, if you know what I mean, he was allowed to go free.

ARGYLE AND BUTE

A quick detour west to the Fort William area where sits the small seaside town of Oban. Seen as a springboard to the islands it has a healthy tourist population and boasts several well-established hotels although some offer guests more than comfy beds and fine dining as I discovered upon reading some recent Tripadvisor reviews. Take for example the 'Premier Inn' where one review stated, 'RM 12O Haunted!' There, the guest described the following. 'Great location, lots of amenities nearby but had an unexpected encounter with a ghost of a white-haired lady dressed in a white nightgown who walked around my bed.' Amusingly the manager had the temerity to completely avoid the subject of ghosts in his reply. Smooth. Another, this time from the 'Muthu Alexandra Hotel,' where one guest stated that during the night she was awoken by the sound of footsteps creeping round the bed. In panic she then put on the light and after being satisfied the room was empty again clicked off the light. Several minutes later the creeping sound started up, which was just the beginning of a very long night.

The former 'Oban Caledonian Hotel' or 'Perle Oban Hotel' as its now known however tops these for consistency of sightings. Reports today are a little thin on the ground however back in the 1990's it was alleged to have a few long-time residents. Several journalists took the plunge in investigating the hotel at the time however the reports were largely flannel and focused on pretty much everything other than the ghost. There was one reporter however who after interviewing several witnesses provided solid testimony. Focusing on room 308, which was thought to be the scene of a suicide, back in the late 1950s, it was thought that a young woman threw herself from the turret after being jilted by her partner. Stories like these abound, and often there is no tangible evidence to support them, and so must be taken with a pinch of salt. Since then, it has been reported that housekeepers do not like entering the room despite knowing nothing of its past. The sightings however are not solely confined to that room as was witnessed by one maid. The worker in question got a little more than she bargained for upon witnessing the figure of a woman polishing a table on the first floor, who then vanished on her approach. Another example occurred in September 1990 at around 11am when Liz Barr, a housekeeper, was tidying room 402. While there she was shocked to see a young woman with blondish hair and a pink blouse standing right behind her, whom she later described as looking from the 1950s. Liz said, 'she was young but old somehow, and looked sad. There was nothing nasty about her. We just stood and looked at each other before she vanished. It wasn't till after she had gone that I felt frightened and ran out of the room.'

Running downstairs, the visibly shaking and white-faced maid, was comforted by staff who after much persuasion returned to the scene. On entering they described the room as uncannily cold and one colleague, Moira Tough, described the chill as hanging in the air for several hours. It was also reported that a luggage rack which had been moved by Liz while cleaning, had been put back in its original location. Perhaps old habits die hard? Another apparition also said to haunt the same location has been noted as that of a young girl wearing a mop cap who has been seen crying on the back stair, which I find sad. Given the infrequency of the sightings, I do hope that they have at last found peace. As a footnote and no doubt completely irrelevant, the hotel was apparently built upon the site of a Llama Park, which I find astonishing.

This next occurrence took place in Skipness on the Kintyre Peninsula and was related to me by a landscape photographer who I met coincidentally while on holiday. He described the location, a rented cottage, as being remote and was owned by the local laird. He told me: 'The place was being paid for by a mate of mine and was an old farmhouse situated in a row of other houses. If I said the avocado bathroom suite was the best part of it, you can imagine the rest. It wasn't the best to say the least, the best part being a large Inglewood fireplace which you could sit inside. The décor was very 1960s and awful. I don't sleep so well at the best of times and frequently get up, so this is what happened on the night in question. It was probably about 3 'o'clock and I decided to do some work on the laptop. After a while I noticed that at the door opposite me now stood a woman with arms akimbo glowering at me. She looked like a Victorian farm worker. I stupidly called out, "I'm sorry do you live here?" She then began floating towards me and came around the furniture and now stood right beside me at the table. She had no legs from the knee downwards. Well, I just put my head down and stared at the computer. I didn't know what to do and it was terrifying. She vanished and I headed for bed and didn't tell my wife who was still asleep. There's more because a short time later something sat on the edge of the bed and then something even lighter sat on the opposite side. I got the impression it was a woman and a kid. Well at that moment I just shouted out, "get the fuck out of here," and the bed rose. Well, I never said anything to my wife till we were on our way home and guess what she told me? She had seen the same woman standing on the landing, who then melted through the door. Well, we had a 4–5-hour drive. When we got back, we were anxious. Not long after we were sitting at our table something like the one, we are now sat at, and on it there was a large book with a raffia type book marker in it. The book suddenly jumped on its side. I am literally shitting myself until I realised that our cat had gotten his claw caught in the book marker which was hanging off the edge of the table and in trying to get away had flipped the book. Some years after I contacted the office renting the property, but they denied all knowledge of it being haunted, I suppose they wouldn't admit to it. There's one other thing. Our cat passed away soon after. He was a big cat and used to jump and pull the handle down on the door which would swing open. One night the door swung open and in he walked, he was clearly visible for a couple of seconds. Both my wife and I saw him.'

Before we reach Fife, we stop over at the Coylet inn on the shore of Loch Eck. This haunted hostelry is perhaps best known for being home to the infamous Blue Boy, whose name reached a wider audience due to a recent BBC production. The boy, the victim of drowning was alleged to have sleepwalked into the nearby loch in the dim and distant past. It has been alleged his wet footprints have since been found within the hotel. A recent witness Christine wrote of her experience online for 'Spooky Isles' and though she did not claim the experience had anything to do with the boy himself, it was certainly unusual. While smoking a cigarette on an exit staircase outside, her partner heard footsteps below. A little perplexed he then called out and she quickly joined him. As they stood listening, they both plainly heard steps moving below. Shining their torch into the storage area below, they saw no one, yet the sounds continued. After some moments, they felt the steps vibrate as something began to ascend the metal staircase. It was then they decided to beat a hasty retreat to their room.

In 2018 the Inn hit the headlines, this time courtesy of the Scottish Sun, whose headline 'Bride Eyed Terror,' described what transpired during a hen night. The article was accompanied by two photographs which had previously appeared on 'Reddit' the year before. One of which was of the bridal party standing in front of the loch. The second image contained an extra guest, the figure of a small boy. Seen peeking over a pile of logs, the party were unaware of his presence until checking later. It is most certainly a boy, but is it the Blue Boy?

To add to the mystery a recent conversation with the current owner Sandra, suggested that the most prolific spirit is not the boy but that of a coachman. Having run the pub for over five years along with partner Carl they have witnessed several unusual occurrences and spoken to many guests who have claimed to see his spirit. Described as wearing a dark long coat and tricorn hat, he has been seen for at least the last forty years. Who he is, remains unclear, but he is most definitely from the time of it being a coaching inn. Along with his appearances there have also been reports of personal belongings being moved in the bedrooms, footsteps being heard and in one instance a guest awoke to find a ball of light floating above their face. The following selection of accounts were related to me by Sandra.

Mostly seen in the back corridor the male figure appears to follow a pattern and has often been seen exiting through the front door which is usually kept open. Perhaps he is following a routine that he undertook centuries ago, but either way his appearances are nothing new, as proven by a guest from New Zealand. On arrival she had been greeted by Sandra and during the conversation mentioned that she had worked there as a young woman some forty years ago. To Sandra's surprise the visitor then asked, 'do you still see the ghost?' Recently another guest mentioned that her grandfather had stayed in a static caravan some years back and had also experienced the same apparition.

I was later told that being a country pub its clientele includes several gamekeepers and fishermen who were described as no-nonsense types. Last be prone to flights of fancy, they too have experienced the unusual with the most common phenomena being the sound of footsteps heard on the upper floor. Mostly heard in the corridor which connects the four guest rooms they have been loud enough to have woken several visitors from their slumbers. In one such case, Mick and his driving mate, who work for the company Olleco, were staying over on business. As regulars they are often given adjoining rooms at one end of the corridor and generally enjoy a peaceful night's sleep. However, on one occasion Mick was awoken at around three in the morning by the sound of approaching footsteps and noted seeing the light from the corridor under his door being blocked out momentarily by a large shadow, as if someone was passing by. Perplexed and a little perturbed he eventually dozed off and, in the morning, asked his companion what he had been creeping around in the wee small hours for. His friend replied that he had done no such thing and had slept like a log. On approaching the owner, he was then informed they had been the only guests there that night. On another occasion a Japanese tourist having left early to catch a plane, left a note on the bedside cabinet for the owners. On reading it Sandra was surprised to find he had written, 'who is the mystery visitor?' after having been woken during the night on several occasions by someone knocking at his door. Again, everyone was accounted for.

Sandra explained that because of incidents like these they have had several paranormal teams visit and the consensus is the building is very active and although the spirits have been described as harmless, they appear to like to play tricks. In one room for example it is common for people to wake to find their belongings have been pushed under the bed to the point where guests must get lie flat out to retrieve. More annoying than sinister it happened not too long ago to a couple from the Netherlands who on hearing of the inn's reputation decided to book in for several days. On leaving they met with Sandra and mentioned how much they had enjoyed their stay, but did indicate they were a little disappointed not to have seen the ghost. Sandra sympathised and during the conversation she casually mentioned that in their room it was common for belongings to be found under the bed after being pushed there. On hearing this a look of surprise came over the guests face who then stated that, that was exactly what had happened on their first night there. Perhaps in the end she got her money's worth after all. The Coylet inn is without a doubt an interesting venue and the building which has changed little over the years, appears to be home to several spirits. On a final note, Sandra explained that old photographs of the inn show that there once used to be a sign hanging outside the front door, which read 'no horses.' I was told this was because horses would often try and follow their coachmen inside, and as a nod to the past Sandra has now hung a similar sign outside, much to the amusement of their patrons.

THE KINGDOM OF FIFE

We now enter Fife where our next destination is the Royal Hotel on St Catherine Street, Cupar, which was at the time a busy golfing hotel, built around 150 years ago. It was in 1978 when a regular guest from Dunfermline was passing by the function room when he was struck by how freezing the area was. Shivering, he glanced into the room and to his astonishment saw a monk crossing the floor before vanishing. Several weeks later the assistant manager had a very similar experience while doing a walk round. While checking rooms and switching off lights he noticed the light in the function room had been switched back on. Puzzled he reached for the door handle and on placing his hand upon it noticed it was freezing cold. He then entered the room to investigate and was stopped in his tracks, again by the figure of a monk. Crossing the room he reached the outer wall before vanishing, before the light conveniently turned itself off. Further sightings occurred and after some research it was found that the hotel was of course built upon the burial ground of an old abbey.

Rothes Halls, Glenrothes is next, where the hall, at the time of the report, was being used weekly by spiritualists from the Leading Light Church. While there they claimed that there were three ghosts within the building. Laren Thomson the box office manager, who was interviewed at the time, described how one technician saw what was thought to be the original ghost. According to one witness he was 'a little bit terrified,' and was noted as 'running down the stairs at full pelt, absolutely terrified, with the blood drained from his face.' Staff however were told the spirit was friendly which must have come as a relief. Typical activity at the time included objects being removed or going missing only to randomly reappear days later and apparitions being witnessed in various parts of the building. They were described as solid, seen in full colour and most interestingly dressed in modern clothing. The first ghost and the one that has been longest in residence was noted as a male with long dark hair and wearing jeans while the second was a female figure. Later, one security guard got something of a shock on spotting her and after going to investigate followed her for some time before she disappeared through a brick wall. He described afterwards how she was dressed in a long skirt in autumnal colours.

Most of the sightings have also been noted as occurring on the upstairs level of the theatre, but the question remains who are these people and what connection did they have to the theatre? The spiritualists, on being contacted, were unable to offer any clues as to who the spirits might have been when alive. There was an ancient cemetery that once sat upon the location, however a more disturbing theory is that one of the ghosts may have been the victim of a murder which occurred in the nearby park, though I am yet unable to verify this. The report ended on a positive note however with the staff accepting that all good theatres should have a ghost or two and why should they be an exception.

Culross Palace is our next port of call in the kingdom of Fife. Situated some thirty minutes from Dunfermline, the village of Culross is today best known as a location for the hit series 'Outlander.' A National Trust property, the palace is one of many buildings owned by the trust within the village and it is no exaggeration to say that as you walk around its cobbled streets it's like stepping back in time. Brightly coloured buildings, forestairs, ancient architecture and a maze of winding lanes eventually take you to the ruins of the abbey which overlooks the Firth of Forth. In a village of this age, one would be horrified if it didn't have the odd ghost knocking about and I am happy to report it does not disappoint. The main two buildings I wish to concentrate on are the Palace and the Tolbooth, though I know from what I have been told there are many others. The village is recognised as the best-preserved 17th/18th century village in Scotland, so first a little background.

The palace was built in two halves the first part being 1597 and completed in 1611 and is lined with Baltic pine brought back on ships as ballast, while trading in the Baltic. They were then painted with intricate designs and patterns while some of the struts for the roof were made from pre-1597 ships timbers making it a unique building. Sir George Bruce, the original owner was an astute businessman who made his money from coal and salt both valuable commodities at the time. Discovering an abundance of coal, he mined the foreshore of the Forth, digging deeper until the excavations eventually found themselves deep below the water. It was there that men, women and children toiled in near darkness while above ships sailed by. It was incredibly hard and dangerous work. The coal was then carried on the backs of the womenfolk who were tasked with climbing near vertical ladders to the surface while a wheel system worked constantly to scoop water out of the tunnels. Back on the surface much of the coal then found itself used to heat large salt pans from which a vast amount of salt was produced, the estuary providing a never-ending supply. Salt was literally gold and with this Sir George become very wealthy indeed and what better way to show off one's wealth than by building a grand home.

Sir George of course was just one of many owners throughout its history and like many great buildings of its age, by the 20th century it was in poor shape, having been rented out to multiple families and tenants who were each allotted a room within the capacious building. Thankfully in early 1932 the National Trust stepped in and purchased the property before renovating it. Knowing of its paranormal reputation I made some enquiries and was put in touch with Linda Whiteford. An employee of the National Trust, Linda has had a varied career in media, working across both radio and tourism PR and is a font of knowledge on the history of the building. More importantly she along with several colleagues have had an inordinate number of paranormal experiences, which she was happy to impart. It was, I was told, so spiritually active that even the sceptics who work there have had their lack of faith shaken. This of course was music to my ears and on visiting was regaled with some very interesting stories, topped off by a rather nice personal experience. Even better, I was kindly given permission to use the material as I saw fit and so have included some for your delectation below.

My first stop was the 'High Hall' now used as a dining room and entertaining space. Situated in the oldest part of the house we entered and found ourselves in a long rectangular room complete with dining table and a grand fireplace containing a series of protection marks scratched into the surround which was thought to ward off evil. The phenomena recorded there has included objects being moved or thrown off tables.

In next doors Bessie's Café for example, it was noted that some years earlier a former worker, well-liked by staff, was at one point pelted by scones which were seen to fly off a plate towards her. It was seen as not being malicious but as a means of attention seeking or merely for fun. None of them ever found their mark but nevertheless, she was no doubt grateful they weren't rock cakes. On other occasions a coffee measuring jug was noted as being seen creeping across a shelf, while staff saw a tall shadow figure. Intense feelings of cold would also be noted particularly on the lower leg. Further phenomena were reported during the filming of 'Outlander' and on that occasion the location manager for the series was given short shrift by an irritated spirit who shouted the words 'Get Out!' directly into her ear. Perhaps the spirits were annoyed at the perceived intrusion or maybe they were just not fans of the show, who can tell. Before leaving the dining room though and again referring to the cafe area it was noted that one of the gardeners, heard what she perceived to be the rumble of thunder before realising it came from inside the building, it was she surmised the sound of barrels being rolled. The area was once part of the brewery.

Another interesting story, but this time from over fifty years ago. In this instance it was told to Linda by a middle-aged visitor, now in her fifties, who as a young child of five had visited the house. While there she experienced witnessing a full-bodied apparition, which had interacted with her. On telling her mum she had been admonished for being over imaginative and for years her experience was disregarded as fantasy. It goes without saying that on speaking to Linda she discovered that others had similar experiences. On her visit she had become bored and wandered off where she found herself looking through a door onto a staircase. Outside, on the landing, she then saw a man walking by who was wearing a musketeer outfit. On his head he wore a large hat with a feather in it and was noted as carrying a sword. As he passed by, he turned and smiled, before winking. In more recent times others have heard metallic clinking and dragging sounds which have predominantly occurred in the attic rooms to which the spirit of the musketeer was apparently headed. It is thought the area was once used as an armoury of sorts and the sound of unbuckling swords, metallic belts and spurs have been reported. I was told that a visiting medium who was wearing a Hawaiian shirt, claimed to have felt intimidated in the space as if he was inappropriately dressed.

Our next port of call is the 'withdrawing room,' which is decorated and furnished in the early Georgian style with wood panelling painted to emulate marble. On one of the walls hangs a portrait of the 'Black Colonel,' John Erskine known for his hot temper and occasional soft side too, who moved from 'Auld Reekie' with his family to give them a better life. Sadly, both his wife and beloved daughter Mary, died from TB within the property leaving him a broken man. It was in this space that both my wife Carol and I had a strange experience when left alone. It was a tranquil room, and we spent several minutes admiring the décor. The sunlight streaming through the widows illuminated countless dust particles and they twisted and swirled, it was quite hypnotic. Carol then asked me to step closer to where she stood, where I found there to be a significant drop in temperature. She then felt what can best be described as phantom fingers running down her spine, a tickling sensation more playful than unpleasant, which continued for several minute. I then experienced the exact same sensation. It was quite hilarious in retrospect, as we wandered around the room trying to escape its clutches. When Linda reappeared some minutes later, she asked if we had felt anything, and when we told her what had just happened, she burst out laughing. It is, we were told, a very common phenomena and the perpetrator is thought to be Sir George. We were told that many mediumistic people have picked up on his presence who have that he was a bit of a ladies' man. It is also thought he is particularly attracted to blonds, which would account for my wife, but what of me? He was obviously 'nae fussy,' I surmised. Other spirits thought to frequent the space include a Little Lord Fauntleroy type figure wearing an outfit of cream and gold brocade who stands and observes proceedings.

Speaking of Sir George, the adjacent strongroom is another area where he has manifested himself but this time as a fully formed figure. The strongroom complete with steel door and incredible three-foot-deep walls would have been nigh on impregnable and we were allowed in though normally the area is roped off. This is due to the ancient, tiled floor therefore visitors are normally obliged to stand outside the room in which they can see period furniture, a jar of quills and a safe. On one occasion a young visitor of around five was seen to stare into the strongroom before ducking under the wire. Once inside she began chatting to someone sitting at the desk. Witnesses including her mother could plainly hear her laughing and giggling with someone. Former guide Brian then came along and on asking who she was speaking to, informed him: 'it was the nice man with the funny white thing round his neck and the hairy face.' The guide somewhat taken aback, then asked them to follow him and taking them upstairs showed them a portrait of Sir George Bruce. 'Thats him,' said the girl, before smiling and waving at him. In the portrait we were shown, Sir George is wearing a ruff. Still in the stockroom further phenomena has included quills being pulled from their containers and strewn across the floor and it was there that tour guide Andy had an experience. Specialising in bespoke tours he was given permission to take a group of five Americans around the building and on entering the strongroom one of his guests let out a scream after her ponytail was ironically yanked, pulling her back across the threshold. Again, in the same area, Rick McCallum, a former Hollywood stuntman and founder of Hollywood Ghost Hunters saw the apparition of a headless man wearing a green period jacket and britches. The apparition was seen to walk across the room and was described as completely solid apart from his head which was fuzzy. In a strange coincidence the very next day the old red jacket which had resided in the room for some time had been removed and replaced by green one. They do of course suggest that spirits may attach themselves to things they owned in the physical world.

The Sun newspaper also got in on the act when representatives from the paper decided to spend the night there. Taking a photographer with them, the small band of intrepid reporters settled down for the night. Sometime later and no doubt to enliven proceedings they decided to try and record evidence by asking Sir George what he thought of their presence. The word 'jerk' was then strangely recorded. 'Well, what about me,' asked Anna the reporter. 'Common.' came the reply.

Before we leave the lairds room however one last story which took place during the filming of paranormal show, 'Spooked Scotland.' Presenter Gail Porter on entering the room felt as if cobwebs were brushing her face and at first assumed that what was what was happening. She was assured by staff the room is kept dust free due to the value of its contents. Was Sir George up to his old tricks again?

The North wing was built in 1611 and contains what has been described as a party room where it is thought debauches of all kinds took place. One would describe it as atmospheric with its dark wood panelling upon which there are the remnants of painted imagery much of which is masonic. It came as no surprise then, to be told that the adjoining room was once used as a masonic meeting place. Next in a smaller ante room it is thought initiates waited before undergoing what might be described as torture, or so it was implied. Awful sensations have been felt there and the bacchanals which followed were described as reminiscent of those of the Hellfire Club. While in this room a presenter from Stirling City Radio heard a loud crash from the adjoining room and on investigating found several Perspex panels had been removed from their frames and were now standing perfectly balanced creating a pyramid shape, a symbol used in Freemasonry. It was while we were there that Linda then demonstrated, how the panes can be easily removed.

Hilariously in the same room Linda's personal investigation team, the '3am Club,' held an investigation. It was while using a spirit board that rather alarmingly the word 'run' was spelled out. The group, rightly a tad nervous, then asked 'why should we run,' before the word 'fun,' was spelt. Who said ghosts don't have a sense of humour?

Less fun however was the sighting of a black mass coming out of the strong room, witnessed by three out of the four team members. It was described as rising from the floor before moving up walls and crossing the ceiling of the Laird's room. Though it takes no discernible form it has been suggested it is an elemental, a spiritual energy that can either protect a place or be harmful to those who might trespass or transgress. It is a spiritual accumulation of all that has been fed into it over the centuries, perhaps long before the house was even built.

It is strange how certain spaces have completely different energies as if the misdeeds of the past are still present and as we toured the atmosphere would go from playful, to heavy. One such pleasant room was the Garden Room or 'Mary's room,' as it has become known, commonly thought to have been used by the daughter of Colonel John. As mentioned, she unfortunately passed away due to consumption and consequently her spirit has reportedly been seen since sitting or kneeling at the window. It's a small room, the four-poster bed taking up most of the space and it is there that visitors have often reported feelings of tightness of breath, supposedly a physical manifestation of the poor girl's demise.

Moving on we reached the principal stranger's room, once used as a bedroom for visitors to the palace. We were told, the activity in this space is wide-ranging and has included reports of a spirit monkey being seen, described as gambolling and clambering across the bed. It was there that an investigation team claimed to have captured several images which showed a two-foot-high figure moving around the room with ease. It was, as Linda suggested, a very bustling port and it was not uncommon for sailors to take back exotic pets. Another more common place animal has also been seen there which is the spirit of a medium sized dog. Friendly of course, as most dogs are, visitors have claimed to feel the canine spirit rubbing itself against their legs.

As we reached the end of the tour Linda then took us to her office where she showed me an astonishing photograph taken when the reenactors of the Clan Ranald Society held a 'Pirates and Redcoats' event. Raising money for charity, the Clan Ranald event attracts many supporters who dress in period costume. On that occasion the house was opened for people to use the facilities including those who wished to change and so there were many people in the vicinity. A few impromptu photographs were taken at the time in which participants held a press up competition in front of the building. Above the proceedings, a resplendent figure in a dark curly wig could be seen clearly at the window, and on inspection the likeness is uncannily like that of the portrait of the colonel which hangs in the same room. It was without a doubt a very intriguing image which I hope one day will be made public. Linda assured me that at the time there was no one was in that area.

Moving on and literally a few yards from the Palace sits the Townhouse, another historic venue. Now used as a shop and gallery, it was at one point the last holding place of 'witches,' kept there before trial. One can only imagine what took place within its walls. Linda, among other staff have described feelings of nausea and people on entering decide to leave quickly due to overwhelming feelings of unease. BBC Scotland presenter Susan Calman visited the several years ago while filming the show 'Secret Scotland,' and was said to have felt quite upset by the feeling within the building.

I hope to revisit Culross at some point soon but for now, the next venue is a block of flats in nearby Tillicoultry. Coming to prominence around thirty years ago, the story featured in the Scotsman when they ran an article on the former weaving mills of J & D Paton. Situated in Weavers Row, the now converted property consists of flats and as we all know nothing annoys a ghost more than a conversion. The ghost, thought to be that of a child who died in the mill, began making itself known by plastering both shower gel and varnish over the unfortunate homeowner's wall. The owner a twenty-year-old bank clerk who was interviewed soon after described a litany of woes including fusing lights and something interfering with the heating system. Naturally upset she was then encouraged to contact a medium in the hope of finding answers which she did.

The medium after perusing the flat insisted, she should tell the child off in no uncertain terms, which she did, despite her reservations. The medium then went on to explain that the flat was being haunted by the spirit of a five-year-old child who drowned in a nearby well. Sometime later she discovered through a local newspaper that another child had also died in similar circumstance circa 1963. The owner resolved to staying there stated, 'the most frightening incident was when I was in my bed about 3am. I always sleep with my head underneath the duvet. Suddenly there was this thundering noise as if somebody was stamping round the room in a circle.' A former worker at the mill, alluded to the fact that the area in which the current flat sits was always creepy and her husband, also a mill worker had on occasion heard footsteps following him while there was no one there. I have at present been unable to find further evidence of the haunting so perhaps the scolding did the trick.

Of all the alleged Poltergeist cases in Scotland, at least in the last century many would argue the most infamous is that of the Sauchie poltergeist which became national news a family in 1960. The location, 19 Park Street, in the village of Sauchie in nearby Clackmannanshire has been well documented and there are several fascinating books on the subject. What makes it so intriguing though is that supernatural phenomena in the area is still, according to reports, ongoing. In the next few pages, I will briefly look at some of these cases but first back to 1960 where occupants, Thomas and Isabella Campbell, welcomed their niece Virginia Campbell to her new home. It is commonly thought that poltergeist activity can be caused by an individual during a period of stress or high emotion and if that is the case then this was the perfect storm. Uprooted from her home, her father and beloved dog remained in Ireland while her mother was forced to work away from home in the village of Dollar. To compound the issue, she also lost her privacy having to share a bed with her cousin Margaret. She was however resilient, and her aunt and uncle did their best to provide a happy home. On the 14th of December of that year a series of events unfolded which were recorded detailing the varied phenomena that plagued the household. This is what was said.

'Virginia was in the house with dad. He said while I was away an apple came out of the dish three times and the clock came off the cabinet and hit Virginia on the nose. A Brillo pad came out of the kitchen and into the living room. Virginia was using the vacuum cleaner, and it went off and the rubber band flew off the handle. A chair tumbled over. There was a little knocking on the big chair. Virginia gave three knocks (on the table) and there were three knocks back. Virginia was pinched on the side and the girls got pinched in bed. The bedcover turned red when it was green. There were noises like somebody walking across the floor.'

The phenomena continued and included witnesses hearing what was described as a rasping and sawing noise and on one occasion a drawer flew open and the linen rippled, 'like a pond in a stiff wind.' Even at school the phenomena continued, most of the testimony coming from Margaret Stewart her teacher. She later described witnessing a desk levitate, doors flying open and a pointer vibrating on the table. Others then got involved including a local minister, spiritualists and the police. Whatever it was terrified the family and was akin to the famous Enfield case occurring some sixteen years later. The phenomena lasted around five months and suddenly stopped. Virginia upon reaching adulthood appeared to suffer no ill effects and was never plagued again by such incidents. The street where she grew up however is still alleged to be haunted and in recent years several residents have claimed similar phenomena to that reported in 1960 is still ongoing. Interestingly most were not alive when the original 'haunting' took place.

This example from the Sunday Post took up the story around forty years later when reporters interviewed Nicola

Benard who moved into the same street in 2001. Having just settled in with her husband and her two young boy's supernatural phenomena was reported within a matter of weeks. She described ghastly smells emanating from an old coal cellar next to the kitchen and soon after her eldest son was wakened on several occasions after having terrible nightmares. He later stated that he was awoken by a woman sitting at the end of the bed. In the aftermath of this his mum would stay with him when he was scared and on one occasion, she too saw the same figure. The room was later described as always having a horrible atmosphere. Appliances would often malfunction, and the kettle was noted as constantly switching on and off. Sometime later she described seeing the 'sheets changing colour,' this of course is interesting on many levels as the very same phenomena was reported to have occurred in November 1960.

Soon after another interviewee, Avril MacDonald related similar tales while living nearby and stated that quite often loud scratching and clawing sounds could be heard against the walls for no discernible reason and that they suffered from, 'peculiar dreams.' However, she had stayed in the property for around fifteen years which would indicate the phenomena was less persistent. Despite this the question remains why is there so much phenomena connected to one location, and more importantly does it have any bearing on the original, 'haunting?' It is an enduring mystery, and the original story was featured in 'Poltergeist over Scotland' by Geoff Holder among others. Later, it was written about in greater detail by Malcom Robinson, author of the 'Sauchie Poltergeist and Other Scottish Ghostly Tales,' both books I highly recommend.

Staying with Sauchie we now have another haunting, this time, the Gartmorn Road poltergeist, which is another interesting case. Given the proliferation of stories the area certainly appears to have had more than its share of haunted houses, quite worrying I would imagine, for anyone contemplating a move. On that occasion the phenomena was investigated by Malcom Robinson and Ron Halliday, (Scottish Paranormal Investigation) who went beyond the call of duty by staying over in the property. Whatever was causing the phenomena however seemed reticent to let itself be known under such scrutiny which was no doubt frustrating for the investigators. Despite this, they nevertheless collected some compelling evidence.

In this instance however it wasn't only one family under the cosh as it were, but three, all of whom lived in adjoining houses, and it soon became apparent that the middle property appeared to be the epicentre. Reduced to living communally downstairs, the residents avoided going upstairs due several frightening encounters. Often loud disembodied bangs and crashes were heard and in one frightening incident, their dog was found bloodied and scared after being locked in one of the upstairs rooms, injuring itself attempting to claw its way out. The question was who put it there? In the aftermath the poor dog would react violently during any attempt to take it upstairs and rightly so.

The three sets of tenants were rightfully anxious as the phenomena ran the usual gamut of furniture moving, drawers opening and closing, and objects being thrown. Perhaps what made this even more terrifying though was the strange and unnatural noises which accompanied the above, included growling and what was described as swishing noises, heard coming from unoccupied rooms.

One of the residents, an eight-year-old boy also witnessed on several occasions the apparition of a man and a woman holding a baby, who he later described in detail to his mother. The child later claimed that the woman spoke to him on several occasions and expressed a dislike of 'next doors dog.' According to the boy, the woman went on to say that she had been responsible for locking it away to stop it biting the baby. The ghost(s) also mimicked others and on more than one occasion different family members heard their loved ones calling out to them but upon investigation found them either sound asleep or even more alarmingly not in the building. During the investigation further creepy incidents were reported including someone, perhaps possessed for a short time, speaking in an unrecognisable voice, and what appeared to be the doppelganger of the mother, witnessed walking downstairs. Despite attempts to communicate with her, the figure retreated upstairs without speaking. The witness finding her behaviour somewhat perplexing, followed her only to find the 'real mother' sound asleep.

Frustratingly the researchers were unable to capture the evidence they were after and so working with local ministers and spiritualists, the house was blessed, and mediumistic help sought. It was then revealed that perhaps the culprit was an earthbound family who may or may not have died in a tragic accident nearby. It's a fascinating story and too in depth to do it justice here, but I recommend further research.

Lothian and Auld Reekie!

Now journeying over the Firth of Forth we enter Lothian and the capital of Scotland, Edinburgh, home to more ghost stories than you can shake a stick at. It certainly has the credentials for a haunted city with its dark history and buoyant tourist industry and because of this it sometimes never lets the truth get in the way of a good story. Despite my cynicism there are of course many genuine and quite terrifying encounters from the city which have been covered extensively in a multitude of books. Below is a selection of tales old and new including the following from Inch house, which I, along with other members of Paranormal Scotland Investigations (PSI) visited earlier this year. A castellated tower house, dating from the 16th century, James Winram its owner, had both his and his wife's initials carved into the original pediment above the door, however since then the building has been expanded on and has an even grander entrance. The current structure was sold in 1946 to Edinburgh Council when it became a primary school before its latest incarnation as a community centre, and a grand one at that. On visiting our guide Kevin, a former pupil, gave us a walk through. It was certainly an experience, and it contains many interesting nooks and crannies along with several alleged ghosts. On the night of our visit, we spent several hours investigating its spiral staircases, cellars and basements in the hope of capturing evidence of ghosts. Rumours had circulated for years about its most famous incumbent, the 'Grey Lady,' who is thought to be the spirit of Lady Gilmour, its last owner. First decamping to a very impressive medieval turret we set up some cameras, attempting to coax the resident, or should I say reticent, ghost to make herself known. Unfortunately, as is often the case, it was a no show, so we headed downstairs to the cellar area with its barrel-vaulted ceiling. It was a little chillier there and as we sat, we heard several distinct sounds coming from the furthest corners of the room.

We then visited the old staff quarters which though more modern were quite creepy. The area was semi- derelict in part and bitterly cold and as we crept from room to room, our shadows played ahead of us before the torchlight. We then entered the old caretaker's living room where disturbingly we came across a massive mound of chewed magazines lying in the middle of the room. The shredded paper, obviously nibbled by mice, was strangely incongruous in the empty room and in the middle one prominent scrap, which they had omitted to destroy, stood out. With grim fascination we gathered round and on inspection discovered that upon that solitary scrap was an image of the actor Benedict Cumberbatch's face, which if you pardon the pun, was very strange indeed.

Afterwards we visited a corridor back in the older part of the building but again nothing out of the ordinary occurred. However, all was not lost as on asking several questions we received a few replies for our troubles. Of course, one could argue that the words we captured may have just been coincidence, but given they were direct affirmations, this seems unlikely. Hunkering down for one last session we now sat in the cellar where on asking out, one of our team Kerrie, recorded names such as Graham or Graeme, Robert and Sarah. This is of course my name and that of my brother, but that doesn't really prove anything.

Some minutes later, while sitting on a small set of stone steps, one of the team Kerrie, felt herself pushed. It was the best physical evidence that was felt during our time there. The recordings, then listened to over the ensuing weeks, produced some compelling evidence including the recording of a deep male voice. Quite clearly the voice of an American, he repeated the words, 'goodbye baby,' twice. It was one of the clearest recordings I have ever heard. Who it was, I have no idea, but we must assume it was someone connected to the building, we hope to find more.

Paranormal investigations are sometimes like waiting for a bus, you wait for ages for one and then two come along at once and soon after I had the opportunity to be part of another investigation, this time in Craigentinny House or the 'Castle.' This great building erected in 1604 for James Nisbet on the lands of Restalrig, was passed onto successive Nisbet Lairds until 1764 when bought by a wealthy quaker, William Miller and subsequently inherited by his son William Henry Miller. A later owner, an MP named Samuel Christy was an absentee owner preferring to spend much of his time in England and the house and sprawling estate slowly became a little less sprawling as it was nibbled away by the ensuing council developments. Despite this, intriguing glimpses of the past including ancient buildings, and ruinous walls can still be found randomly dotted throughout the estate. The castle today survives and is being put to good use as a community centre and is quite unique, possibly the oldest community centre in Scotland, though certainly in the oldest building. But is it haunted? Quite possibly given some of the evidence recorded. What is most interesting though is that it does not feature on any top ten list of haunted locations in Edinburgh which for me is very refreshing. There had of course been several investigations in the past and hats off to those involved for their efforts and their findings. The ghosts, according to reports have included that of a green lady, a staple of most castles, the figure of a woman seen hanging from a tree, several male figures and disembodied sounds of marching. The latter it has been suggested harks back to the time when the centre was used as a drill hall.

Our contact was Vikki Cavanagh who kindly allowed our group to spend an evening investigating. On arrival we split into two teams, collected various pieces of kit, cameras, cat balls and then went our separate ways. Our group focused at first on two rooms, a small basement office and the games room before going outside the premises. Al fresco investigating is always fraught with danger, random noise pollution being the most common issue but given what transpired in that area we felt it was at least worth a try. It was there during WW2 that an entire wing of the building was destroyed by German bombers. This incident tragically claimed the life of the building's caretaker. As the evening progressed, I recalled that on my initial visit I had felt uneasy in the games room in which the figure of a man had been reported. This was our first port of call but despite my own expectations nothing happened, and I had for my sins made assumptions based upon the queasy sensation I had felt before. Strangely the more I hoped for something to happen the less it did, and soon a quiet desperation sank in. Despite this we carried on and stuck to our plan, made more difficult by hearing what appeared to be positive noises coming from the second group. While chatting to my wife Carol afterwards she was able to give me a brief account of their evening and by all accounts they received some great evidence from the get-go. With great responses to questions and lights being switched on and off upon request it sounded like an investigator's dream. It was all very positive, and I suppose proved a point that ghosts can't be in two places at once. Maybe their energy was more attractive to those on the other side. It happens.

Despite our own shortcomings we did however capture some interesting voice phenomena which ironically, was recorded outside despite our misgivings. Once there we found the street and surrounding area quiet, so we then decamped to the area where the bomb had struck and sat on a low wall near the perimeter of the building. While sitting, one of the team, John, then enquired if anyone was present and a brief conversation ensued with him asking questions such as, where was the spirit from and did it know Leith? On playback it was found that an impressive array of answers had been recorded, all delivered in a strong Irish accent. It was all going swimmingly until the spirit took umbrage to a certain question and told John to 'Fuck Off!' Somewhat taken aback on hearing this, we would no doubt have complied had we heard it at the time. All in all, a very interesting evening but as with most investigations one can never expect miracles.

On another note, an impressive mausoleum, known locally as the 'marbles' can be found nearby. Once standing on a commanding position atop a nearby slope it is now surrounded by modern bungalows. It is the last resting place of one William Henry Miller, and his burial chamber is alleged to be anything from between 17.5-50 ft below the surface. The reason for this is mundane, likely because of a morbid fear of body snatching, but it was rumoured that he was a vampire, buried deep to keep his marauding corpse locked safely away. Why anyone would come to this conclusion is baffling. In the 1940s for example Miller's grave was again subject to scrutiny when a policeman on doing his rounds made a startling discovery. Interviewed many years ago, Bill McDonald, described what happened to his colleague while patrolling the street adjacent to the 'marbles.' On that occasion, he noticed the door to his tomb was ajar and on entering played beam of his torch down the shaft. Shocked to see what he thought was someone moving below he did not wait to gain a better look and slamming the door he ran. No doubt a trick of the light, but it was enough to resurrect the story as it were for at least a little while longer. But the story doesn't stop there, as Miller was also rumoured to have been a woman, which if true would have made him the first ever female MP. Why did this rumour start in the first place? Well tenuous as it might appear he was described as not having a beard, was frail and softly spoken. That could account for a good proportion of the population I would imagine. Whatever the truth of the matter the poor soul seems much maligned.

Before we leave Craigentinny though, one last story from a longtime resident, Mark. It's a strange tale and would have caused me to question the motivation of the witness had I not known him personally for some years. He is down to earth, a genuinely decent person, and to this day cannot explain what he and a friend saw at the back of Craigentinny house while playing when he was a child. Alerted by the approach of what they thought was someone walking towards them, they hid behind a hedge. When the figure came into view, they were horrified to see that although it walked upright its face was described as that of a werewolf type creature. On passing, they noted, it appeared to be looking around for something and on turning its head to the side, Mark described seeing a very prominent snout. Hardly daring to breath, the two kids remained frozen until the creature reached the end of the lane, where it paused and again appeared to look around. The boys were by this time beside themselves with fear and so deciding it was now or never, bolted without looking back. He later told me that at that age, he had no idea what a werewolf was, but it had long shaggy hair and a long snout and was solid looking. Later while having a walk around the area Mark took me to the location and described to me how different it looked back then, the hedge they cowered behind for example had now long gone.

Now a brief stopover at another beautiful Edinburgh building, the former Craiglockhart Catholic Training College for teachers. This grand building was initially owned by the Craiglockhart Hydropathic Company but became a convalescence hospital during the great war specialising in the treatment of traumatised soldiers. Its most famous, 'guests,' were the poets Wilfred Owen and Siegfried Sassoon. After some two years it was then acquired by the Order of the

Sacred Heart, firstly used as a convent it then became the training college, with both a boarding and day school attached which ran from around 1920 until 1986.

Now owned by Napier University I recently spoke to Vivienne who works in the library who has recorded many of the ghostly encounters that have taken place within the building. Unsurprisingly some of the most notable reports feature the apparitions of nuns, but there are others. Witnessed across campus and the library, formerly the swimming pool, in one instance one such figure was apparently seen walking through a wall near the 'Rivers Suite.' Later a joiner saw another similar apparition on one of the upper floors. I was also told that staff claimed to have had a feeling of someone being behind them while walking around the building and in another incident one cleaner spotted an elderly woman walking along the corridor towards the Hydra Café, before it was open.

There is however something more destructive at work as staff on arrival one morning found a bookshelf, which had been hammered into the wall, tipped over. On another occasion an interior glass panel was also found to be inexplicably smashed which had been intact the previous evening when security had locked the building. At other times books were reportedly found to have fallen from shelves, which could not have happened naturally. Vivienne stated that they had been placed flat on their respective shelves, with none of them overhanging, therefore there was no reason they should have fallen, unless physically taken. She then told me about Gail, a long-term employee who had worked at the coffee servery for many years, who had described to her an incident that took place when the building was a convent. She said that at one point one of the nuns had hung herself, and in the aftermath of the tragedy the room had been bricked up. When Edinburgh Napier acquired the building, they opened the room up again and since then cleaners have claimed to have heard doors opening and closing when there is no one there. Other reported phenomena such as lights being switched on and off randomly and of course occasional sightings of black clad figures were also commonplace. I admit there is something a little creepy about the idea of a phantom nun, and the idea of meeting one unexpectedly while going about one's duties in such a cavernous building would be an unnerving prospect.

According to reports, visitors to the building have also encountered the spirits of long dead soldiers. The following account was reported by Joss Cameron and was recently featured in John S Tantalon's book, 'Tales from the Crypts of Auld Reekie.' In it she described visiting there as a child with her mum. She stated that on one occasion while she was heading to the main building she looked up and noticed a figure in an army great coat standing in the tower above before he promptly vanished. She later described seeing the same forlorn figure on several occasions. On making enquiries as an adult, she was told that the access to the tower had been blocked off many years before due to the number of past suicides. The building, as I previously mentioned, had at one point been a convalescent home for those suffering from mental stress and shell shock while fighting in the Great War. Wilfred Owen, once resident there, had at one point christened it 'Dottyville.'

Still in the company of Vivienne and Julie from Napier, I was passed on some further stories, this time regarding another university property this time at Craig House on Craiglockhart hill. A beautiful mansion built circa 1565, it replaced its older namesake which was destroyed in the rough wooing (when Henry VIII sacked Edinburgh) Typically going through several changes it became a psychiatric hospital in the 1880s and remained so until purchased by Napier, just over a hundred years later. Many students were no doubt in awe at the splendour of their surroundings on studying there, its wood lined rooms, grand hall and staircases no doubt an inspiration. In 2013 however the university sold the property, which was then developed into, you guessed it, housing. A move lamented by many.

Described in Cassell's 'Old and New Edinburgh,' as a 'weird looking mansion,' it literally consisted of three villas which were intentionally joined together to give the appearance of a country house rather than an asylum. I have only seen photographs of the interior, but the great hall was quite stunning and ornate fireplaces adorned many of the rooms. In 1972 it was renamed the Thomas Clouston Clinic but was shut around twenty years later.

It has, or at least had several ghosts befitting a building of its age. The one most widely discussed was the 'Green Lady, 'and though her identity remains steadfastly elusive, she was reportedly seen on several occasions. I was intrigued but on investigating I found that the poor thing had nary one decent sighting to her name. Despite this, there has been other more tangible phenomena as reported, by recent Napier staff members. These included people smelling the unmistakable odour of cigar smoke, someone hearing a baby crying in the attic and the sound of a piano playing. Possibly the best piece of evidence however was the sighting of a young man in a long leather coat, with long slicked back hair who was seen entering a toilet but never came out. Who he was has remained a mystery, perhaps the lost soul of a former student or worse still a patient.

Still in Edinburgh, but now on Princes Street we arrive at the Royal British Hotel whose ghostly credentials came temporarily to the fore when featured in a book from the 1970's by Hans Holzer. Travelling across Britian in search of ghosts, Holzer was, and still is, recognised as one the greater paranormal researchers in modern times and a prolific author. He wrote, that upon reaching Edinburgh he decamped to the hotel where he was joined by an old friend Elizabeth Byrd, who as we know from earlier had previously stayed in Leith Hall. She subsequently wrote about her own experiences, one of which took place in that very hotel. It was, as she later found out, the scene of two fires which on both occasions caused fatalities. Fire number one which occurred in 1971 was the result of deliberate arson by a recently employed chef, Robert Docherty, and the fatal enquiry report found he had deliberately set fire to a box of waste wallpaper in an occupied room. He was of course caught and during sentencing his actions were described as wicked and reckless. Unmoved by proceedings he remained impassive giving no indication as to his motive. The victim, a female guest from Glasgow, had no connection to Docherty and was unfortunately in the wrong place at the wrong time. He was jailed for nine years at the High Court in Edinburgh. Robert Collins Docherty, 24, married with a young child had only been working at the hotel for only three days when the incident occurred. Several years later, in 1973 another fatal fire broke out this time claiming the life of a Welsh rugby fan.

In the aftermath, it was found that many of the hotel fire extinguishers did not work, and escape routes blocked off.

During their meeting Elizabeth recounted a story that occurred around a year before when she met with a book dealer friend at the hotel. While there she left to use the bathroom and on entering the ladies was overcome with a horrible feeling of dread causing her to flee, though at the time she had no knowledge of the previous tragedies. It was an intense and terrifying experience which left her feeling sick and eager to leave. Had she picked up the energy of those past events?

It is hard to say but reading on I was astonished to find a further revelation, in which the author claimed there had been a historic fire which had left 200 people dead! Obviously, this was news to me, and I suspect many others. A brief check revealed nothing of this nature ever took place and I can only assume that this was a huge oversight by the author, rather than an attempt to pull the wool over anyone's eyes. Later Elizabeth's friend claimed the ghost or presence felt in the bathroom had nothing to do with the fire but rather a suicide. She stated a housekeeper had come to a particularly gruesome end in the room and claimed the residual energy of that grim passing had been absorbed into the walls. Either way it gave me a brief shudder.

Speaking of haunted toilets, there is one in Edinburgh's alleged most haunted pub, the Banshee Labyrinth, in Niddry Street. Supposed to be the favoured hangout of a ghost named 'Jock,' his motivation is open to speculation though he appears to get his jollies by lurking in the smallest room, taking great delight in terrifying customers. Now I am generally sceptical of these types of stories unless there is any evidence, and having never used the haunted facilities in said pub, I found myself at a crossroads. However soon after several guests from my Old Town tours obligingly told me the following after visiting there.

The first, a student from the Netherlands, claimed while in the cubicle the bolt on the toilet went from open to close with great rapidity as she sat inside. She said she was genuinely scared and peeking under the door saw she was the lone occupant of the bathroom. Her friend then corroborated the fact, saying that on returning to the bar her friend had asked to leave. There have been several similar encounters including one from my wife who on visiting the ladies described the toilets as creepy and felt as if something was present there. Later, a couple on my Old Town tour asked if I could suggest a convivial pub and I recommended they go there. They said they might, and I left it at that. On the next day I was taken by surprise when the same couple approached me on the Royal Mile and enquired as to why I had not mentioned that the toilet in the Banshee was allegedly haunted. Somewhat taken aback I sheepishly replied I had forgotten to, which was true. She then told me what had happened after they took up my recommendation and she described that while washing her hands there, something had wrenched the bag off her shoulder. It was a forceful tug strong enough to undo the pin which held it onto her lapel. I asked why it had been pinned on and she told me that while recovering from a recent operation her husband was obliged to pin it there to stop it falling off as she was unable to use her hands properly. It is no exaggeration to say that afterwards they both left the premises rather hastily.

Now back to 1835 when Maria Theresa Short, an entrepreneur, opened the Camera Obscura as an attraction on Calton Hill. Forced to close it several years later she then relocated to 'Outlook Tower,' the present-day site of the camera. It was then eventually taken over by the great Sir Partick Geddes, town planner and all-round philanthropist, who opened it as an urban study centre where all were welcome, and many got their first look at the outside world through the lectures and exhibitions he presented. He was great man. After his death in 1932, the building changed hands before ending up, in the spirit of its founder, as an attraction based on illusions. Maria, the original owner who apparently died in the building is thought to be one of several ghosts who are still present in the building as investigators have claimed there are multiple apparitions. Conveniently next door, the infamous Ragged School, also stood and it came to prominence when featured on 'Ghost Hunters International,' some years ago. It was an interesting watch, taking the subject seriously unlike most other 'ghost' programmes and in that episode, they investigated the loft area of the building. They appeared to find some intriguing evidence in what is now, the Camera Obscura shop. Keiran, who I have known for many years was a former employee at the venue and he was happy to provide the following report which took place in the camera itself. Keiran explained, that on one occasion he was with a group of visitors who were sitting in a half-moon formation. While there he became aware of a white, small, child sized shape out of the corner of his eye. At first thinking it was just a reflection on his glasses he turned to the group who appeared puzzled at his increasing discomfort. He told me later that it felt like someone had invaded his space and so after the tour he asked a colleague to sit with him in the same location out of curiosity. While there he called out to see if there was anyone present and later described sensing an unusual atmosphere. Convinced he had a paranormal experience he began asking around and soon several reports surfaced including one from a cleaner who reported hearing a child's voice say distinctly in their ear, 'can you help me?' Other areas of interest were noted as being near the mirror maze which led to several cleaners being anxious to work there as icy cold sensations were also commonly reported. On one occasion Keiran heard someone whisper the word 'Shh!' loudly in his ear. Co-incidentally his colleague Isaac also heard the same voice at the same time, though both thought the other was responsible. Sometime later a cleaner received a fright after finding a half empty bottle of apple juice lying in the middle of the floor. Muttering to himself, he bent down to pick it up only to have it forcefully slapped out of his hand. He said afterwards that he was struck with some considerable force. Now heading back down the Royal Mile we reach South bridge and at its head, The Bank Hotel.

It has in recent years changed hands however around twenty years ago it hit the headlines, due to its alleged haunting and the article detailed the spiritual hijinks which allegedly took place there. It made for interesting reading and the main witness Linda Morrison, a former worker, claimed that while servicing rooms there she heard giggling from inside a locked suite. Knowing the room should have been unoccupied she investigated but found it empty. On another occasion a visiting writer from London experienced something a little more alarming on witnessing a ghost in room number five, where he resided, later describing the figure as being crouched. He stated that it had creeped from the ensuite bathroom towards the bedroom window before vanishing. Sometime later a German tourist described seeing the very same apparition. Management at the time claimed, that despite some scepticism, there were too many sightings to discount the possibility of it being haunted. The building which had been a bank when built in 1923 was described as having a creepy atmosphere in places particularly on the second and third floors where strange voices had been heard frequently. Keen to find out more I contacted the hotel regarding the stories but so far, I have not been cordially invited to look around.

Going back in time now to 1965, we head to Pendleton Gardens, again in Edinburgh. In this instance the spirit, thought to be the former homeowner made itself known in several ways, only stopping after the intervention of two self-described local amateur mediums. Despite a lack of faith in their own abilities they still managed to clear the house as it were, so kudos to them for their efforts. It is also curious to note that the spirit, somewhat reticent to make an appearance, took nigh on two years to show itself, something of a record in these cases.

The first indications that something out of the ordinary was afoot began with the homeowners noting a strange crackling sound coming from the fireplace despite it not being lit. This aural treat occurred in different parts of the house. Further unaccountable noises then occurred including the sound of a dog barking, a kettle boiling on the stove, despite no kettle being present in the room and thumping footsteps. On investigation, the witnesses claimed that doors would then literally be slammed in their faces. On another occasion the bathroom door, half open then swung fully open on their approach. Something it appeared was intent on attracting their attention.

Soon after unexplained knocking was reported on the walls and while lying in bed the householder heard footsteps clumping up the path towards the front door, followed by a sharp volley of knocks. The occupant's wife and mother both investigated and on running downstairs found no one at the door and the path empty. The spirit then began to move objects, like the rug being taken from the bathroom and found on top of the bed or an ashtray removed from the bathroom during the night. According to reports most of these events took place while the owners were away for the weekend, which they did quite regularly, but on returning home found the house in disarray. In one bizarre occurrence they found a large piece of wood, the back of an old gramophone, lying flat on the floor, despite it being securely propped up against the wall. Perhaps you might assume, as I did, that vibrations from the nearby road had caused this, but not so, as it was again found to be lying on the floor despite being secured behind two chairs. Afterwards they could only speculate as to what had the dexterity to do this as both chairs had not been moved. Whatever it was obviously liked playing games, but was it malicious? Further phenomena such as the loud meowing of a cat heard coming from the kitchen soon followed and they found their own cat sitting transfixed by something in the middle of the room that wasn't there. It was reported that the phantom cries had not come from their own pet!

After some deliberation, a visit by two mediums was arranged and on looking around the premises they announced that the spirit was that of an elderly ginger- haired lady, who had become ill and ended up in hospital. They also stated that there were some objects within the house, or at least in the deceased woman's lifetime, which was associated with freemasonry. The owners no doubt suitably impressed with this revelation explained that when purchasing the house, the seller had been a ginger haired lady whose mother had recently passed away. The owners then further corroborated the mediums claim by stating that when they had taken up residence, they found in the attic some items relating to a masonic lodge which had belonged to the elderly lady's late husband. The mediums then politely appealed to the spirits better nature, asking her to relinquish her hold on the property. The former owner not realising till that point, she had passed on complied, and the haunting ceased soon after. If nothing else, it proves that not all spirits deliberately set out to terrify the living and It's usually our reaction I suspect which is at fault.

Here is an example of one such positive experience which was told to me after one of my Edinburgh tours. On that occasion I got chatting to a former local now living in Aberdeen who related the following which took place in his student days. This is what he had to say: 'when I was a student, studying at Edinburgh Napier, I used to live in a large flat in Dumbryden, Wester Hailes. It was a large ex-council flat with four rooms. At the time, I lived alone and only congregated in one room, to conserve the heat. Some of the windows in the flat were broken, so were always left slightly a jar. During the winter, I'd find that the cold was so bad that I would need a blanket constantly, to stay warm. One night during December, I came home after work and all the electricity had stopped working, it turned out that the power grid had shorted and the whole street was without power. I was tired so I decided to just call it a night and fall asleep on the couch. During the night I was woken up by a weird feeling and found I was lying on my back, directly facing the ceiling. When I opened my eyes, I could see an elderly lady standing over me in a comforting way. I quickly stood up and tried to adjust my eyes to the darkness and looked round and the presence was gone. Quite shaken by the experience, but in disbelief, that this was something other than my eyes adjusting to the dark, I fell back asleep. I slept for a little bit longer and suddenly had the same strange feeling. I was lying on my back again, facing the ceiling. I opened my eyes and suddenly could see the same elderly woman standing over me staring at me. I lay there for a second to take in what she looked like and noticed that she was quite frail with wrinkles on her face. After the second experience, I couldn't go back to sleep and ended up staying up all night, until the power came back on.

A few months later, my dad passed away. It had been a long time since I was in contact with his side of the family and afterwards my uncle gave us lots of photos of the family. I'd never seen my grandparents up to that point, and to my surprise found that my grandmother had the exact same face as the presence that I saw that night. In some strange way it seemed like she was looking over me and making sure I was ok, like a type of guardian angel.

A great wee story from the King's Theatre which featured in 'Edinburgh After Dark,' by Ron Halliday is next. The theatre currently undergoing a refurbishment has had its fair share of creepy tales attached to and so I am curious to see what happens on its reopening. Spirits do not appear to like change, so either they might move on or if not show their displeasure, my money is on the latter. It was noted that one theatre goer got a little more than he bargained for after attending a play. At the interval he went to the bar but despite being there previously, he found himself lost. Now heading upstairs, he soon came to a dead end and a little perplexed, began to retrace his steps. It was then he noticed a woman walking up towards him. Passing him on the stairs, he was shocked to see she was floating above the steps and wearing old fashioned clothes. On passing she then went straight though the wall. Running downstairs, he blurted out his story to his companion who at first thought he was joking. Who the mysterious figure remains unclear as he felt too embarrassed to ask if others had reported a similar experience.

Back on the Royal Mile for this next story, which was related to me by an ex-policeman, whose colleagues witnessed the apparition of two young children while patrolling. On the night in question, it had been snowing heavily and by all accounts its thick blanket lay across the High Street inches deep. The officers one male and one female were no doubt cursing their luck for having to be out on such an inclement night. As they made their way toward the Tron Church, they were arrested, if you forgive the pun, by the sight of two young boys wearing old fashioned clothing who appeared to be playing on the steps of the church though they made no sound. The officers momentarily glanced towards each other before striding purposefully towards them. What the hell were they doing out at a time like this? The boys at first unaware of their approach suddenly appeared to notice them and scurried away, heading down nearby Niddry Street. The startled officers now in pursuit turned the corner mere seconds later only to be met by an empty street and in the grand tradition of any great ghost story, there were no footprints.

Later, on returning to the station and having decided to recount their experience, the shaken officers were met with incredulity. My source being one of the only ones to believe them listened intently. The officers, he told me, were genuinely perturbed by their experience and described the boys as being young, wearing caps and tweed like jackets. Who the boys were is anyone's guess and to my knowledge they have never been seen since. It's a good story made more so by the wintry conditions in which it took place, and even better by a chance meeting with the daughter of one of the policemen on duty that night. Coincidentally or not, I was telling the above story recently to a group in the Waverley bar. At the end of the event, I was approached by a member of the audience, named Linzi. She told me that one of the officers at the station that night had been her dad, and his colleagues had not been taken seriously. Personally, I was glad the story was corroborated.

Prizing ourselves away from the High Street we now find ourselves in Tollcross and again looking at another vintage tale, this time from the 1980s. The location was Coasters, a popular venue at the time which contained three separate bars, The Outer Limits situated on the ground floor, The Bermuda Triangle and The Barbados Suite. It was around that time that a series of articles appeared in the local press which I read avidly. It would appear liquid spirits weren't the only kind to be found there, and you guessed it, those interviewed were cleaners. Their experiences were well documented at the time and several articles were written about the phenomena which included random puddles of water appearing from nowhere, glasses being broken and strewn across the floor during the night and the sighting of shadowy figures. One witness even described seeing a 'vacuum which danced by itself,' we've all been there. It was further stated that the phenomena appeared to be most prevalent around the Barbados Suite. On January the 2nd of the same year it was reported that neighbours heard the terrified screams of a woman coming from the premises which prompted several people to try and gain access. The ensuing investigation revealed nothing. The papers then interviewed three cleaners who happily recounted their experiences including a Mrs Hetty Graham who witnessed a strange figure while having her break. She described it as, 'drifting back and forwards before it just went away.' She then bolted from the room. Her colleague, Tina Stewart then described a vacuum cleaner which was seen to operate by itself. I have heard similar reports several times including that of a friendly child ghost who asked the cleaner 'what is it?' Perhaps then, a spirit from the past might be fascinated by modern technology.

Later the former Manager Rick Protheroe suggested that the ghost could perhaps be that of a young girl who was allegedly meant to have perished in a fire in 1922. Further investigation however found no evidence of anyone dying in such circumstances. The medium who visited however, was convinced a young man was the culprit, who remained earthbound to the area. It was also reported that another club, this time Tokyo Joe's, was reputedly haunted. The manager who appeared keen to share his experiences while working there was interviewed when the local paper ran the story. This time the ghost took the appearance of a tall man wearing a cape who was seen to frequent the club after hours. One staff member at the time was quoted as saying, 'we sometimes held seances after the bar had closed where all manner of things would happen including chairs moving by themselves. Sometime later a local reader contacted the paper with her own theory suggesting the spirit might be that of a young lad who disappeared from Morrison Street during the Second World War. Again, frustratingly there is little chance of discovering the truth of the matter though it seems unlikely a young lad would have worn a cape. Was it coincidence however that both clubs were situated back-to-back but in different streets?

The following account took place in 2004 in Comely Bank Grove, Edinburgh and was related to me by one of my fellow guides, Sjoukje. It serves as a reminder of the little surprises one can encounter when renting. Edinburgh properties at the time did not remain on the market for long, which was best described as buoyant, and this was the situation she found herself in having newly arrived in the city. Struggling to find a suitable flat she was delighted on viewing one property in one of the nicest areas in the city, Comely Bank. The flat which had been newly renovated was described as beautifully stylish, a cut above the usual bargain basement offerings and so when the offer of a tenancy was approved, she couldn't believe her luck. The excitement however did not last long as after around two weeks of moving in, the first of several unsettling experiences occurred. On one occasion for example the built-in wardrobe door was seen to slowly open of its own accord, granted not necessarily the first sign of a haunting, still it was a little unusual. Unconcerned at first, she surmised it could have just been the fixtures settling, however when it began happening with other doors her suspicion grew. 'I then began to find lights had been switched on in rooms where I was convinced, they hadn't been,' she later told me.

After a month a waterpipe then randomly burst behind the shower which flooded the flat, afterwards she stated, 'again, this could have been explained away with bad plumbing, but I always felt I was not wanted there, like I was unwelcome and recalling the feelings of being watched I had to endure, still gives me the chills to this day. The thing that I always remember the most though was when I was awoken at about 4am one morning by a loud scratching sound on the front door, not like a cat scratch, it was much louder like it came from human fingernails. The noise lasted for around five minutes while I lay terrified in bed.' Unable to stand it any longer she crept tentatively to the peephole and on looking out saw nothing. At that moment the scratching stopped. Bolting back to the safety of her bed she then phoned the police in panic. They listened politely and promised to have someone look which they did, the next day, by which point she had already checked outside, finding the door unscathed. Strangely though, she discovered that one of her wellington boots was missing. She stated, 'the police called late next morning to see if I was alive, which was good of them. They seemed unimpressed and suggested the boot had probably been taken by a drunken neighbour.' A quick round of enquiries round the houses produced no further clues and as of today the wellington remains missing. Perhaps a neighbour took it as was suggested, but it appeared unlikely given all were elderly or professionals certainly not the usual suspects in cases of theft. This was the final straw and after a mere six months she left, moving ironically just around the corner where she then resided peacefully.

We now find ourselves in Leith at a property on Prince Regent Street which I read about on a Facebook group. In the post a tenant in one of the properties described several frightening encounters. Occurrences such as a hatch in the attic crashing shut unexpectedly, mirrors falling off walls frequently, and candles being blown out all pointed to poltergeist activity. It came as a bit of a surprise however when several contributors claimed to know the property in question, as it had been the scene of a murder which took place some years back. The circumstance from what I gather were both unpleasant and sad and so I won't provide further details but suffice to say it is fairly apparent this is likely the cause of the haunting. One person following the thread later stated that her late brother also stayed in Prince Regent Street, though couldn't recall the exact number. Be that as it may it was claimed that after coming home one night he took off his boots and ten minutes later was terrified to see them 'walk across the bedroom, while accompanied by a strong smell of tobacco.' Afterward he was described as running from the house, refusing to stay there ever again. Another resident in the same block then claimed that strange phenomena had also taken place in her flat. While there she described the atmosphere at times as being foreboding and regular occurrences such as cupboard doors flying open randomly and the TV switching on by itself were common. Their young baby would also wake up screaming, nothing unusual in that you might say, but the mother claimed it would occur coincidentally when the phenomena took place. To compound it all her five-year-old daughter was scared after seeing the figure of an old lady sitting in a chair by the window. There may be more to this story yet to come and certainly judging by some of the responses several flats in the vicinity appear to have been home to something out of the ordinary.

Not being one to have covered too many stories of white ladies or indeed ladies of any hue in the past, I succumbed to temptation as this tale fascinated me because of the volume of sightings. In 1964, renowned psychic Elizabeth Byrd who features elsewhere in this book decided to visit 'Woodhouselee,' a then semi ruinous house in Edinburgh. Accompanying her was a small group of like-minded individuals including Ian Groat, a local gunsmith. He had claimed to have had several uncanny experiences at the property and knew the area well, so Elizabeth something of a magnet for ghosts was delighted to tag along. For those that believe a spirit can attach itself to the fabric of an old building, despite it being moved, this is a good example for 'Woodhouselee' had been erected using stones from its original namesake, situated some miles from its then current location. The original structure, according to local tradition, had been haunted by a 'White Lady' and was allegedly demolished due to a proliferation of ghostly occurrences. Somewhat fanciful as it was more likely for practical reasons. Either way the lady was thought to have moved with the stones, having been seen in the vicinity of the new building, though never inside, her wanderings confined to the grounds. Local workers at a nearby stables for example were interviewed at the time and several attested to seeing the figure. The stories were also verified by locals who used the area for walks. But the question was, who was she? Scotland is littered with tales of ladies of a similar ilk, think the 'Ghosts of Motley Hall,' but in this instance she might have had a name as it was suggested it was the spirit of Lady Ann Bothwell, the original mistress of old 'Woodhouselee.' Legend has it she met her end by being cast into the snow by her husband's enemies, naked. It was further said that she herself did not die from the ordeal though her child did. The resulting breakdown and subsequent search for her missing child continuing for centuries.

It had all the requisites of a classic ghost story and so Elizabeth and her companions, after undertaking a reconnaissance of the area, settled down in the cellar, amongst the fodder stored there. It was in poor condition by this point and was described as 'having large chunks of masonry falling from it and the roof had caved in though the grand stair was intact though rather perilous.' Looking at the photographs one can see online it was a tragedy that the building was destroyed but I will get to that soon. After a two-hour vigil they were rewarded by the appearance of a white blurred figure which could be seen through the crack of the cellar door, from where they remained hidden. It was described as moving backwards and forwards for five minutes before vanishing. During the time it made no attempt to enter the area where they hid and the witnesses who included a Mrs and Mrs London all agreed upon what they had seen. It was a most fortuitous visit, though no photographic evidence exists of its appearance.

Further investigation found that the British Army had used it during the Second World War and had invested a large sum of money on the building where they installed heating. It was then used as a prisoner of war camp. Interestingly well at least according to the story, sentries at the camp kept accurate records of their patrols and in a three-year period it was noted that there had been 14 entries relating to the appearance of the 'White Lady.' who on one occasion was challenged by a sentry before vanishing. She was however never seen inside the house. After the 1964 vigil the house was sadly demolished over the course of a weekend and upon the area a chalet was erected for the son of a local lord who conveniently owned the estate. It was around this period that Elizabeth Byrd made further enquiries to the estate manager who in the absence of the landowner allowed them to visit the chalet. It was to an extent, or at least implied, that the chalet was a glorified holiday home. Above the fireplace it was noted that a stone frieze from the original structure was now embedded and upon it carved the legend, 'Occultus Non Extinctus.' meaning the occult is not dead, a peculiar motto to have in one's home, particularly given the period. The question however remains, does the 'White Lady' still wander the grounds of the estate?

I read about the following many years back and it's a strange tale even given the parameters of the subject. It unfortunately involved a lone witness, named Tom Alder, so there was no one to back up his claims. Given that, it's a vivid description of what may have taken place in the 1970s. The date being nonspecific causes one to wonder at the veracity of the tale, but like the author who first recorded it there is level of trust in the telling. One night while passing Gorgie Cemetery near Slateford Road the witness glimpsed movement within the graveyard which lay beyond the glare of the streetlight. Assuming it was someone walking around he paid little heed, particularly as he had chosen that route on many occasions. However, that night would be different as he was to soon find out as his gaze was arrested by a misshapen figure. It appeared to be wearing a cloak of some description and further recounted that another figure began to rise out of a grave. This he described as female and wearing a corpse's garb. Frozen with fear he felt that his presence had now been detected and the cloaked figure turned towards him. Now getting a clearer view, he noted that it was human shaped but with spindly arms and legs. The female figure then pointed at him, at which point he screamed. Running around the church along Harrison Street he avoided the usual route and on arriving home looking somewhat dishevelled was quizzed by his wife. Naturally she seemed unimpressed accusing him of drinking though in fact he had only had two pints. It was some considerable time before he retook that route, but whatever it was did not reappear again and as far as we know his sighting remains in isolation to this day What was it? Something demonic, an elaborate prank, who can say, and after forty years it looks unlikely to be solved.

An obscure haunting from the Broughton area next, on the site of the long-gone zoological gardens. Once home to tigers, monkeys and other exotic creatures it was demolished in the 1800s and the remaining hall, one of a group there, including, Powderhall and Logie Green, was supposed to have been haunted as most halls should be. Broughton House, because of its high walls and expansive gardens attracted much speculation from the populace, none more so than from a local father and daughter, Violet and Robert Chambers. They led a bohemian lifestyle and had recently moved into a row of newly built houses which were on the edge of town but now sit within Broughton today. Back In 1845 however there were many interesting places to explore and Violet, who became author Violet Tweedale as an adult, would describe them in her books in later years. Her father Robert, who she obviously adored, would often undertake midnight rambles, looking for ghosts. He had an artistic temperament, was fun, and judging by the authors account did not adhere to the mores of the day. She later said, 'Broughton house was commonly reputed to be haunted though no one knew by what, my father and I would be fascinated and often creep around the property at night on illicit ghost hunts.' She went on to describe how her father would often stay up working late and then suddenly sit upright before announcing that they should visit the house. His daughter, around six years of age at the time would then excitedly grab her coat before rushing for the door. Now creeping in the shadows in the garden of Broughton House they would keep vigil in hope of seeing something. Perhaps they didn't really want to see a ghost but were content to stand in the shadow of the mature trees surrounding the property, or bathing in the glow of the moonlight, but either way six years later they did. It was on a bitterly cold November night, with scudding clouds obliterating the moon, that they once again stood in the grounds. The blinds of the property were drawn and the occupants, oblivious to their nocturnal visitors slept soundly. Traversing one of the paths, Violet who remained nearest to the wall was suddenly alerted by the sight of a woman with a pale countenance and two strands of black hair running toward them. She was moving at what was described as a frantic pace and as she got nearer, they noticed her bare arms were outstretched in front of her. Young Violet dove behind her father in terror, and he quickly stepped aside as the ghost flew by, though not a sound was heard upon the stones as she passed. Her father in a pique of curiosity then swiftly followed leaving the terrified youngster in their wake.

Following as best she could she eventually found her father panting by the gate who on getting his breath back related how the figure had vanished as he was about to touch her. Who the lady with the black hair was has remained a mystery and despite further visits she never appeared again. The house of course and the grounds no longer exist but one must wonder, had any others seen her?

Still in Edinburgh the following occurrences took place in the infamous South Bridge vaults, perhaps one of the most haunted locations in the city. Here is what I was told. 'I visited Edinburgh with my ex-partner and decided to do all the tourist stuff, the castle, open top bus, and a ghost tour. The most interesting was the underground caverns underneath Niddry Street, a stone's throw from the Royal Mile. When visiting the caverns, the tour guide asked the men and women to stand in two lines parallel facing each other and switched off the lights, so that we were in total darkness. The area was cold and eerie with moisture dripping off the stones. When I looked to my left, I could faintly see each person standing in a line, as dark silhouettes. Suddenly I could see another person standing in front of one of the tourists, looking directly at them. I thought for a second that the tour guide had planned someone to jump out and scare us, but as I looked closer, I noticed that the silhouette would change from a solid shape of a person to a ball of static. The figure then stood in front of each person and looked directly in their face from about an inch away with a threatening, aggressive stance. The weird presence then reached me, and I could see the silhouette directly in front of me, looking me in the face. I could feel its presence and felt intimated by how close it was standing. I had to pull my face back. I continued to watch the silhouette as it moved to the end of the line before it walked into the darkness and faded away. I personally don't believe in ghosts and my scepticism, thinks that the silhouette was my eyes adjusting to the darkness, but at the time it felt very realistic, like having a nightmare that paralyses you in your sleep.'

The vaults are thought to be haunted and of course there are many candidates as to who the spirits might be. As a refuge for the poorest of the city there has undoubtedly been many deaths in the area, some natural others not so. The 'Watcher' or 'Mr. Boots,' is probably the most documented apparition however there is one area that is allegedly thought to contain something a little more out of the ordinary, this section containing two abandoned Wiccan Temples. The first, initially used by The Source Coven of the Blue Dragon, was eventually abandoned and though locked is now a feature of the tours. The second room which is smaller, and more rustic contains a stone circle in which it is claimed a demonic entity has been captured. On ghost tours or at least the one I attended guests were invited to step inside to see if anything happened. I have in all honesty spoken to many people who have witnessed this over the years and surprisingly a fair proportion have taken a bad turn whilst many others don't. It is perplexing, however I was told on good authority some time ago that the entity in the stone circle story was created to add a frisson to proceedings, so are the reactions of guests then psychosomatic? Maybe not, as a further conversation suggested that the entity is genuine. It is however not contained within the stones but rather was inadvertently 'allowed in' during a ceremony in which a mirror created a doorway. A terrifying prospect indeed.

But now for some stories, the first supplied from a guide called Kieran, who had the pleasure of working there. He told me that while conducting tours within the vaults over extended periods of time it was not uncommon for guides to experience certain unusual events shall we say. At different times this had included rapid changes in temperature and hearing inexplicable noises such as knocking or rattling and on occasion human voices. These voices were noted as whispering, speaking random words, screaming and shouting. On one such occasion, while leading a tour, Kieran described hearing a woman's scream whose pitch sounded like a roller coaster, starting softly building to an ear piercing crescendo and then fading away to nothing. He told me it sounded like it had come from a throat that was straining, the vocal cracked with exertion. Alarmed to say the least the Kieran manfully continued with his tour. Afterwards an American woman approached him and much to his surprise said it was disappointing that he had never mentioned the scream. Kieran, somewhat taken aback had assumed he had been the only one to have heard it. It was then the rest of the group spoke up, each describing the same sound, each keeping silent, afraid of being ridiculed. A collective experience of course is worth its weight in gold and a further discussion with a colleague proved it was impossible for anyone to have been in the vicinity who may have caused this. Who was responsible for the scream is difficult to answer but it is known there were several murders committed in the area, and very possibly many more that will forever remain unwritten. One potential candidate however could very well be the spirit of a local prostitute, Mary McKinnon, who is alleged to be present in the vaults having been hung nearby for murder.

On a second occasion the same guide described entering what is commonly referred to as the dark vault and in doing so placed his group against the wall. As he shone his torch around the room, he became aware of three wide eyed French visitors at the far end and moments later he was 'rushed by a shadow.' Somewhat startled he quickly played his torch towards the group convinced the three tourists were trying to play a trick but found them still rooted to the same spot with a look of fear upon their faces. Could it have been the infamous Mr. Boots or the Watcher? Soon after another guest in the very same area refused to enter one of the rooms because, 'a woman in a white dress stood there.' There was of course no one visible but a woman matching her description had been reported as being frequently seen there. I was told that the guest who was described as burly, tattooed and looked like he could take care of himself, appeared nervous. The guide sensing this assured him there was no one in the room, and that no one would be playing tricks, so the guest grudgingly entered and stood with his back against the wall. Keiran then told me that despite his assurances the visitor remained agitated throughout and at one point looked emotionally upset by what he claimed to be the presence of the woman. But who was she? A local prostitute named Elizabeth is one potential candidate who it is claimed was lured to her death in the shadowy confines of the South Bridge. Another possibility might be the previously mentioned Mary McKinnon who lived at number 82, the South Bridge Tavern, a notorious brothel of the day. On one occasion while protecting her girls from an over-exuberant client she killed him accidentally in the altercation. Whether he was rich, or poor was irrelevant as she was a prostitute and on the lowest possible rung in society. A plea of self-defence was therefore thrown out and the poor woman shown no mercy, being hung nearby. Her restless spirit is said to still haunt the area where the tragedy of her passing took place and so joins an impressive roster of potential candidates.

Still in the South Bridge I had the good fortune to be passed on the following firsthand accounts from another former guide, Tonks Brown, and was told that her tours, on occasion, ran between the Greyfriars Kirkyard and the vaults. It's a hard job at times as I can testify to, and the guides must be conscious at all times of the wellbeing of their guests. Sometimes things happen unexpectedly, so one must always think on one's feet, but what if they are under threat from something unknown and potentially dangerous? The following are examples of events which left both guides and guests terrified. Of course, some say the whole thing is psychosomatic and is merely a physical reaction to good storytelling, after all the atmosphere in the vaults is unique. But what if there's more to it? After reading I am sure you will have made up your own mind. The first incident Tonks described took place on a daytime tour notable for a trendy looking guy who had clearly been dragged along by his partner. Despite his lack of interest, the tour started normally with the guide explaining they may encounter 'cold spots,' and as it could be a spirit drawing energy from them, it might be advisable to step aside. With the initial introduction over they then headed to vault number five. This vault is the one which guides falsely claim is the most haunted, the reason for the deception being to eliminate 'experiences,' which might be psychosomatic. The real haunted vault however is number four and it was there the fun began. Once there the disinterested guy then claimed to be standing in a cold spot and so as was mentioned at the beginning was advised to step out of it. As he did so he received a hefty punch in the lower stomach for his trouble which sent him tumbling backwards, then cracking his head on the arched wall. No doubt trying to remain cool he quickly regained his composure and despite the guides concern insisted on continuing. For the remainder of the tour, he then stood next to the guide and upon finishing in the torture museum, the guide took him outside and asked how he was. Incredibly he responded by saying: 'I don't believe in this shit' which left the guide speechless. A firm sceptic he no doubt put it down to wind and an uneven floor.

Moments later they were then interrupted by one of the young girls who had been on the tour as a birthday treat, not the best of ideas the guide later conceded. The girl who she judged to be around ten or eleven then asked if it was normal on tours to feel like someone had put their hand up your t-shirt, claiming to have felt someone stroking her back. Tonks then replied that it could be something spooky but suggested that it was more likely to have been one of her friends playing a trick. The girl then replied that it couldn't have been as she had been standing at the front the whole time, which on recollection was true. Obviously a little anxious, Tonks then suggested that once above ground she would have a look to which the girl agreed. Once outside the girl then lifted her t-shirt revealing several long dark scratches down the length of her back, like cat claws. Anxious of what she had seen the guide then played it down by saying the young girl must have been the poltergeist's favourite. Goodness knows what her family must have said on hearing the news. Afterwards Tonks excitedly related her experiences to a colleague, who remained nonplussed. The phenomena were by all accounts a regular occurrence as she was to soon find out.

The following took place some months later and is described in her own words: 'In the torture museum at the beginning of the tour I turned my back on the group and then, thud! one of them was on the ground. Now this is weird because you can normally tell when someone is about to collapse but there was no sign. So, I ran to her and when I got about a foot from her, she started to make this noise. Now I've got friends with epilepsy, and I have heard all the weird noises a human can make. Over the years I have tried to replicate this sound, and I can't. It was such a horrendous sound it made me stop in my tracks and back away from her. After a couple of seconds, I realised I was the one supposed to be in charge. So, as I touched her, she opened her eyes and looked around. I said, "are you ok," and told her she had fainted and that she was lying on the floor. She said she was and then insisted on continuing the tour. Then on entering one of the vaults, I put my candle on a lip on the wall and as soon as I had done so, one woman entering the room collapsed, her knees passing under her. Luckily her partner caught her in time as it was a concrete floor. She was out cold and again when she recovered said she had never fainted before. "Great," I thought, not even five minutes in and two people have fainted. Now standing in the haunted room and about five minutes into one of my stories, this huge guy just suddenly screams and leaps out of his skin, and we all scream as well. I then asked him what happened, and he said a drip from the ceiling must have fallen on him. We then all broke out into laughter because we were so nervous and started calling him a "big jessie," and things like that. Afterwards I take them into the non- haunted room and get them lined up with men to the right and women to the left. I then get into position, and I am about to start talking and as soon as I open my mouth there's this animalistic shriek, like an animal being peeled and its coming from the wall that separates us from the actual haunted vault. Of course, all the women scream and run away from it, and I also screamed and ran away. After a moment I pull myself together and say, "who did that," and then a deep rumbling man's voice, from behind the wall where I know there are no people says, "Me." We end the tour right then and go up to pub where I tell the rest of the stories. I tell them I am sorry and if they feel cheated, they can come back to the office in the morning and get a refund. I just felt we were getting a lot of warning shots. On leaving someone says, "you should get an Oscar for that performance, you looked genuinely terrified." But it was real.' Afterwards the onsite safety officer, Terri, surprised to see the tour finish so early asked the reason. While explaining they heard a coughing sound coming from behind them and on turning saw the massive guy from earlier. Obviously having heard their conversation he then stated that although initially he had thought the whole thing was 'bullshit,' he changed his mind when forcibly grabbed in the collar bone and tugged. It was that sensation which had made him scream. Considering this, Tonks was accompanied that night on the final walkaround while blowing out the candles. Hats off to her, I am not sure, even in company, I would have relished the prospect.

There were numerous other incidents two of which resulted in what can only be described as a physical attack. In the first, the guide felt as if there was a pair of hands around her throat causing her eyes to stream and for her choke which unbeknownst to her had left vivid mark. On finishing her shift, she then headed to a nearby club no doubt grateful to be with friends and on arrival one asked what had happened to her neck. Heading to the bathroom she then discovered a large weal which looked uncannily like a noose had been placed there. It then remained evident for some time before fading during the night. Similarly on another occasion a second physical attack took place in Greyfriars at the black mausoleum. A creepy location, it has no connection to' Bluidy' George MacKenzie, the alleged ghost, whose mortal remains are buried nearby but is nevertheless thought to be haunted. There are certainly numerous, books, podcasts, programs claiming to tell the real story but frankly they raise more questions than provide answers. Nevertheless, physical attacks liken to those in the vaults are most reported. On that occasion, Tonks felt nothing out of the ordinary and on finishing went to catch up with friends. Sometime later she received a shock after going to the bathroom and noted there were thirteen scratch marks across her legs. Strangely there had been no physical indication of it happening while standing in the black mausoleum.

On another evening, in the same location, this time while taking part in 'Ghostfest' (a short-lived festival dedicated to all things spooky) another incident took place. On this occasion the group led by Tonks was in the company of a well-known historian, famous for being in the television program 'Most Haunted' and during the proceedings they held an EVP session in the vault. Electronic Voice Phenomena may or may not record 'ghost voices,' depending on your belief, but it is thought that perhaps spirits can communicate this way. I am not completely sold on the idea as was Tonks but despite her reservations she participated, asking the spirit or spirits to tell her something that no one would know, what was her real name. There was no forthcoming answer and so someone else was then given the opportunity to ask something and though the question was unrelated to Tonks, the voice was heard plainly to say her name. It was something of a revelation. I have visited the vaults myself on several occasions and in fact stayed overnight there during 'Ghostfest' and I was witness to nothing on that occasion, but on others, well that's a different story. Suffice to say I am certain there is something unpleasant in the vaults and quite possibly at Greyfriars Kirkyard and I salute those who work there daily or at least those sensitive enough to be troubled by it.

Now leaving Edinburgh we venture into the Lothian region where there is no shortage of uncanny tales. The following selection starts to the west of the capital in the town of Livingston where several years ago the local authority was asked to help rehome one of their tenants, due to a ghost. Adamant that his home was haunted, not by just by one spirit but rather five, his account of events reached the local paper. Many readers of course assumed the householder had exaggerated events in the hope of getting a move, however the Sutherland Place home had recently been refurbished and the tenant Mark, liked living there. According to his testimony all was normal until some renovations took place, soon after things began to occur on almost a daily basis. Phenomena described included the stereo being switched on at around 4.20 in the morning despite being switched off. On one occasion some five minutes after this occurred, he described seeing a sort of 'white blur' at the end of his bed which turned away before disappearing. It was, according to his account, around the same height as a human. His partner Leah was also terrified when an invisible entity held her down while in bed. Although this could have been a case of sleep paralysis it was still a traumatic experience which previous sufferers, will testify to.

News spread and a previous tenant confirmed on interview that he too witnessed ghostly happenings during his five-year tenancy. When questioned he stated that he did not report any of the incidents as 'people would think you're a nutter.' He similarly claimed that his experiences included feelings of a weight pressed upon him and sightings of a figure being seen at the foot of his bed. Mark no doubt frustrated at the lack of urgency then contacted a local medium who after a quick once over proclaimed the house was haunted by up to five entries none of which thankfully could be described as evil. The ghosts, according to the psychic included an elderly couple who appeared to be from the Victorian era. When interviewed she said, 'There is nothing particularly evil, although one was a bit rude, and he swore at me.' I must admit this made me laugh. Mark however found nothing to laugh about and as the council was moving at a glacial pace on the matter he upped and left, decamping to the sofa at his girlfriend's parents' house. He further added that he would be writing to his MP in due course, though I am not entirely sure if they would have been au fait with such spiritual matters.

Still in Livingston, and to another house this time in the appropriately named Dedridge estate. These three storied properties were thought to be so badly haunted at one point that not one, but two exorcisms took place, with the tenants eventually rehomed by the council. In this occasion it was thought that the poltergeist activity was centred around lodger Lorraine Ronaldson, who, if the stories are correct, was subjected to a frightening physical assault which included being dragged across the living room with 'blood spurting from cuts and slashes which suddenly appeared on her throat and face.' Six similar attacks had previously taken place according to an article which appeared in the local papers in 1987. On the back of this Livingston Development Corporation quickly arrange for tenant the Avril Perkins and her two young children to be moved.

Why the lodger was targeted is unclear but at varying times a male voice was heard to shout obscenities, gas taps were turned on and ornaments thrown across rooms. It was described as chaotic and the phenomena strikingly familiar to many high-profile poltergeist cases. It was at the time investigated by the late Archie Roy, a renowned expert in the field of paranormal investigation who after studying the case conceded that unlike some previous cases, it was unlikely to have been a mass hallucination. The two exorcisms which took place afterwards were carried out by both a local minister and an ordained medium. How successful they were is still unclear as is the fate of the lodger and frustratingly the story just petered out as many do, leaving us to wonder whether it was the property or the person who was the catalyst.

Now onto another appropriately named location, Gorebridge, where sits the grand Borthwick Castle famed for its haunted Red Room! Borthwick castle dating from 1430 is a Scottish tower house whose previous guests have included both Mary Queen of Scots and Cromwell, the former seeking refuge within the castle. It was said she then dressed as a page boy slipping from the castle unnoticed before making her escape. Now a high-end hotel it is used for weddings and events but some years ago when in its original form, one could rent single rooms. It received and no doubt still does get great reviews with one visitor on TripAdvisor remarking how the guest book was full of comments regarding ghostly and unusual experiences. In 1978 the Dalkeith Advertiser published an article which suggested the spirit was thought to be that of a servant girl who fell pregnant to one of the lairds, who was then tortured and murdered for her troubles in the Red Room. Because of this, the castle has for some time had its fair share of occurrences, with guests claiming to have experienced unnatural freezing temperatures and hearing scratching. One such guest, a writer, had a very sleepless night after hearing footsteps leading to her room followed by frantic scratching and in the morning several notable marks were noted as being found on the door. Another potential spirit is thought be a former chancellor who after embezzling a large sum of money was caught by the lairds' men and as punishment burned to death. Either way the activity back then was so prolific it was rumoured a priest from Edinburgh was asked to perform a blessing. Did it work? Perhaps not as some recent reports suggest there is something still residing there.

In a recent blog, a well-travelled individual documented a frightening experience which took place while staying at the castle with her boyfriend. In it she stated that on arrival there she found the atmosphere quite heavy which was present most of the day. After dinner they then retired to the Red Room and got ready for bed. She later claimed to have been awoken by the sensation of being pulled on both arms which felt as if she was being pulled out of bed. Now awake she noted that the room was pitch black and she could see nothing. Settling back down she was again woken by the sensation of someone trying to pull her into a sitting position. Throughout her ordeal her boyfriend refused to awaken despite her best effort. After a long sleepless night, she told her hostess what happened who replied that several woman guests have gone through the same. One even claimed to have seen a sad looking girl on the edge of the bed. Strangely on each occasion their partners could not be roused. It's a very intriguing story but one doomed to bear no more fruit as on contacting the hotel I was told, albeit very politely, that the current regime does not like to discuss anything of a paranormal nature. Strangely on the night I was looking at some stories from the castle, my wife had a weird experience and felt as if she had been visited by the spirit of a young lassie who touched her arm during the night.

Dalkeith is our next stop, where a haunted fire station on Abbey Road resulted in a blessing taking place. Recently speaking to an ex-fire service employee, now a volunteer at the Museum of Fire in Edinburgh she told me that around twenty years ago a series of supernatural occurrences took place at their place of work. Formerly the location of an abbey as the name suggests, sightings of a phantom monk were reported soon after work was done on the building. Firemen were reportedly subjected to a series of terrifying events with disembodied screams reported and loud banging and knockings being heard from no discernible source. Terrifyingly one fireman sleeping at the station awoke to see the face of a ghostly monk looking down at him which was protruding from a nearby wall. Due to the ongoing phenomena a team of spiritualists were soon called in described as members of the Angel Gateway Spiritualist Church, who then performed an exorcism. It was said that it was organised behind the back of the powers that be, at least according to what I was told, but I cannot verify this. Either way the blessing then took place in which the leader of the group claimed the spirit was that of an earthbound monk, Thomas Howard, whose terrible crimes kept him bound to the physical plain long after his death. I spoke to several firefighters recently who knew of the story. One told me that someone from Blue Watch had taken what they thought was a picture of the spirit which at one point had been pinned up in the station, but its location is unknown today. He told me they had named the spirit 'Tam.'

What crimes he had committed remains unknown, but an account of the night's proceedings suggested that the lead spiritualist was forced into a kneeling position with her hands folded across her chest. The monk then communicated that this was the position he himself had forced upon his victims and further stated he had dabbled in the black arts. Who his victims were was never elaborated upon, but after some time it was said the apparition left the building and moved on.

Back in time now to 1974, where the location was the Armadale 'Highlander Hotel', in Lothian, which at the time was run by new owner Jim Sibbald. Whether he knew anything of the buildings reputation I am unsure but soon after he described seeing the ghost of a bald man in a brown robe. The ghostly monk prone to being mischievous allegedly terrified staff including Elizabeth Hutton by grasping her ankles while she closed the bar. It was described as a very frightening experience. Later several guests, witnessed the same figure who on that occasion provided them with a party trick by walking through a wall. In another incident it was reported that a local photographer was hired to take pictures of damage which had been done to a bathroom by vandals. Setting up his tripod, he then focused his attention on photographing the damaged tap not realising at the time that he had company. Afterwards at home he began to develop the images and noticed something peculiar as there appeared to be an odd reflection on the taps surface. Curious, he magnified the image and upon it he could clearly see his own reflection in the tap but to his surprise a second figure was also noticeable standing directly behind him. It was the figure of a man with a bald head, wearing a brown robe. He later said. 'I could see my own reflection, my tripod and the man. I could make out his eyes, eyebrows and moustache. He also stated that he would be more than happy to show anyone who disbelieved, the print for themselves. I wonder what happened to the image. Other customers also noted nocturnal visitations including that of a woman in grey who was seen standing at the foot of a bed, while another claimed to have seen a pair of eyes staring at them, which she later described as floating on their own. In the bar glasses were frequently seen to move by themselves and in one instance a terrified staff member allegedly handed in her notice after witnessing a painting 'fly across the room.' Someone else who needed no persuasion that the building was haunted was musician John Connell. John whose band 'Hollis Brown' were booked to play in the lounge, later described that while running through their set, he saw out of the corner of his eye the figure of man wearing either brown robes or a cloak. He immediately stopped playing and despite being a practical person could provide no explanation of what he had just witnessed.

Now in West Lothian our next stop is Bo'ness which sits seventeen miles northwest of Edinburgh close to the Firth of Forth. It has of course, like most towns do, a smattering of creepy stories and legends attached to it. Regarding this I was passed on this story by Stuart Simpson who provided some historical or should it be hysterical information about the ghost alleged to haunt Kinneil House. It's a great wee story which I enjoyed reading. This what he said. 'My great uncle John Simpson was custodian at Kinneil House for many years. He was something of a "character" and used to regale visitors with tales of drinking tea or playing cards with the ghost of Lady Alice Lilbourne (a previous owner) He claimed she cheated! He was also at the centre of the great ghost scare in the 1960s when hundreds of people were turning up every night in hopes of seeing something. The "manifestation" seems to have been audible rather than a sighting though, for in the end, "an owl with asthma" was taken away. Other suggestions (as to the hauntings) were attributed to the sound of the Gil Burn running echoing through the tunnel under the big house. The legend is that the good lady jumped out of the window into the burn whilst it was in spate. I think it was the Daily Record who first did a silly piece on the story with my late uncle John, posed sitting in an armchair looking like for all the world Alfred Hitchcock while reading a book, "Best Ghost Stories" (bought of course by the reporters). There was a caption, "Me? I don't believe in ghosts." Between the owl story and the Record story interest then died down. Is lady Lilbourne still haunting Kinniel House? Incidentally I see from time-to-time people referring to the "white lady." I believe this name was made up in relatively recent years as in all my lifetime she was referred to as simply 'the ghost.'

STIRLING

Historic Stirlingshire, boasts many great ghost stories, including several from its famed castle. One of the finest in all the country, it looks down upon the famous battlefield of Bannockburn, which in 1314 saw Robert the Bruce vanquish the English oppressor, Edward II. Much like Edinburgh its historic, old town, has many wonderful survivors from the medieval period. On visiting Stirling Castle, I was hugely impressed and as part of the visit we were given a tour around the building. It was very interesting though I was particularly interested in hearing a few ghost stories, which I had winkled out of the guide. She appeared quite happy to tell me, though I got the impression that Historic Scotland who look after the property are little more reticent in promoting its spookier aspects. Why, I have no idea as a castle without ghosts is positively shameful. On asking if she had any personal experiences, she mentioned that on one occasion she thought she had heard kids crying and on another heard footsteps walking behind her. Perhaps, the area which has the creepiest reputation though is the gallery, which at one point was a nursery. There have been several 'incidents' in this area including those involving visitors. Take for example the time when a mum and child were walking in the gallery when she felt a small hand grab her own. Initially thinking it was her son she continued walking, until suddenly he ran ahead of her. She said later, her hand was still being gripped by that of 'a child.'

In another instance a couple getting their bearings claimed that they were given very helpful advice by a soldier. Later, they mentioned this kind act to one of the guides who informed them there had been no soldiers present. It was also noted that on many occasions, service dogs have reacted badly to certain areas, barking, whining and refusing to enter, their sensitive demeanour picking up which many cannot. This of course is just the tip of the iceberg and I daresay with patience there are many other stories just waiting to be discovered.

A classic trope next and one might well believe it the work of fiction if not for the fact I met the witness in question to discuss his story. When he started the conversation with, 'I know this might sound like I am making this up, but....' I knew he was telling the truth. The story was told to me by a local Edinburgh man on a daytime history tour I was conducting in which both his wife and brother-in law also attended. They both backed up his claims. The incident, he recounted to me took place just outside Sheriffmuir on a rain lashed night while the witness and his two companions were driving. Ahead of them at the side of the road stood a bedraggled figure huddled against the elements and though initially they drove past, one of the passengers suggested they stop. After a few moments deliberation they slowed down allowing the stranger to enter the car.

This is what the witness said. 'I started the car up and began driving. We quickly realised the guy in the back was a bit strange to say the least as on several occasions he called out for me to slow down, and that the next bend was dangerous. The atmosphere was a bit off, and everyone was silent. The guy's demeanour was odd. Further along the road he shouted out "be careful this is where I died," and at that point, we were all desperate for him to get out. He then asked us to stop and said that this is where he wanted out and so I slowed down. He then climbed out, slammed the door and was gone. We felt relieved and quickly began talking about the guy and what the hell was up with him. We then reached the destination of my backseat passenger and on arrival he asked if I could take off the childproof locks. I suddenly realised they had been on all the time so how had the stranger gotten out. I reasoned that maybe it had malfunctioned at that precise moment though it seems unlikely. After a brief discussion we then realised none of us could describe him, yet he was sitting in the same car as us. That is a true story.'

Glasgow and Beyond

Cathedral House Hotel is our first destination in the 'The Dear Green Place,' that is Glasgow. An interesting building it was erected in 1896 as a halfway house for women prisoners who had just been released from nearby Duke Street Prison. The discharged prisoners were then helped to find gainful employment. Described as being 'very commodious' the halfway house must have been luxury compared to the poor conditions and harsh regime of the prison itself. Today it has been suggested, at least on certain platforms, that ghostly children are still at play within the building. To back this up it has been suggested that a woman, after serving her sentence, was reunited with her children and subsequently drowned them in the bath, afraid to lose them again. Though the story remains unproven it is horrible to think it might be true. It is known however that twelve women were executed in the vicinity, including Susan Newell the last woman to be hanged in Scotland who was found guilty of strangling a paperboy, and it has been suggested that she may be one of several spirits still present within the building who are said to brush against people's legs.

Of course, times change, and some years ago the building was bought over and refurbished into a trendy hotel and restaurant. Approaching the current owners to ask if anything of note had happened since the change of ownership, I was told politely that they weren't interested in discussing such things, given the hotel is more boutique than 'bootique,' today. Despite the current setback I managed to gather a few nuggets from previous intrepid explorers which I have included below.

The first story that caught my eye concerned rocker Suzi Quatro who after being interviewed in the papers claimed to have seen a ghost while staying there. The manager was duly informed but what he could do about it was anyone's guess. According to another report a guest noted several strange occurrences while residing there, the most interesting being after he and a group of friends returned to the hotel, after a trip to the Necropolis. As only one of them was an actual resident, the others left soon after. While sitting in their car before heading off, they noticed their friend through the hotel window, standing on the staircase and could clearly see another figure next to him. Curious, they then phoned him to enquire who he had been talking to. Somewhat surprised by the revelation he assured them he had been alone. Not the sort of call you want to get just before retiring for the night. He later claimed that he thought he could hear children singing nursery rhymes being sung as he was in bed but rationalised, that perhaps it had been a dream, or something heard in a semi sleep state. On a final note, there have been several guests at the same establishment who have also reported seeing a woman wearing white, however given the current situation it is unlikely we will find out more.

Still in Glasgow, the Hilton is not your typical haunted hotel, well at least not architecturally. A tall modern tower, it certainly does not give off a creepy vibe, yet several guests have claimed to have seen an apparition there, or perhaps two. The haunted area, according to reports, is ironically on the thirteenth floor, which has been unlucky for some, having witnessed the spectre of a woman with long blonde hair. The bar also boasts a few spirits ahem, including that of a man though his description is at best vague. Another hotel is the Grand Central where again there have been reports of the sighting of several apparitions. It is rumoured that one is that of a maid who committed suicide and the other a chef who fell seven stories to his death. Again, difficult to prove or maybe I just haven't come across the correct information yet, but a present I have found nothing to support those theories. Whoever they are they appear to be like getting up to mischief which seems to be a common trend. Are ghosts bored I wonder? Anyhow one of their specialities is interfering with the fire doors reopening them once closed.

Still on the theme of hotels two friends of mine Fiona and Malcom Smith had an uncanny experience while stay at the Millenium Hotel in George Square some years back. A grand hotel, known at the North British Station Hotel it was erected between 1807 and 1818. Sold by British Rail it was known formerly as the Copthorne in the 1980s. Inside it still retains a certain grandeur and was noted as having an old blocked up entrance which once led to the railway station as was common with such hotels. Having undergone various changes in the preceding years it would appear there are a few guests who may never have checked out. Now back in room 310, after a day out in the city, the couple retired to bed. In the middle of the night Fiona was woken suddenly by the sound of someone raking about in a cupboard. Now lying there listening, Fiona described the noise going on for some time initially thinking that Malcom had gotten up to look for a paracetamol. Moments later she then realised he was still in bed sleeping. Soon after she dozed off. In the morning, she began to describe what had occurred to which her husband interjected by saying he had experienced the very same thing. In his account he also woke and described hearing the floorboards creaking as if someone was walking around followed by rummaging in the bathroom. This was accompanied by the sound of an old-fashioned wardrobe being opened and the sound of someone looking for something. Darting from bed under the assumption someone had broken into the room he found nothing. On leaving the next day they debated whether to mention their experience, and when asked how their stay had been, Fiona replied, 'interesting.' She then asked if the room had a history and it transpired, they were not the first to have had a similar experience. The person on reception then went on to say that some time back a night manager sleeping over in one of the third-floor rooms woke to find two Victorian children standing at the foot of his bed. The couple concluded that perhaps the sounds they heard could have been attributed to that of curious children. As far as I am aware there has been little written about the hotel which alludes to it being haunted, but I think after their experience it is more than deserving to be thought of as such.

A housing development at Queensland Court and Gardens is our next location where one resident Gary, recently posted his experience online. He stated that when his daughter was just born her crib was next to his bed. He was dragged from his sleep one evening by hearing his former partner screaming, 'get away from her.' On asking what she had seen she claimed to have seen the shadow of an old man, sitting and looking into the crib who was nodding his head. When she screamed the figure disappeared but not before she saw a 'black shadow swooping away.' On enquiring they discovered a previous tenant, an old man, had been found dead behind the door. Later, a second bizarre incident occurred when he heard a noise on the landing outside his home. Peeking through the spy hole he saw nothing. As he continued to look his ex-partner who was now behind him asked what he was doing. Glancing back, he asked her just to go back to bed. To his surprise, seconds later, his partner then shouted through, asking who he was speaking to. On going to speak to her, he then realised she was wearing completely different clothes!

On the B763 Dalmarnock Bridge which spans the Clyde, there were several reports of the apparition of a young man about thirty years of age, wearing a navy-blue coat, black trousers and sporting a crew cut. One witness wrote down his account in 1972 describing his encounter. While walking Dalmarnock Road in July of that year he was drawn to the sight of a young man standing on the bridge looking upriver. With a jolt he realised that he was possibly going to jump so he quickened his pace and found himself shouting "No Don't!" at which point the man jumped. Reaching the edge literally a second later he was shocked to see the man had completely vanished, with no sign of anyone in the water. Afterwards while recounting the tale, perhaps he took solace in the fact others had witnessed the exact same cycle of events for years.

Alexandra Parade Dennistoun is the next destination in our Glasgow stop off, this time to a flat shared by three students. Unluckily for them, in May 1998, they got on the wrong side of a previous occupant who just happened to be dead. John, who was the main witness, was at the time in a relationship with one of the tenants, a Greek student named Lia. He described that she had a large room to herself at the front of the house in the top floor flat while her two French flatmates, Miriam and Alex shared a smaller room. Being a long weekend, the young couple had taken advantage of the holiday and travelled to London to visit Lia's sister before returning at around 6.30am on the overnight bus. A strenuous ordeal at the best of times so on arrival the couple were exhausted, and after dumping their rucksack on the floor flopped into bed where they soon fell asleep. John told me, 'I remember the room was darkened with heavy curtains, but the light was still shining in around the edges. Lia's bed faced straight onto the bedroom door which had frosted glass on it, you couldn't see through it but could make out shapes. I was trying to sleep on the inside of the bed nearest the wall when I had a feeling of being watched. Lia was snoring beside me, so I propped myself up on one elbow and looked at the door. Through it I could see the shape of a person and thought we had woken up one of the French girls as we hadn't exactly been quiet when we arrived. I lay back down but again I had the feeling of being watched so on turning to face Lia I saw over her body the figure of an older woman coming from the door which was closed and floating towards the middle of the room. All the while she was frantically gesticulating to the rucksacks on the floor. I remember she looked annoyed, I shook Lia awake and said word for word, "Lia there is someone in the room, but I don't know who it is." Lia stirred and glanced over and said calmly. "Oh, that is the lady who used to live here, I have felt her, but hadn't seen her, don't worry John, go back to sleep I will talk to her." So as weird as it sounds, I thought to myself, "ah good Lia is dealing with it," and so drifted off to sleep only to hear her say, "thank you for visiting us I know the room is a mess, but we will tidy it up later, we are very tired and need to sleep, thank you." Thinking back, it was as if she was chastising the entity.'

On leaving for studies early in the morning John waited patiently all day for her return. In the meantime, it transpired that neither flatmate had heard or seen anything unusual. On returning Lia explained that her family back in Athens had the ability to see spirit and that she had felt the woman's presence around the flat on several occasions. The French students were however a little spooked at the revelation.

Jonh stated: 'Even after 26 years this experience is still one, I can strongly visualise. I still see the lady and how annoyed she was, with her frantic arms; she didn't have any legs that I could see. She was a blend of shapes and what I can only describe as dark clouds. I think of her being in her 70s or 80s but her face I can't describe just her shape and her arms moving up and down.' Afterwards Lia said she could sense her on occasion but nothing solid ever manifested.' She was at the end of the day just a house-proud ghost attached to the property and perhaps unwilling to let go.

The idea of a haunted hospital to many is the ultimate nightmare. The following submitted by Mary McLellan took place at the Western Infirmary Glasgow in 1975 and the details first documented by respected investigator, Andrew

Green. On the night of the incident Mary, a ward sister was setting up some equipment in a room facing a well-lit corridor when she became aware of a tall silver-haired man wearing a blue dressing gown standing near the doorway of the ward opposite. He stood still and silent for a moment and on glancing back he had gone. Thinking nothing of it, she assumed he was a patient who had just gone back to bed. Almost immediately she was surprised by the ward nurse who came over to her. She was very upset having seen the figure also, who she recognised as a patient who had died two days previously.

In another hospital, this time the Glasgow Royal Infirmary, a young nurse described that some years ago while walking along a corridor on the top floor she became aware of a ward sister walking towards her 'As she walked by, I said: "Evening Sister," then I realised I could see her only from the knees up.' A case of shifting floor heights, I would imagine, terrifying, nonetheless. Still in a hospital, this time the 'City,' where it was claimed an exorcism took place after builders disturbed something while demolishing an old part of the ward which was thought to be part of an old workhouse. While working there several workers heard cries from another part of the ward and went to investigate, finding themselves locked inside an area which was in the process of being demolished. Who or what had mysteriously locked the door was never resolved, perhaps it was an ill-judged practical joke? Or was it? Either way a tragedy was narrowly avoided when the door was unlocked, the men narrowly escaping the impending demolition ball. Afterwards and due to further unexplained incidents, they demanded that a priest be brought in, or they would not work there.

And now to the 'Gibson Street Poltergeist.' Possibly one of the most famous ghost stories of recent times gained a new lease of life after featuring on Danny Robins podcast, 'Uncanny,' where his supernatural sleuthing is a refreshing change from the usual jump scares and celebrity hysterics. What makes this story even more intriguing than most is that it has a direct link to the previously discussed Glen Luibeilt bothy incident, both involving the same witness, Phil Macneill. Though the bothy incident was a terrifying experience, it was made worse by the fact than on returning home to Gibson Street he had perhaps brought an uninvited guest with him. For around six months after returning to Gibson Street he felt uneasy and the thought that something negative had attached itself to him was never far from his mind. He later reported finding a cross made from old newspapers under a carpet alongside some accompanying bloodstains which was to say the least unnerving. He also stated that on discovering those surprising artefacts a bulb somehow unscrewed itself from its fittings and fell to the floor, smashing. Coincidence? Perhaps not! Phil went on to claim that a series of incremental weird goings on eventually prompted him to leave the property. Afterwards a former tenant then made contact and described that while living at the same property his flatmate had been thrown out of bed. A researcher later uncovered that in 1851 a child lived at 39 Gibson Street who was called John McAlpine the same name as the man who took his life at Luibeilt!

It is worth remembering though that strange goings on in Gibson Street were nothing new as suggested by the following report dating from 1958. Reading the newspapers of the day this is what the July 14th edition of the Glasgow Herald July 14th had to say on the matter. To say the reporter was sceptical would be an understatement and the acerbic tone of the article made me chuckle. This was his opening salvo. 'Three American students, inexperienced no doubt in the life and aura of the Glasgow tenement have given up their tenancy of a flat on Gibson Street, which, they are persuaded is haunted. They have heard things which have convinced them that they shared their dwelling with a poltergeist, a mild, murmuring elemental, that sometimes turned off the radiogram and occasionally pushed egg boxes and breadboards off their kitchenette shelf. It is a wordless visitant that mumbles in two voices, but never so distinctly that the listener can distinguish what it is trying to say.'

He continued, 'The disembodied voices, and the acoustics are much more considerate in one of the neighbouring streets in Woodside. A colleague who lives there has been both instructed and entertained by his "haunting" in which the words and sense of the ghostly conversation are perfectly clear. These manifestations are also convenient because they have a set pattern and timetable. The voices, question and answering in rising notes, begin just before midnight, perhaps three times a week. Half an hour later they dwindle and fade. The listener may then settle down to sleep undisturbed for five or six hours, and if he wakens, rested and sharp of hearing just before seven o'clock in the morning, he can pick up the conversation where it left off. It ends always with a sharp thudding noise like the slamming of a front door.' He then mentions an all too familiar pattern with, 'one of the voices defending and the other attacking in a recurring debate on domestic extravagance.'

Still in Glasgow but on a more series note, the following stories, all featuring city museums were related to me by several long serving members of staff who were gracious enough to share their experiences. The first venue is the beautifully designed Scotland Street School, now a museum. What a great building, very atmospheric and of course imagined by one of Scotland's greatest designers, Charles Rennie Mackintosh. Built between 1903 and 1905 it contains several classroom constructions with each displaying different periods in time. It has for many years garnered a reputation for being haunted and there have been sightings of at least two apparitions seen on both the 1st and 3rd floors. The encounters described at time as being quite terrifying, have involved both staff and visitors. The cookery room thought to be one of the most active areas has also been the scene of poltergeist type activity with objects frequently moved or thrown across the room. There have also been several investigations within the building and strong evidence was captured. Phenomena has included witnesses smelling the unmistakable odour of strong tobacco and seeing shadow like figures moving along a corridor. Visiting mediums supporting the teams, have also picked up on the names of both children and former staff members one of whom was described as quite a nasty character who enjoyed instilling fear into his charges. One can only imagine the residual negative energy that is now ingrained in the building.

I spoke with one member of staff recently who has worked across several museums for many years. His name is John Irwin, who along with his colleague Angela Short provided the following personal accounts. It goes without saying that evidence you are about to read certainly backs up the building's reputation. John described the following, 'The cookery room is on the top floor of the school and was for the first time going to be used for an Empire Biscuit decoration workshop. The room hadn't been used for making food in a long time as far as we knew. The two learning assistants who were preparing the room were standing at the double Belfast sinks and one joked, "I wonder what the ghosts feel about us using the room for this," as he said it the red carbolic soap which was stacked two high between the sinks went flying off and landed on the floor beside them. It was as if a hand had swatted the soap off the stand. The cookery room always seems to be a hive of activity, numerous staff throughout the years reported hearing furniture being moved and scraped along the wooden floor. Most times when they went to investigate nothing had altered but one staff member admitted that he had on one occasion noticed that the table and the cooking implements had been moved out of place, and he was the only person in the venue. The west side of the building on the mezzanine level (which is between the ground floor and 1st floor where the lift is) always had a strong smell of pipe tobacco. It was so distinctive I could smell it every time I was in that area. I looked for potential sources, but it was only in that area. The original plans showed it would have been the staffroom and could not be smelt when in the lift.' John's colleague Angela then added the following which she experienced while working at the school. 'I would often smell a rose/flower perfume on the 1st floor that my manager was in. On the top floor you could smell pipe smoke, like someone had walked by smoking a pipe. On the ground floor in the cinema room there was always a feeling that you shouldn't be there and to get out, I hated that room. One morning around 7.30 myself and Lily the cleaner had just come in. I started to do the 'opening up' and Lily offered to help. I was in a room on the half-landing ready to unlock the door from the inside. I then heard Lily singing on the stairs, on the other side of the door. As I opened the door, saying "Lily do you ever stop singing," the lights on the other staircase went on and there was Lily waving to me from behind the glass in the opposite stairwell. To say I was a bit spooked was an understatement, I asked her if she had been singing and she said no. She then asked if I was ok as I was a bit white. I told her I heard a wee girl's voice singing and then copied what I had heard before Lily finished off the song. When I asked how the f**k did she know that she explained she heard the wee girl sing often, and it was always the same song. Lily was a very small, lovely old lady, who spoke with a very girly/youthful voice. If you had spoken to her on the phone, you would have thought she was a wee girl. Later I was in the lock up in Scotland Street School and the only person in the building. I had done my rounds making sure every window was closed, all the doors locked, and the keys returned to the key box and all the lights off apart from where I was on the ground floor. As I was waiting for my shift to be finished, I thought I heard a door opening and so waited to hear if there was anything else, but there was nothing, A few seconds later I heard someone walk into the staffroom directly above. I immediately got my keys and made my way up to see who it might be in the building without me knowing, but the staffroom door was locked, no lights, no sound, nothing. I went back down and five minutes later the same thing but louder, someone was walking into the staffroom over to the window and then stopping. I then decided to creep up the stairs, in case someone was trying to prank me and as I went up the stairs the silence was deafening. I opened the door slowly onto the landing, no one was there. As I went along the corridor, I could hear what sounded like a conversation taking place behind the staffroom door. Remember there were no lights on, and I was the only one in the building and I thought I was going to catch my colleague pranking me. I carefully put the key in the lock and threw open the door, to find no one there. The muffled conversation stopped and all the hair on my body felt like they were standing on end, like the room is charged! I made a very quick exit locked the door and bolted down the stairs. After my heart has returned to normal, I realise it's still only 17.35 and I have another 25 minutes of my shift left. About 10 minutes later I again hear some stomping in the staffroom as if they had big boots on. I left 15 minutes early that night.'

Another venue reputedly haunted was the old Transport Museum where the museum centrepiece had been a recreation of a 1930s street, complete with cinema, shops and an underground railway station, where there had been reported sightings of shadow-like figures and the sound of footsteps. A security guard in the early 2000s was reported to have been doing his rounds in this area when he thought he saw someone moving ahead of him. Calling out 'hello' he was surprised to hear the same word in response, but this time from a child's voice. The experience was described as unnerving.

Angela, who was the main witness to the following was just 17 at the time and it certainly made a lasting impression, again proving that those most likely to see a ghost are those not actively seeking them. Her encounter took while she was cleaning in the old cinema which was described as spooky as hell. This is what she said. 'We used to clean the museum on a Tuesday, and I was told at the time it was supposed to be haunted. While hoovering I had put all the seats up and was making my way along row-by-row hoovering. I got to the bottom of either the 2nd or 3rd row, and I noticed a seat was down. I pushed the seat back up and carried on and when I got to the bottom the same seat was down. The seat wasn't loose or broken as they all stayed upright unless you pulled it down and sat on it, as the springs were tight. I laughingly said, "ok if there is a ghost show me a sign," and all the seats on the first row bounced down and then back up. I have never run so fast out of a place in my life.' Definitive proof of something playing tricks or malfunctioning seats? My money was on the former. To add to its reputation the building had once used as a mortuary during World War Two during the blitz. In more recent times however, the museum relocated to a new purpose-built venue, where perhaps it lost some of its charm. Do the ghosts of the old transport museum still make their presence known despite the buildings change of use? Only time will tell.

A further story from John now, but this time at the Burrell in Pollok Park (one of the most prestigious art collections in the UK gifted to Glasgow by philanthropist Sir William Burrell) 'In the old Burrell collection I remember seeing a photograph taken on an analogue film camera, back in the 2000s, which a visitor took in the Hutton Rooms. There was a streak of light sitting in one of the antique chairs which had the outline of a person on it, but the issue was that the section was roped off and inaccessible. In Kelvingrove Gallery there have also been at least three members of staff who have witnessed a lady walking down the east turret stairway on the upper level. A very level-headed member of staff who doesn't believe in ghosts does admit to always having the fear put into her in what is now the Scottish Gallery. She had no explanation apart from feeling like she was being watched whenever in specific rooms. The overnight shift, this was at least twenty years ago, reported many times hearing internal doors slam closed, the rattling of chains they used to have on certain ones, footsteps and noises that couldn't be explained. There was even a figure seen sitting on a bench in the main hall. They thought someone had been missed when clearing the building for closing and so went up to wake the sleeping figure, when they just disappeared.'

John's colleague continued. 'My dad used to be a shift man at Kelvingrove and would often pop in to see him after closing time, I remember I was about ten and we were in what was called the control room. The stairs leading up from the 1st floor to the ground floor were directly above this room. While talking to my dad we heard someone come down those stairs with a heavy foot. I asked him if his colleague was back, and he said probably. We waited for him to enter the control room, but he never appeared. My dad then phoned down to the basement where his other colleague was and discovered they were both together and no one had been upstairs. On other occasions I heard the same kind of footfall while in the control room and used to run out to try and catch them, but there was never anyone there. Whenever you went up the east turret of the building you would always feel like you were being watched no matter what time of day or night.' Glasgow museums are among the best and I was grateful for these contributions.

Moving out of Glasgow, our next destination is in Wishaw the venue for Meridian Knitwear. The large rambling premises once home to a large work force was featured in several newspaper articles in 1981. Accounts described a ghost thought to be that of Willie Primrose who had died in the factory some 45 years previously in somewhat mysterious circumstances. Keen to find out more I did a little digging and discovered that he was thought to have been accidentally locked in the basement of the building on a Friday, before his body was found the following Monday. How he died is uncertain, but his playful spirit is thought to have remained in the building. It is no doubt easy to let one's imagination run wild in such cavernous spaces but as can be seen the following interviewees appeared genuine in their belief.

The factory manager Mr Woods was first to step up to the plate stating, 'I've been in the factory when some of the machines started operating with no one at them and the power switched off at the mains.' Whether the spirts intention was to impart some message or just create chaos is uncertain. One girl apparently working in the canteen had the lights go on and off and fleeing for help ended up in the administration office refusing to go back. Of course, most researchers wouldn't necessarily jump to the conclusion that a building was haunted because of some flickering lights for obvious reasons, but perhaps the following is more persuasive.

In one of the most frightening incidents, witnesses saw a face at one of the windows in a stairwell which had locked doors at both ends and thinking initially that a worker had somehow gotten themselves locked inside, they quickly investigated but of course it was empty. Mr Shields, another interviewee, claimed that both he and his wife also witnessed machines being switched on and off when the building was empty. He further added 'We hired a watchman last year to spend the night in the factory while the roof was being repaired. He was an ex- Royal Marine commando.' On arrival Mr Shields was startled to find him sitting on the front steps refusing to go back in. 'He wouldn't say what had frightened him, but he didn't even stay to collect his pay.'

'We saw a Ghost at the Co-op.' was the headline in the Wishaw Post 1966. The Co-op ghost as it became known was witnessed by a group of teenagers and resulted in the police being called out to the building in Russell Lane. On being interviewed later one policeman was quoted as saying, 'we are not sure what action the teenagers expected us to take in apprehending a ghost.' Nevertheless, that conundrum was solved as the ghost had vanished before the police arrived. The witnesses who were later interviewed stated that at around 11pm a group of them were hanging around the car park when they saw what they thought was the apparition. Corroborating each other's story, they describe witnessing the figure of a woman who appeared at one of the windows in the gable end of the building.

Anne Renkevic speaking on behalf of the group stated, 'we were in the car park when we saw the figure of a woman up at one of the windows. She had short blonde hair and had staring eyes. Everything about her was white and as we watched she waved her hand at us as if she was asking us to come up to her. The hand seemed as though it was coming through the glass despite the window being closed. There was, as they argued, no reason for anyone to have been in the building at that time of night. One of them went on to say that a mutual friend had told them that the room where the ghost was seen was used for storage and therefore no one should have been there. Anne, obviously made of sterner stuff claimed to have returned to the scene later and saw the same apparition, she also claimed that people laughed at their accounts.

Moving on we come to Kilsyth in North Lanarkshire, between Glasgow and Stirling. It was there a very creepy set of circumstance unfolded, centred around a young family, the Canavan's, whose home was situated on Kirklands Crescent. The property adjacent to what was described as an ancient graveyard, had according to reports been plagued by several apparitions. These included sightings of an elderly man and a young boy whose connection to the property was never substantiated however one can only assume that at some point they may have been grandfather and grandson. Either way it was noted that their nightly ramblings culminated in a blessing taking place by a local priest. Cynics claimed in the aftermath that the story had been fabricated to help the tenant secure a move to another council property but on reading of the circumstances I am not so sure. Having moved there in September 1992, after taking over the tenancy of the house, all seemed normal at first. Her two children Christopher and Danielle were very young, and the two-bedroom house was spacious enough to suit their needs. It was noted however that the house was prone to extremely cold temperatures even in summer. It could of course have just been a house that remained obstinately chilly, it happens, but when taps began turning on and off in the middle of the night, well that was something entirely different.

Classic poltergeist activity soon followed, and on several occasions while returning home after spending the day out they would frequently find the house in disarray with toys and personal belongings scattered across the floor. Several neighbours then alluded to the fact that the house lights would often switch on and off by themselves when there was no one at home. Others would mention that the sound of a boy crying could be plainly heard while there was no one in. This of course further unsettled the family.

Soon after the first sightings of the ghosts themselves were witnessed. On one occasion for example the tenant's sister was staying over and during the night awoke to feel an overpowering sensation of someone watching her. Glancing upwards she witnessed a wrinkled face looking down at her. Springing from the bed she then bolted from the bedroom and ran into the living room where she cowered in shock. Sometime later upon returning to the bedroom she stated, 'it was freezing.' The man she saw was later described as having grey hair and wearing glasses, he was very drawn with big eyes and wore a very blank expression.

Another incident soon followed and, in this instance, the witness Patricia, was woken by the sound of long fingernails scratching outside her bedroom door. When interviewed later she said, 'I am terrified in my own home. I am so afraid I refuse to be left alone in my own home.' Following on from this her son then saw a man who he described as hiding in the closet, prompting the family to partially move out, preferring to stay with family and friends. In desperation they then approached their local church for guidance. A priest, Father Jeremy of St. Patricks in Kilsyth later confirmed that he had performed a blessing in the house and indicated that he was waiting to see if it had worked, suggesting that the next step would be an exorcism. As far as I know this never took place.

Now in South Lanarkshire we pay a visit to, the Applebank Inn, a near neighbour to the infamous Broomhill House. This derelict mansion and wooded area around it, are both reputed to be haunted by a ghost, 'the Black Lady.' It is one of those unique story's that continues to grow and gather further reports and recent findings suggest that the once generic monikered ghost has been given a name. To add to the mystique there is also an alleged curse attached to the spirit. Broomhill House now ruinous is little more than a few partial walls, now reclaimed by the forest that surrounds it. However, one part of the structure has since been removed, a lintel, which was repurposed and placed within the nearby Applebank Inn. According to locals and staff it has attracted the unwanted attentions of a terrifying apparition.

The story of the house gained prominence by featuring in a 1963 edition of Fyfe Robertson's 'Tonight,' show where the legendary reporter interviewed a young paranormal investigator, Tom Roberton. In the show Robertson was shown attempting to perform an exorcism on the ghost. On viewing it does appear a little quaint however the psychic was firm in his beliefs. It was, he said a cursed area, and to add some weight to his argument around the same time the location manager sadly died in a car crash. Was it a curse or just a tragic accident? Probably the latter but the story persists and to this day people tread lightly around the subject. Today thankfully due to the efforts of people like Helen Sykes secretary of the town's historical society, much meat has been added to the bones and story with or without ghosts remains fascinating. The then owner of the house, Captain MacNeil Hamilton on returning from duty in Ceylon brought with him a Ceylonese woman as a servant, which in the early 1900s was, shall we say, unusual. You can imagine the reaction. Two years later the 'Black Lady' as she became known vanished and has never been heard of since. Where did she go, she could hardly have gone unnoticed? Was foul play involved? Unthinkable as it seems, perhaps an illicit affair had ended in murder. Whatever the truth of the matter, since the disappearance her restless shade is said to haunt the area. Fascinatingly, Helen Sykes later discovered that her own grandmother worked at the house at the same time as 'the Black Lady,' and has since found her name, Sita Phurdeena. Some remain convinced that she still haunts the area and reports indicate she, or at least a figure of some sort, has been seen at the windows of the inn. It has also been noted that locals have a healthy respect for the story and many regulars have claimed to have witnessed supernatural phenomena in the inn and in the area surrounding the ruins. There was also an image taken some years back which is purported to be that of the ghost, which was eerie to say the least.

To the west of Glasgow in Renfrewshire we arrive at Paisley, which is the fifth most populated town in Scotland. A town famed for its weaving mills, the famous Paisley Pattern being its greatest export. It's an ancient settlement whose ghosts have been seen in locations both old and new and include a spate of sightings at the Piazza Shopping Centre. The events that unfolded around thirty years ago were featured in numerous articles and one of the ghosts was thought to be that of a monk, who they named Henry. Dick Blyth, a former caretaker at the centre was interviewed at the time and described the apparition as being friendly. Mr. Blyth believed that the monk was upset at the sound of modern trappings such as fire alarms and would make frequent appearances to show his dissatisfaction when they were tested. Many wondered why the spirit of a monk should be present, but research proved that on the site stood an ancient Monastery and gaol. 'My hair stood on end the first time he appeared,' said Mr Blyth, a practicing spiritualist. He went onto claim that the spirit still thought of the area as his home. One woman however was not so accepting and during one of his appearances fainted in shock however according to the caretaker there was no malice intended. Others within the complex remained unconvinced and were sceptical of the happenings however more accounts quickly materialised this time coming from nearby 'MacKay's.' a three storied fabric store situated within the Piazza. During an interview one employee Joan Convery, concluded that their ghost, might have been an old gaoler from when the towns prison stood there. Why she thought this is anyone's guess and his appearance was a little tenuous to say the least, resulting his presence being felt. The witness further claimed that although she couldn't see the spirit, she felt he was a man who was just a bit nosey and wondered what was going on. She then described admonishing him for trying to frighten people and being the compliant sort, he apparently left. Unsurprisingly other staff members including her manager at the time remained unconvinced.

More compelling and again in Paisley was another haunting, this time centred around 'Cantons,' a furniture store, built on the site of the Glen Cinema. The cinema was the location of one of the worst civilian tragedies in Britain, when in 1929 around 70 children died in a mass panic. Ironically the cause was a smoking film cannister and not a fire. The town to this day rightly remembers the tragic circumstances and for many years survivors would gather to pay respect to their friends. Considering this awful tragedy, when the cinema was eventually demolished and replaced by Canton's furniture store. Because of what happened next, we can only assume, that those emotions may have been imprinted on the area as several ghost encounters have been reported. Most of those recorded took place some twenty years ago and were reported in the local news. The frightening encounters which terrified the then current staff included lights switching on and off, objects mysteriously disappearing and randomly reappearing, and the sound of footsteps being heard frequently.

It was noted that some of the Glen cinema had still survived up till that point though hidden behind a partition wall in the furniture shop. The newspaper who initially reported this, the Paisley Daily Express, was given a tour and were no doubt surprised to see the stage, curtains and part of the original ceiling. One of the salesmen stated that on one occasion his boss had gone down to the basement to fetch something when he was aware of footsteps tailing him. Thinking it was one of the staff he turned to speak but found no-one. On other occasions lights which were switched off at the end of the day were found to be back on when staff arrived to open in the morning. One staff member described seeing dusty footprints stopping directly outside a locked room that was never used. The most common phenomena, at least according to the report was hearing children's voices and the sound of footsteps.

Another location in Paisley, the Reid Kerr College also had similar problems which threatened to disrupt their students' studies. Alan Carstairs a former lecturer claimed that for some time strange phenomena had been plaguing his department, which included the sound of heavy footsteps coming from within a padlocked building, dramatic falls in temperature and heavy vats of glaze being moved around at night while no one is present. The art and design lecturer went on to say that some of the phenomena defied explanation citing the example of a huge vat of pottery glaze being found in another classroom despite the rooms being locked. They were, he added incredibly heavy to lift. In another incident he was alerted by 'violent knocking' at the door to his classroom only to find no one there. 'I opened the door and there was a huge rush of cold air. When I went back into the classroom which had been very warm, I found it to be freezing.' The building, a former nursery, was taken over by the college in the 1970s.

I spoke recently to Roddy, an administrator for the 'Oor Wee Toon,' Facebook page, Paisley. The site focuses on local interest stories and history, though I contacted them due to the number of alleged haunted buildings in their vicinity. He told me the following which was centred around his home which he bought in the early 1990s. The house built in 1927 in the Glenburn area was distinctive due to the 'cartwheel gates,' at the front and the owners fell in love with the place very quickly. There was one issue however, it needed a complete refurbishment as nothing had changed too much since its original owners the Fyfe's had it built. The Fyfe family had owned a well-known local garage, 'Potties,' and were a well-liked couple. This is what I was told, 'Mrs Fyfe had apparently passed away in the house and so much was needing done by then including rooftiles, kitchen, bathroom, plastering rooms. We removed fireplaces and chimneys except one where we installed a new fireplace with grate tiles and new living flame gas fire, a porch, new windows, and doors. The renovation took place at nights and weekends, whenever there was time, and it took two years before we moved in. Whilst proceeding with the work we were constantly having debates as to who was moving the tools especially seeing as we had stored most of them in one room, which we locked before we left. Doors were found to be opened when we knew they were shut and a whole series of unexplained events took place which we accused each other of and denied.

Strange occurrences continued and we often heard noises like doors opening and closing but on checking everything was before. I would get phone calls from my wife while on nightshift and would have to come back because she heard banging noises and footsteps coming from the attic. I drove from Erskine on two occasions just to check the attic. I just joked about it saying it was Mrs Fyfe letting us know she was still around.

One night after a couple of years it was chilly, so we had on the gas fire. I happened to look at the flames and noticed the blackening of the firebrick at the back, I asked Sharon what she could see. She said it looked like a woman's face which is exactly what I saw. I then took some photographs of the silhouette in the blackening, and we had a laugh about it saying Mrs Fyfe had decided to reveal herself after all these years. Soon after we were telling visitors about the event and how we hadn't heard of Mrs Fyfe since she revealed herself and to confirm what we were talking about, I went to find the photo I had taken only to find they were not in the place I left them, though all our other photographs were still there. To this day I still cannot find these photographs and we never heard of Mrs Fyfe again though we believe she has now accepted us living there.

AYRSHIRE

This story some fifty years old took place in Irvine, the year being 1971. The McDowal family and their six children were the unfortunate recipients of a haunting that attracted some press coverage at the time, resulting in the intervention of the church. The ghost, described as that of a woman was often accompanied by both sound and smell which must be said is unusual. Prior to her manifestations a sickly smell which would permeate the air. It was also noted she would sometimes speak in a voice, 'like a whisper.'

But who she was and what she wanted to this day remains a mystery, but her appearances coincided with a string of bad luck which according to the report saw all six children having to attend hospital at varying points. Perhaps it was just a coincidence, however what could not be denied was the appearance of her spectre, seen on several occasion. Their house on Merryvale Road, was a typical council house, same as its neighbours but when first moving in the feeling of something not being quite right was with them from day one. Pictures would randomly fall from walls despite being securely fixed and unaccounted noises were heard. On day three the lady of the house was shocked see a full-bodied apparition. She was quoted as saying; 'I saw this thing; it was an old woman in a long white gown with lace on the sleeves and around the neck. It was not a shadow but substantial.' The figure was subsequently observed on numerous occasions. Walls would shake abnormally; stamping was heard, and extraordinarily cold temperatures felt in the wake of its presence.

After consulting a local minister, the house was then blessed three times to no avail. They then called in a spiritualist from the local church who despite their best intentions appeared to then aggravate the spirit who displayed its displeasure by further appearances and the phenomena continued unabated. Unfortunately, I cannot comment further on the story and to its outcome but what is interesting is a former resident Rebecca Fisher, claimed she had experienced similar phenomena during her eight-year tenure.

THE BORDERS

Now in the borders our next stop is the beautiful town of Peebles where some years back two Brisbane bar workers traveling to Scotland in search of a White Christmas, ended up getting a fright Christmas instead. Andrea Pratt and Veronica Doyle started work at the Cross Keys pub as seasonal workers however were unaware of certain stories connected to the building. The ghost which haunts the premises is presumed to be its first landlady Marion Ritchie who died in 1822. Having been so attached to the place she has never left and is thought to wander the halls and rooms of the establishment. There have certainly been many eyewitness accounts. Things kicked off as it were one Saturday at around 1am when after a long shift they retired to their room. While lying there they noticed the handle of their door rapidly turning. Assuming at first it was the bar manager Gordon Saunders trying to frighten them. The rattling then started up again prompting an investigation in which they found nothing. Ironically, Mr Saunders had also heard the same rattling at his door and assumed it was caused by the wind. Afterwards one of the girls armed themselves with a golf club, possibly one of the most ineffectual weapons against a ghost. Later a loud crash was then heard coming from another part of the hotel and after a debate they agreed to investigate, finding nothing. On returning to their room, they found it locked, resulting in them having to sleep in the corridor. An inauspicious start to say the least. Of course, a loud crash does not necessitate a haunting and perhaps a combination of nerves and an open window could account for what had taken place, but what of the following? The volume of a new cassette recorder for example was described as moving up and down by itself. It was later said that in the 1970s an investigation captured what was believed to be the voice of Marion Ritchie on cassette. Bizarrely it was said to have sounded like 'Mickey Mouse.'

Another story from Peebles, this time in the Town House which sits opposite the pub. In this instance the ghost is said to be that of a baby whose spectral cries have put the shivers up the spine of successive caretakers. One former town hall foreman Peter McCorkindale stated upon hearing it, 'It's something I will never forget as long as I live. I just ran like hell whenever I heard it.' The story goes that decades ago, on the night of a dance an irate wife turned up with a baby in her arms to retrieve her errant husband. No doubt taken aback to find his wife there, he was confronted and in the ensuing melee the baby fell to the floor, where it struck its head. The interviewee admitted that it may have just been a story however he was adamant that the crying phenomena was real and had been witnessed by several former workers. He continued; 'There's a side door at the town hall where you go down some steps to go in. We had to patrol that area and go around and check the building. On several occasions I would hear this sound like a child wailing and strangely enough it was usually always around midnight.'

Now another haunted hostelry but this time the Traquair Arms in the village of Innerleithen. This story first featured in an article from the Press and Journal in 1993, when owners Hugh and Marian Anderson were interviewed. Both described witnessing a woman with a sad countenance wearing 19th century clothing and her hair tied in a bun. On two occasions the apparition was clearly seen walking through a solid wall. It transpired that the building, then around 188 years old, was in a previous guise a coaching inn, and guests over the years reported many strange occurrences. On one occasion for example, a visitor asked the bewildered owner if they 'had any creatures floating around' though quite what they were referring to is anyone's guess. On being questioned, they claimed to have felt something touch them while in their bedroom. Despite this, the owner's wife remained convinced their apparition was friendly and probably being playful, however she admitted that her dogs got very upset by her presence. The Scottish Society for Psychical Research were convinced enough by the reports to investigate further.

Old Gala House in Galashiels is our next stop where my wife and I visited in September 2024. On leaving we stopped and spoke to custodian, Keith, who looks after the building. Never one to miss an opportunity we enquired if it was haunted, and he told us it allegedly was. There has for example been several mediums who have visited the building one of which claimed to have seen a male figure. The spirit was most notably seen standing on the right of the dining room. He then took us to the oldest part of the building which is now a meeting room. It had a strange atmosphere, and we were told that one person using the room had left abruptly saying they just couldn't be there anymore because of a bad atmosphere. On leaving Keith told me that a visiting medium had stated that the spirits were happy he was looking after the building, which in my book is the ultimate seal of approval. It's a great building and though not awash with stories it certainly retains an interesting energy. I hope one day to find out more.

No another road story and one that takes place in what is commonly thought to be one of the most supernaturally active stretches of road in Britain, the A75 Kinmount Straight or 'Ghost Road.' Why it's so haunted remains unanswered but numerous witnesses have described a wide range of apparitions for decades. These have included sightings of figures on horseback, an eyeless hag, a man carrying a musket, a white lady crossing the road near Kinmount House and a Roman legion walking in formation only visible from the knee up. Most recently sightings have included that of an elderly man in a tweed cap standing beside a bus stop and on approach he has been seen to vanish. An impressive roster indeed and in a recent interview with a local he described several contemporary sightings. The gentlemen in question Bob Sturgeon, conveniently living near to the road, had up till recent times ran a roadside snack van at Carrutherstown, near to the haunted hotspot. He stated, 'There was rarely a week went by without somebody telling me about some experience, usually along the Kinmount Straight.' His van, described as a refuge for those who had parked overnight in the nearby laybys, was popular with long distance drivers, and would appear that many were keen to get things off their chest after having harrowing experiences. Later he stated that drivers were not the kind of people to share their stories or invent things for no reason.

One of the most common sightings according to Mr Sturgeon, was the appearance of groups of dejected and bedraggled people, carrying bundles and puling carts like medieval camp followers. He further said, 'One man was so shocked he gave up lorry driving altogether, and I never saw him again.' It was by all accounts a terrifying experience. On reading it appeared that upon waking at three in the morning whilst parked at the Kinmount Straight he saw a parade of people pass by which went on for ages. Afterwards he was described as just frozen and in an awful state which affected him badly.

Further equally horrifying reports, include those from the Millers who were driving home on the A75 when a figure suddenly appeared in the road ahead of them. Described as a man in a hessian sack the figure held a rag in his hand towards them. They of course slammed their brakes on convinced they would hit him, but nothing happened. A cursory search found nothing before they reported the incident to the Annan constabulary. Again, a similar tale but this time from driver Donna Maxwell who along with her two children was travelling near Swordwelling when a man described as being in his mid-thirties and wearing a distinctive red top and dark trousers stepped in front of her car. Instinctively slamming on her brakes, he vanished on impact. The story made the headlines in 1997 after a subsequent police search revealed nothing. Who the apparitions are and what their purpose is has remained unclear, however it's a miracle than none of the drivers involved were injured themselves.

Perhaps though the most infamous tale from the area is the following. It has been well documented, and I first read this in Peter Underwood's, 'Gazetteer of Scottish Ghosts,' though it had been in the public domain from some years prior. Taking place in April 1962 on the same stretch of road between Dumfries and Annan, it involved two brothers, Derek who was twenty-two at the time and fourteen-year-old Norman, who afterwards recounted a terrifying encounter. The journey up till then had been uneventful but as midnight approached, they found themselves on that infamous stretch of road. From out of nowhere the pair were then startled by the appearance of a large hen which flew at the car before disappearing at the point of impact. Barely recovering from the shock, they were then taken aback by the sight of a woman wearing rags who ran towards them with outstretched arms, her face contorted angrily. Again, on the point of impact she vanished. The brothers were then subjected to a stream of spectral figures lunging at them from the dark which caused them to brake frequently and according to their testimony they spent the next half hour trying to avoid hitting a multitude of spectral figures. The eldest described feeling compelled to keep his foot down as one would in the circumstances, being terrified to stall, yet cringing on each impact. Later they described the figures as generally ragged, and poverty stricken in appearance, with some of their faces twisted in anguish while others raised their arms in despair. The ghostly retinue was bolstered by a myriad of phantom animals too which included horses, chickens and goats. Eventually, the driver became aware of the taillights of a truck just ahead of them and though much relieved to see something tangible he realised a collision was inevitable. Unable to apply the brakes he warned his brother to prepare for the worst and on bracing themselves struck the van before it too vanished. Slamming on the brakes the pair then sat in shock for some time before continuing their journey. Thankfully the rest of their journey was uneventful, and the pair soon arrived home. One stated afterward that they did not possess any psychic powers and therefore could find no explanation for what had happened. On reading I wondered if the van was a replay from a previous crash whose occupants weren't lucky enough to avoid that straggling horde of spectral creatures? It was said in the aftermath that perhaps witchcraft had supposedly taken place in the area however that stock excuse for anything out of the ordinary does not bear up to scrutiny. The truth is no one knows though perhaps some more earthly horrors took place in the past.

On a final note, I hope that you have enjoyed the journey through my country. It is without doubt a land of myths, legends and ghost lore and all the better for it. I am still fascinated by the subject and like our ancestors enjoy sitting by a warm fire, hearing of the experiences of others. We all have tales to share and there were several I would have liked to have included but the information at present was not forthcoming. There were also others that were perhaps a little scant in detail however that does preclude them from any future publication. There will always be intriguing stories out there to be unearthed and as I collect them, I hope one day to take another journey through Scotland's Haunted Heritage.

BIBLIOGRAPHY

- Aberdeen's Haunted Heritage: Graeme Milne
- Tales from an Edinburgh Tour Guide: Graeme Milne
- The Haunted Neuk: Norman Adams
- Haunted Scotland: Norman Adams
- North Edinburgh Nightmares: John S Tantalon
- Tales from the Crypt of Auld Reekie: John S Tantalon
- Hidden Haunts: Scotland: W J Gilbert
- The Sauchie Poltergeist and other Scottish Ghostly Tales: Malcom Robinson
- Is anybody there? Stewart Lamont
- Ghosts over Britian: Peter Moss
- Great British Ghost Hunt: Hans Holzer
- Edinburgh After Dark: Ron Halliday
- Poltergeist over Scotland: Geoff Holder
- Scottish Ghosts: Dane Love
- Gazetteer of Scottish Ghosts: Peter Underwood

INDEX